# HEART OF PETRA

Heart of Petra

To anyone who's experienced a church split
and to those who've caused one

—fix your hope that one day
He will purify our lips and we will stand
shoulder to shoulder.

# HEART OF PETRA

## BREAKING BONDS BOOK 2

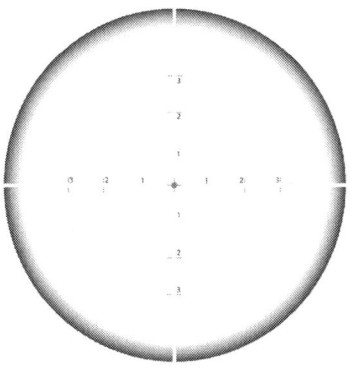

## HILAREY JOHNSON

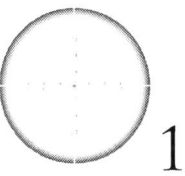

1

Whoever heard of an insomniac with a pajama fetish? I swipe my hand down the leg of my lime-green cotton PJs, but it doesn't help steady them, and I still need two tries to adjust the telescope.

With a deep breath, and a double check at the lock on my bedroom door, I'm able to slow the skipping in my ribs. It's amazing how blood and heart vessels work together, pumping day and night, even while people sleep—well, while most people sleep. An insomniac doesn't have the pleasure of dreaming during the seven hundred and twenty minutes our sun shines on the other side of the world.

I twist the focuser on my telescope clockwise—a bit too far, back just a hair. Perfect.

Returning to my love of pajamas: Seven sets of long-sleeve, long-pant outfits wait in my bottom drawer in two neat piles. One drawer up contains nine matching shorts-sets, twelve nightgowns and one baby-doll nightgown my parents don't know I own.

Shouldn't the comfy fabric and freeing cut of nightclothes start to filter into all daywear? Maybe this is where my obsession began. The cotton, polyester and spandex blends create some of the most luxurious sensations. I wish I never had to change into the heavy fabric we usually use to make my clothes. I don't mean people ought to walk around outside in their lounge pants, with slip-shod manners as though they don't respect the society around them. But if someone could invent a style that felt like pajamas—I'd order from that catalog.

Now that my space probe is set, I can stretch out and wait for the earth's rotation to progress and pretend I didn't get my sister's email.

Pretend Ava didn't leave us.

One o'clock in the morning is when it usually gets good. Until then, celestial bodies will ballet across the chasm of oxygen-less dark. The place where God has gone to prepare a palace of many rooms.

Of course, that isn't where I look.

Neither do I strain to see down in the city, praying in vain for a glimpse of the sister who wouldn't listen. I haven't done that for years. Until tonight.

Ava wanted to tell me why she left, and why it's been so long since I've seen her. She wants to know if I feel the same as she did when she lived at home.

Even in the semi-dark, I'm distracted by the bumblebee-yellow paper, the YWAM Discipleship Training School application sticking out from under my Bible. The black letters, "Youth With A Mission," buzz in my brain as I read. I finger-trace the script of my full name: Leah-Patrice Petra Jones. I don't feel the same as Ava—at least not enough to defy mom and dad. To leave my family.

I lift the paper and take time to match the corners, creasing the center. It isn't exactly disobedience that I kept the filled-out form after my parents said, "No." I filled it out months before mentioning the idea…and it would be wasteful to throw it away now. It could be used for scratch paper or something.

"Oh God, thank you for this day, thank you for your provision, please put a hedge…" My mind and eyes wander to the ambient glare of downtown Reno lights diminishing the glow of stars. Up here, on a hill overlooking the city, it's like I have sky above and sky below. I'm trapped—suspended in stasis.

After I finish creasing the YWAM application, I start to tear the paper. Three centimeters into the act, there is the heat of regret deep down in my core. I slide the paper into my purse. Maybe I'll get the impulse to toss it sometime away from home, and I won't be able to retrieve it like when I am here.

"I'm ready for an adventure, God. Whatever you need to do with me, whatever you want from me." My words flit off into the void as I'm distracted. That always seems to happen when I pray.

It's weird to be so tired and yet unable to succumb to such a simple, natural function as sleep. "How can I be still before you, God, when my mind races like this?"

Doesn't Psalms say he grants sleep to those he loves? The thought makes me gulp.

When I can no longer hold it in, air strains for release against my teeth. The sound of a sigh crescendos like a sonnet in my lonely bedroom. Never mind, it is enough that I have eternity ahead—I've probably misunderstood the meaning of that verse. Dad is adamant about not taking verses out of context.

A knock at my door.

I scramble to open it before I'm asked why it's locked.

"Leah?"

"Yes, ma'am?"

"You can say 'Yes Mom,' too." She takes a deep breath. "You're up late."

"I'm sorry."

"I didn't mean…" She leans in to kiss my cheek. The smell of her Oil of Olay night-cream reaches me before she does. "You sleep with your blinds open?"

I don't look at her but try to answer offhand, arbitrarily. "Yeah, I'm a little warm. I was just about to open the window a crack."

"You know Dad doesn't want your window open at night."

"I thought that was only because I used to sleep on the first floor. Second story now, won't it be fine a crack?" I cover the tension in my forehead by lifting my eyebrows. "Just a breath of wind off the Sierras. It's January and still doesn't feel like winter."

"Okay." Mom's nose wrinkles up for a moment and she looks so pretty. Maybe I should borrow her night cream.

Just to show her how little the window needs to be cracked, I walk over and lift it less than an inch before closing the blinds with flair.

"G'night." She starts to turn. "Are you coming to first service?" The question comes like a belated thought, but I'm sure it's what brought her up here.

"I'd rather not, Mom." Sitting through Pastor Thompson's sermon twice is not the problem. It's doubling up the thirty minutes of boring singing where I have to stifle a hundred yawns.

"Dad loves having your voice with ours on the worship team."

I hesitate — still living in stasis.

"But beyond that..." Mom's eyes smile although her mouth stays still. "Actually, Pastor Thompson will be out of town and Dad is very excited for the substitute to meet our whole family."

"All right." Definitely why she came up so late. So we finally get to meet the visitor Dad's been spending so much time with. "I better get to sleep then."

"Yes, get your beauty sleep, Leah."

I huff. "I need beauty sleep?"

"No, darling. You don't need any more beauty, and that's the truth."

She leaves while my cheek still tingles from her second kiss. Truth? I relock the door and angle my telescope uphill—parallel to the ground behind our house.

Like Jacob's wife: weary Leah—the unloved. Wouldn't a beauty have a husband by now? My mom and sister are beauties. They both had husbands and kids by my age. Ava-Nicole was the prettiest one of us all, but Dad said it was her lust for the world which made her run away and bow down to an institute of humanism.

Truth.

The day the man I loved married a stripper, I knew everything my parents had ever told me was a lie.

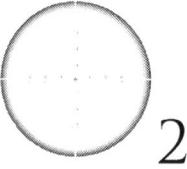2

"Bye, Leah!" Mom calls from the entryway at the foot of the stairs.

"Wait a sec, please. I'm coming." The thick tweed-colored carpet absorbs my feet like loose sand. I teeter down with my suede boots in one hand and my plaid pea coat in the other. I know I look about twelve years old in this coat but my mom always goes on about how hard it was to find one, in my size, in plaid. Guess, I should've told her eight years ago I no longer wanted to be a fuchsia Scotsman — probably it's too late now.

"No, honey. Wait thirty minutes and drive your own car." Mom stands on the tile, shoulders drooping and feet huddled together, as she buttons her brown, puffy coat. "We've a business meeting today after church."

A business meeting with Pastor Thompson out of town?

Her eyes search out her buttons while she continues. "Drive your own car so you don't have to wait for us." When she finally looks up it isn't directly toward me, but at the painting in the entryway. The thirty-six inch canvas consumes the wall and anyone who hasn't seen it before. Mom looks at it like a critic.

"I've grown to hate that picture."

"Artists never appreciate their own work, Mom."

She turns and leaves without saying goodbye. I start after her, wanting to cheer her with a quick hug, but when I reach the bottom of the stairs the cold tile seeps through my socks and I change my mind about rushing out into the morning chill.

I shut the door and lean. Mom's painting is the first thing you see when you leave the world and enter our home. Our sanctuary, Dad calls it. Even though it wasn't a sanctuary when Ava needed it.

Maybe it's a little weird that we have a painting of a broken woman behind bars overpowering our entryway. Mom painted the picture right after she came to know God in college and dropped out. It was one of the only two possessions my parents had when they married. My mom had her painting—a visual reminder of who she was before Christ. My dad had an antique pocket watch—a family heirloom from the Civil War period.

"It's one thing to be lost and come to Christ— quite another to know truth and turn away." As far as I know, that was the last thing Dad ever said to my sister.

Truth again.

As I walk up the stairs, I ignore the sets of family photos on my left and keep my eyes focused on "Captivity" until it's impossible to see the painting at all. The reds and darks do contrast with all the other colors in our house, but I've never seen our home without it prominently displayed.

Since I have a little time to kill, I walk straight to my telescope. Chances are, no one will be up at seven thirty on a Sunday morning, but I can check. I'm not surprised the guy who waits tables and comes home late has his blinds closed. What does surprise me is Lucas. He's about my age, criminal justice major at UNR, I think dad said. He doesn't normally live with his mom and stepdad — they must be out of town because their cars have been gone for several days. Lucas has a girl over. She isn't wearing much. They move like lovers as they make breakfast together. It isn't really spying. I mean, their blinds are pulled all the way up.

The minutes go by quicker than I realize and I find myself running out of the house. I've missed first service for sure, but I'll miss Sunday school too, if I don't hurry. Lateness shows disregard for others, but I drive calmly anyway. Better late than not at all.

The church lobby resembles a grocery store the weekend before Thanksgiving. I pinch my lips together trying to look rushed so no one will stop me as I weave my way through to the College and Career Sunday school class. This is the only time our whole congregation is together—the hour wedged between first and second service.

Up ahead, I see Dad turn as he holds the door for Mr. Blake. I drop to one knee, pretending to tie my shoe. They're boots, so I rub the toes clean instead. I'm sure Dad didn't see me. What am I doing arriving late? If he noticed my tardiness, I'd never get to skip the eight a.m. service again—or worse, I wouldn't get to go to the College and Career Sunday school class anymore. It hasn't been that long since I convinced him to let me attend this group. In high school he didn't want the "world" to taint me—or me to have access to it, I'm not sure which.

Was youth group what tainted Ava?

I slip into the crowded room and feel a puff of stuffy air escape through the doorjamb behind me as I push it closed.

"Leah, I'm glad you're here." Truitt Ridgemann's singsong is led and chased by several strokes of his guitar. "Would you be a dear," he continues. "Lend me your ear?"

I can't help but smile. Several other twenty-somethings are speckled throughout the room in easy conversation so unlike the other Sunday school classes. Truitt continues picking a pleasant melody as I take the seat next to him. "Yes?"

Marta Miller, a petite girl with silky dark hair leans over to get my attention. She starts mouthing the turkey sound "Gobble-gobble," with hilarious, widened eyes. Her boyfriend, Liam Blake, joins the fun—less discretely. Marta always picks a characteristic in other people to ridicule. For our Sunday school leader, it's his saggy chin.

Truitt focuses on his hands, lost in the chords instead of answering my "Yes?" I shake my head at Marta when she and Liam don't let up. I wouldn't say Truitt has a turkey neck—but his chin does seem to disappear when he looks down. Truitt might be attractive if he lost a little weight.

I wonder what Marta says about me.

"Since Hayden..." Truitt looks up quickly and I wonder if I gasped. "...is on his honeymoon." I notice a few people lean in. It isn't everyday that someone from your group runs away with a girl who took off her clothes for money.

Truitt's oblivious, either by innocence or design, to all of the eavesdroppers. "He asked me to take over his gig at the women's prison since he and Sparrow..." Truitt pauses, I think to wait for another reaction from me. I disappoint him with a placid face. "...are occupied." His eyebrows rise.

The noise in the room returns to the previous hum as conversations resume. "Are you going to?" I ask, trying to ignore Marta still making fun of Truitt. Someone as beautiful as her shouldn't pick out flaws in others so frequently. I get up and move to Truitt's other side so I can't see her.

"I've helped out before, but I need a backup singer." He lays his guitar flat on his knees and turns toward my new location. "And I don't know how many people will show up."

I must look confused because he enunciates his next words. "Leah, would you come with me, after service, to the women's prison? In Carson City, about twenty-five minutes from here." Truitt's earnest eyes pin me back with their grassy light.

I know where Carson is, my aunt lives there. Why did he ask me directly? How can I wiggle out?

"God told me to invite you."

I laugh. This is a joke in our group. Not that we take communication from God lightly, but could you imagine if someone could hear the voice of God, and tell you what to do?

"I'll..." I look down at my brown corduroy dress. At least I'm wearing something rugged, casual. "I'll ask my dad."

"Great. Can you drive?" Before I finish a hesitant nod, Truitt victoriously picks up his guitar and begins to lead our worship. Ugh, more singing.

Most of the people in our young adult group leave church after Sunday school or they lag, and talk inside this room. Very few sit under Pastor Thompson, but consider Truitt their leader. Even if I didn't sing, I could just imagine the backlash of asking my dad to skip second service too. Truitt discourages everyone from skipping today.

"We have a rare opportunity this morning. Since Pastor Thompson is on vacation."

"Hrump."

I can't tell who made the sound. It shouldn't

surprise me though. Sometimes the college group feels like a different church, but when I hear a complaint like this echoing from the sanctuary, I remember that most from our group have parents who are members.

Dad said there's been murmurings like "What kind of pastor takes vacation during a recession, when some in the congregation are losing their homes?" Our family's only income is from the church as well—maybe that's why we haven't left town since we went to my brother's wedding five years ago.

"We have a guest, his name is Barkley King. He served as a director for twelve years at the International Messianic Seminary in Israel. He's a dynamic speaker and I think you would all benefit a break from my uncultured, sloppy sermons." There are a few smiles. Truitt is not a trained orator, but he has a good heart and the most essential element for a leader: a sense of humor.

I follow Truitt into the sanctuary as people start to trickle in.

My mom and dad stand by the sound board with the tech guy—or rather a technologically-inclined kid named Josiah. Josiah smiles up through braces and pimples. Does every high school freshman wear the same cologne? I can't help but smile back. He's had a crush on me for years.

"Lower, yeah, good." My dad says, pointing. "Keep Truitt's microphone right there." He looks up at me with a smile. "Mornin' sweetheart, you look nice." I sidle up and receive a sideways hug and kiss on the forehead.

"Morning, Daddy." He nods and presses his lips into a greeting toward Truitt but doesn't say anything.

"Missed you last service." He makes his point without even looking at me.

A response is not needed. I cannot change the fact that he's disappointed I stayed home.

There's an edge of excitement in the sanctuary today. Tingles dance on my skin like the second before the ski lift scoops and your feet leave the earth. The energy follows us onto stage. The microphones are arranged different from normal. Truitt's is set back a little more and Mom and I flank Dad in the center stage. I would trade with Truitt if I could; I live in a fish bowl enough as it is, being a pastor's daughter.

When Dad first came as worship pastor, we didn't know it was a package deal—that all of us were expected to sing too. But people say they love the worship. I think one reason everyone enjoys it so much, though, is Dad really knows what he's doing with sound and balance. He's a great performer. Plus, he's always on time, and there's never anything unexpected. That's why he doesn't let anyone else ever sing with us except Truitt and he never allows Truitt to introduce new songs. It isn't Dad's fault I can't concentrate and I have to turn my head a dozen times to hide my yawns.

That's a default in me.

Dad's body language is dramatic, reverent today. A sweet peace lifts with the first notes from the piano behind us. I wish I could let go and sing instead of concentrate on my pitch and dad's cues. If I could feel the words, instead of focusing on the archaic language and slow tempo…if only worship wasn't so tedious.

Adventure.

The word is whispered in the quietest place of my soul, as though my secret longing is answering a call.

A call to adventure.

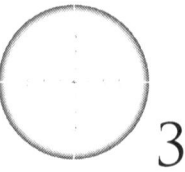

3

Mom and I take the front row. I maneuver, like usual, to sit furthest from the pastor so my parents are angled away from me instead of looking past me at the podium. When I was young, and inattentive, I would get a pinch or a lecture about eye contact. Of course, I'm not a child anymore, but just in case—I don't want to be pinched.

Dad gives announcements. Nothing is ever new: the ladies are having a tea, the food bank is low, we need more help in children's ministry.

"I'm honored to announce Barkley King..." Dad goes on about qualifications and I casually stretch my neck to gaze around the room. We're full. It seems most people from first service have stayed. Marta's family, the Millers, and the Blake family—two reasons I prefer second service—are still here. Our guest speaker must be...

The applause bursts like thunder. No trickle of indecision. The entire congregation claps like it was a collective exhale of anticipation. My hands seem to be just as eager.

"Thank you. I am honored." His accent is not British, not Australian, but similar. I've never heard it before. "Let us ask the Lord for his good blessing."

Dad slips in next to Mom, and I make sure he closes his eyes before I openly study the pastor. He is tall, has caramel skin and thick, black curly hair. He also has the kind of face that would make the average person buy any cream, hair product or cologne he represented. Words roll over his tongue and I'm moved by the intense sincerity, evident even with his eyes closed.

"For the first few years of my life, I stuttered." He goes on about being the only son of wealthy parents and traveling in the Mediterranean and Northern Africa. His stutter was an embarrassment to his parents, "So I frequently sang rather than spoke." There is a rumbling lilt and his sentence climbs into full-blooded song.

"Amazing Grace, how sweet the sound." And the sound is sweet. Golden and thick, his voice pulls others to join. By the, 'but now I see,' part, everyone is singing.

"The good Lord saw fit to remove my stutter, to heal my words..." And his words pour over us. Dad turns slightly and gives me a wink. "So I knew whatever I said, however I used speech—it would be for Him."

Too quickly, service ends. I reach to pluck my Bible from under my chair and before I can stand, Dad says, "Leah?"

"Yes, sir?"

Dad holds one arm out toward me. "Pastor King, this is Leah."

The pastor extends his hand. His warm fingers grip the tips of mine instead of a hand-shake. He steps back as I stand. His heels snap together softly and his head dips but then his eyes return to mine. His are like black walnut: dark with brown swirled in the iris. He smiles as though he already knows me, or knows a joke we share. "Your father has told me so much about you."

I can't help but look down, hoping the warmth I feel is not turning my face pink, even though I know it is. My parents smile proudly.

"Pastor King," someone says.

"There is only one who is both king and priest." Everyone within hearing distance laughs with him.

The pastor turns, but angles himself so I am at his side and not behind him. In fact, his arm is just behind mine. If I bent my elbow, we would touch. This makes my limbs feel as shaky as when I skip breakfast. I make eye contact with everyone and smile, but focus more on my breathing than the conversation.

The sanctuary doesn't empty in the usual way—as though people are famished or the playoffs are already half over. The congregation mingles, talks and shares hugs. The room still hasn't cleared when Dad and several of the elders start to congregate together with Barkley King.

Mr. Blake stands with his hands on his hips and feet planted apart. It acts as a barrier to his body space and even his wife waits three feet from him. Maybe he isn't perpetually angry and it is just his ruddy coloring. "Let's get this over with before everyone's starving." Mr. Blake crosses his arms and I change my mind about the angry thing.

Mom puts her arm around me and gives a squeeze. "We'll be a while." She directs our pace toward the entry hall more hastily than feels natural. "Don't wait for us to eat lunch. Dad and I will probably go out. We'll see you later this evening." Her words are pronounced and rehearsed.

Dad, Pastor King and several of the men have already disappeared. I stand awkwardly alone as mom follows a stream of men and women, most I've known my whole life, down the hall to the meeting room.

"Ready?" Truitt approaches from the side.

"Oh, I forgot to ask." I start toward the room but I can actually hear Mr. Blake's agitated voice through the closed door. Dad would not appreciate me entering that room while they have a business meeting in progress. I'm always curious since not even Mom will divulge what kinds of things go on in there.

Once, when I was seven, I hid under the table during counseling. A woman just talked and cried and begged my dad for help with a foster boy named Jamal. The most significant part I remember was boredom. I couldn't wait to show my dad how still and quiet I hid. When she left, I popped up to scare him. It was one of the few times I can remember a spanking.

I'm a little big to hide; I'll need to find another way to listen.

"What's that expression for?" Truitt nudges me.

"I don't think I can go."

Truitt's coat collar is turned up; his left arm holds a stack of a dozen paper Bibles and he straddles a guitar case on the floor. He wiggles his right pinky finger in his ear canal, scraping and looking at it. Scraping and looking.

"You forgot to ask your parents?" He wipes his pinky nail on his jeans and readjusts the Bibles.

"Why aren't you in the meeting?" I ask him.

"I avoid meetings of all kinds, anyway. But…" His eyebrows leap to meet each other in the middle of his forehead wrinkles. "It isn't like I'm a pastor or something."

"You're the college leader."

Truitt laughs and bends to pick up his guitar. The top two Bibles drop from his stack. He retrieves them quickly but when he bends for the guitar again three more shoot out. I can't stop laughing as he alternately drops and retrieves Bibles almost for my enjoyment alone. He finally pins the top of the stack with his chin.

"Let me." I reach for the guitar case handle.

Truitt rolls his eyes but lets me take the guitar. "I'll see if Joey's still coming. He can swing by and pick me up first. Can I borrow your phone?"

By the time I say, "I didn't see him this morning." Truitt is already into a conversation.

"Sorry, man. I hope you feel better. No, no problem. Are you sure? Yeah, I could use a ride."

What kind of person has friends who would get out of a sick bed to give them a ride? "Truitt," I interrupt him. "I can give you a ride."

Truitt hesitates in contemplation. "Nah, Joe. Rest. I got it covered." Truitt hangs up and hands me back my phone. He angles his head and looks at me through his left eye only. "Are you sure? I can call someone else." He looks down and his already small chin disappears into his neck. "There's no reason for you to drive me out there if you aren't going to stay. Maybe I should cancel the whole adventure. The women are going to be disappointed anyway when they find out it's me filling in for Hayden's guitar and Sparrow's flute."

Adventure?

I look back at the room where my parents are meeting. "I have the whole afternoon free."

I prayed for opportunity—for adventure. Should I cower if this is what God sends? It isn't like I'm disobeying my parents—since they don't know I'm going.

"Naw, my dad loves it when I get involved in different ministries." Of course he prefers me helping in the nursery or singing at the convalescent home.

"If you're sure…" Truitt pulls the guitar from my hands and pushes the double swinging doors wide open with his foot, allowing me to walk out first.

"Let me help."

"I got it." He squeaks with dramatic strain. I laugh and lead the way through the nearly empty lot to my Jeep. With a quick glance back, I verify that everyone still here is at the meeting. Maybe I should have invited someone else. Dad isn't going to like that Truitt and I drove such a long way together, alone.

"Rag top, cool." His voice has a hardness though. He doesn't think it's cool. He stretches while he walks and his large, pale belly makes an appearance. Dad will understand—we aren't bending courting rules. I'm driving with a youth group leader (whom I am not attracted to) for a ministry.

I take the guitar back and scoot the passenger seat forward. He reverently, or somberly, sets the Bibles inside. "You don't take corners too fast? Rollovers are common in Jeeps."

"No." I want to add 'Thanks, Mom,' but he actually looks a little anemic. "I've never had a ticket of any kind. I'm a slow driver."

"I've seen you." He grunts as he climbs into the seat. His largeness is accentuated in the small cab. "Glad we didn't take someone else, I'd never fit back there." Truitt points to the back bench where even I feel like my knees are in my chest if I sit there.

Still, it probably would be better if we were taking someone else.

"There's the lever. You can scoot back."

"I know you're a slow driver." A metal gear sound and a clank interrupt as his seat slams back with his weight acting as a horizontal gravity. "A cautious driver. Why do you think I asked you to go with me today?"

"I thought it was because God told you to." I don't even try to hide my smirk.

"I would like to hear God's voice like that…" It almost sounds like he finishes the sentence with the word 'again.' "But I don't think God would tell me to tell you something he didn't confirm with you."

So which is it? Did I hear God say "adventure" to me this morning? Or am I being rebellious by driving somewhere with a man, unaccompanied? Is that how it started with Ava? One compromise led to another until she was excommunicated from her family?

"You didn't want me to come to the women's prison because I'm so godly, or my voice is exceptional, but because I'm a good driver?" I start the engine, tempted to peel out of the parking lot. I'd never get the courage though, especially in the church parking lot.

"Those other things are true, but aren't mandates for serving in a prison, if you know what

I mean," Truitt says.

"You don't think a leader should be godly? set apart? above reproach?" As soon as I say this, I know they are my dad's words. Not mine.

"All I'm saying is that in a prison—they're just glad you're there."

At the stop sign on the way out of the parking lot I double check all of my mirrors and wiggle in my seat to make sure I'll be comfortable for the drive. "Well, a leader should still be—"

"I'm not the college leader." Truitt articulates. "You know how to get to Carson?"

"Yes." I turn right onto South Virginia. "Not the leader? You just direct it, lead worship, teach, pray—"

"Well, I guess I'm the only one who teaches." He slides his feet from his loafers and I want to crack my window but it feels too obvious an insult. He rubs dingy white socks together like a cricket does his legs. I'm relieved when he pushes his feet back inside his shoes and the foot odor dissipates. Truitt looks at his fingers, or feet, but since we started, he hasn't looked out the window. "But I'm not the leader," he says again.

"I kind of remember my dad saying Pastor Thompson asked you to head it up."

"But I made it clear with him that I was happy to do a Bible study with them until they hired someone full time."

"And our group has grown over the last year since you started," I say.

"Yeah," He smiles at me then looks away, distracted. "Watch the road."

"So, just an unemployed volunteer, nothing more?" I pull my purse near and rummage for my tingly Burt's Bees lip balm.

"Ten and Two, Leah."

"Huh?"

"Your hands. Ten and two." He pulls my crocheted handbag from my fingers and points at the numbers to an invisible clock in front of him.

"Sheesh, Truitt. I need my chap stick. It's in the outside pocket, right…"

"Fine…"

"Just yeah, there…"

"For you, my lady," Truitt holds up a hand like a traffic cop. "I will enter this uncharted water, this no-man's land you speak of. I shall reach into the abyss for you." His hand curls into a fist until only his pointer finger is extended. "If…you keep your eyes on the road."

"Deal." He hands me the tube and I smear it on quickly. A light peppermint scent freshens the air. I concentrate on the somewhat-newly widened freeway and drop the lip balm in the door cubby next to me. I want a drink of water but I don't want to freak him out again.

"So your dad hasn't mentioned hiring another youth leader?" Truitt sets my purse on the floor.

"I think as far as I'm concerned, we already have one."

He looks past me, but not really outside my window. "I never set out to lead."

"Well, all men have to lead. As a husband first and then a father."

Truitt readjusts my purse so it isn't on its side. "I will..."

His mouth moves but I can't distinguish his words. I'm starting to get annoyed by how often he does that. "You'll what?"

His voice is low, stern. "I'll never be a father."

The mood shifts. In an uncomfortable silence I concentrate on the simple, barren scenery that is high-desert Nevada. Never a father? Certainly that isn't by choice.

"I don't want to live if I can't have kids," I say.

Truitt's smile is more like a shrug of his lips. "You'd be a great mom, Leah."

"I can't imagine doing anything else with my life." Suddenly I see a flash of bumble bee yellow paper. My parents said no to YWAM. A girl should go from her father's house to her husband's house. And Ava's fate waits for all daughters who are led astray.

"You have a back-up plan?" Truitt is back.

"What do you mean?" A sensation almost like pins and pricks of fear touch my temples. My parents won't be pleased with anything else but for me to be a wife and mother. The plan worked for my sister Anne-Marie. Even my brother married young and started making babies to fill his church.

"If God has different plans, or God's timing isn't the same as yours?"

"I just want to get married and have kids. Is that so much to ask?" Once I say it, it doesn't feel as powerful. "Although…I have thought…about…" Just tell him Leah. "YWAM."

"Fun. Good program." He looks at me with such tenderness.

"But my parents would be pretty disappointed if I didn't get married." Maybe they're already wondering if I'll ever fulfill my duty to "create a godly legacy."

"I wish you all were as I am, Paul said. Unmarried," Truitt speaks gently.

Tan-gray landscape whooshes by. We turn through a low rolling hill pass and descend into Carson City. "It is not good for man to live alone." I answer.

"Well, it's not like you don't have time. What are you? Eleven years old?"

"Funny, Truitt. Twenty."

"Well, don't think twice for at least a decade, maybe two."

"How old are you?" I ask.

"Twenty-six."

The bags under his eyes and shiny silver specs near his temples suggest more years than twenty-six. "And yet you've already decided not to be a father."

"I had plenty of kids in my class when I

taught." He concentrates on the dashboard with a wistful smile.

"What grade?"

"High school, history."

"You didn't decide against kids because of high schoolers?" I prod.

"Have you thought about going to college?"

Okay, he doesn't want to talk about it. "My parents," How should I phrase this? "They don't want me to go to college. They feel it's not a good idea for a woman to enter marriage with debt."

"That's wise." He's sincere but I can tell he weighs his words like a pastry chef measures flour. "A man shouldn't bring debt to a marriage either."

"Good point."

"You could save, work part time. Go slow."

"I have a small home business." Though really it's just updating websites for people my dad knows.

"Are you saving money?" he asks.

"I have five-thousand dollars." Enough to have my pick of any YWAM Discipleship Training School in the US.

"Good for you."

"I don't have any expenses since I live with my parents." Why does that feel like a confession? "And that isn't likely to change." At least not until I leave my father's covering for my husband's.

"Turn here, Leah, there's the sign."

Nevada Department of Corrections.

I'm still in stasis—even here—a prison in

front and my unmet expectations behind.

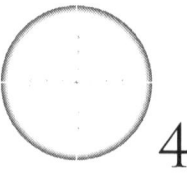4

It's ridiculous how my heart trots when we pull into the Warm Springs Correctional Facility. The low-key coloring and architectural austerity glare at me through symmetrical windows. I've never received a parking ticket—not even a stern look from a police officer. Still, I can almost imagine what it would be like to enter this wide clean parking lot, look at prison walls and government signs, and know I couldn't leave until others made the decision for me.

We turn through the parking lot and I get a better view of several rust-colored guard towers that make me think of lighthouses. Razor wire circles the top of the enormous chain fence like a boa constrictor waiting for another exhale.

We park and pull the Bibles and guitar from the back. Beyond the fence there's movement in a few of the opaque windows. I raise my hand, feeling stupid. Why not wave? Would it be better to pretend I don't see anyone?

"I'm glad you came." Truitt easily carries the Bibles stacked in one hand and the guitar in the other. It makes me smile even more about the show he put on earlier.

"Since visiting hours are not on Sunday, we usually get a pretty good turnout." He starts to whistle the tune to a vacation Bible school song: I've got a river of life, flowing out of me...

The line about opening prison doors sticks with me as we walk through the double door entrance. Neat containers of fliers line the wall on the right offering government subsidy with titles like: "SNAP," "Medical Programs," "Social Security" and "H1N1 Flu tool kit."

It takes us a while to fill out forms, get copies of driver's licenses, submit Truitt's guitar case for a search and walk through the metal detector. Even so, when I find myself shivering in a slate-gray plastic chair as women in orange jumpsuits trickle in — I'm not ready.

The room could be any economically built structure, like a school or a DMV. Dingy bricks painted or faded to a death-pallor gray provide walls in a perfect rectangle. Most of the women have the puffy-eyed look of someone who recently woke or has been crying. Without makeup, their faces are blotchy and uneven. Still, no one looks as frightened as I feel. Why am I here? I should have thought more about what my parents would have wanted me to do.

"You know Sparrow, don't you?" A familiar

girl with shaggy, brownish hair stares down her bony nose at me.

I want to rise from my chair to shake her hand but she's standing so close I can't without bumping into her. She rolls and unrolls a magazine with a picture of Christian singer—I can't remember the band.

"I met you at Walmart, late one night."

"Is your name—Are you Cori?"

Cori seems surprised that I remember. An almost sincere smile touches her lips before it returns to a sardonic line. Her once shiny, blonde cut has dulled and grown to her shoulders but I still see Sparrow's friend in the skinny, angry girl before me. Cori scratches at one of the many red sores on her arms and looks at Truitt.

"So Hayden and Baby really did it?" Cori rolls her eyes at him. "Sparrow. Hayden and Sparrow got married." Her patronizing expression makes me feel ridiculed even though she directs it at Truitt.

"Yep."

"White dress, cake, rice…the whole bit?"

"Actually, we blew bubbles—we didn't throw rice."

Cori turns to me when I say this and I feel like I just interrupted the adults. She scratches her arm, and looks at me the way my mom looked at her painting this morning. This girl is the reason Hayden and Sparrow started the prison ministry. Most of the other women glare at me with something like suspicion and distrust. Some seem to recognize Truitt and tentative waves and smiles begin to outgrow the glowers.

I look down and check to make sure I don't have food on my clothes after the scrutiny of a few women, four in particular, who are talking louder than everyone put together. Their mannerism and vocabulary seem too manly at first but since they each look as tall or as large as Truitt, it fits in a way. A very young, mousey-looking girl shuffles in. The bags under her eyes show a bluish cast through her pale coloring. When she sits off to the left, in an un-crowded section of chairs, several jeers erupt from the group of bigger women.

Truitt starts to strum his guitar. I've never sang songs to God in any place except in a church. If I felt a spectacle before, I am on HD-TV now — naked. I'll do what I always do, keep in sync with the leader. In this case — Truitt. I'll pretend the women aren't here and just think of Truitt.

The four women simultaneously stand, file through the chairs and sit behind the mousy girl who entered last. She looks uninterested but still scoots forward in her chair. Truitt's guitar playing ceases and Cori's confrontational voice distracts me from the group.

Cori points to the cover of her Christian magazine. The word pornography is partially covered but still obvious. "It seems there are just as many men in the church who are addicted as non church — or as you say 'secular'." She says the last word so derisive I feel like she could be any of the girls in my youth group talking about secular music or something equally heinous. "Have you ever looked at porn, Truitt?"

A few girls nearby laugh, or catcall. Truitt turns pinkish and clears his throat.

"Ohh, he has," a woman with dozens of braids sticking out of her head like a porcupine sings out.

Cori stands on her chair. "Did you know, uh?" She calls out like a dramatic television evangelist. Cheers erupt to encourage her. "Most ladies, uh, only produce one film. According. To. This. Article. The experience is…" She flips open the magazine and runs her finger along the words, "The experience is so painful, horrifying, embarrassing, humiliating for them that…" Random inflections and arbitrary pauses interrupt her hell-fire sermon, "They ne-vah. Do it. Again!"

"Preach it, sistah!"

"Get down from the chair." A guard.

The laughter is almost contagious because of her Elvis Presley gyrations and anemic figure. The guard who gave the warning steps forward from where he was leaning on the wall. Cori levels her finger down at Truitt while she lowers to a squat. "Does that turn you on?"

He looks from side to side and then back at her. "It is wrong to take without giving. Men should protect, not steal." Truitt stands and I get those goose pimples of awareness from when I sense the

Lord working. He speaks about sin and forgiveness, how every sin has already been paid for. They are listening!

"Every sin, except murder." Cori's maniacal voice halts even the slightest movement. The room becomes ethereally quiet. Truitt is just as—no, he's more shocked than anyone.

A woman with milk and tea colored skin and a long brown braid diagonals the room. Her low-heeled Mary Janes clack clack with a rhythmic pulse. I sense that everyone else is waiting for Cori, but I can't take my eyes off the woman and her sensible, black uniform skirt.

"And now, behold, I speak unto the church." Cori's voice echoes like she has a microphone. "Thou shalt not kill; and he that kills shall not have forgiveness in this world, nor in the world to come. And again, I say, thou shalt not kill; but he that killeth shall die."

That's not in the Bible.

The woman with the clacking shoes stands at the door where we originally entered and looks directly at me. She indicates "come," with a precise swipe of her pointer finger. I look behind me to see who she signals. Truitt fixates on Cori until I rise. He's pale, like he'll pass out. He reaches out and places his hand on my elbow.

I turn back and the woman is gone—but she wanted me to follow her.

"Die, murderer!" A prisoner screams and Truitt's hand flinches, his grip pinches my arm.

Does he think they're yelling at him?

I bend my elbow and have to wiggle out of his grasp. When I find his fingers, I clench his hand. It seems like everything happens in slow-motion, but I know it isn't. At the same moment a throaty, war-like cry erupts from one of the big women. The group leads a lioness-type attack on the lone, mousy girl. They flank her just as the leader reaches her. Truitt stands so quickly it knocks back both of our chairs. An off-tune twang echoes as his guitar crashes to the floor.

Truitt runs toward the door, my hand still in his, but I watch behind us as the room bursts with flashes of orange jumpsuits. It looks like someone is sprinkling Kool-Aid on a hot, oiled pan.

Orange hits me from the side and explodes in my face as both color and pain. I don't recognize the woman attacking me and bizarrely concentrate on how ugly her face is, filled with so much fury and hate. Truitt pulls the attacker from me while her arms flail. They strike the air, his face, his gut.

He pushes her roughly; she lands on her backside with a grunt that rumbles into a roar as she stands and charges toward us again. Truitt turns and crouches, football-style, so that she strikes his shoulder with her own stomach and momentum. She falls back again and this time we don't stay to see what her next move will be.

Once we're out in the hall, the scraping metal of chairs, raging voices and the scuffle-sound of bodies crescendos so I cannot hear Truitt speak.

"What did you say?"

"The way we came is locked and—" A siren slices his next words. The hall we originally entered is a series of automated detention doors and the first one will not budge no matter how he pounds on it.

We head down the other hall, deeper into the prison—in the direction of the cells, I think.

As several people with riot shields approach and run past us, we press against the wall. The woman with the Mary Janes steps around the corner. "Follow me." She mouths. I lurch toward her but Truitt's hand holds me back.

"What?" I try to wiggle my fingers free.

"Where are you going?" Popping and then a hissing sound cuts him off. He tries again, louder. "Wait…here!" He jogs away and peers around the door where the Bible-study-turned-riot is happening.

I turn back but the woman is gone. The noise in the room changes from aggressive to confused grunts and moans. The fracas hedges us from behind and a stranger leads us onward.

Truitt gags, then sneezes and stumbles back to me. "Gas!"

"How do you know? Did you smell it?"

He shakes his head and coughs instead of answering. His eyes are leaking—so is his nose. The only thing I can smell is multiple sweaty armpits, but I don't doubt it's gas because of the way Truitt gasps. The clumsy sound of my voice proves my lip is as fat as it feels. In fact, my whole jaw is hot and tender. I have to turn my head to look straight in the direction where the woman was last. Truitt grabs me again.

I shake him loose and run around the corner. "Leah!" His voice fades under the noise of my panting and the faint clack-clacking of Mary Janes. The electric buzz of a detention door sounds ahead and I reach the threshold before it latches shut. I hold it until Truitt is panting and gasping several feet behind me. It swings wide when I push it and then dart ahead. I want to turn back to see if Truitt made it when I hear the door slam shut, but a wheezy pant close behind signals that he still follows me. He tries to speak but doesn't seem to have the lung capacity to run, breathe and yell above the sirens.

We enter a classroom-type place. Desks and computers sit in rows, and a bookshelf lines one wall. We scan in a comical, disoriented way, using our whole bodies to look instead of turning just our heads. Maybe Truitt's vision is obscured like mine.

"There!" Another detention door is closing.

He reaches it first and holds it for me as I pass through. In the next hall, I trip and crumple like a demolished building. My right arm juts out to stop me. I hear my own scream as though it comes from behind a closed door. I'm not sure if it is my wrist, elbow or shoulder. Maybe the pain is from all three.

Truitt moves as though he would pick me up, but he labors just to bend.

"Come on, Leah, keep moving." He tries to pull me up.

Where? The showers, cell blocks...solitary confinement area?

"Something's broken." I've never felt such intense pain.

Truitt jumps up and checks both doors on either end of the hall. "We're trapped anyway. Stay seated. Let me see your arm."

I don't lift it but arch my back a little to offer my right side to him. He can look if he wants—it isn't like he's been a ton of help so far.

"Tell me if you feel pain." He touches, pokes and squeezes my bicep, forearm and wrist. I call out, but not from pain. Framed in the glass, just beyond the door, peer several irate faces.

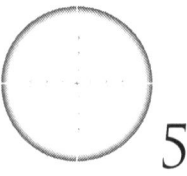5

The door buzzes. Truitt jumps to his feet and stands in front of me. I close my eyes and brace myself as people rush into the room.

"How did you get here?" The voice belongs to a man—not a female prisoner. I open my eyes and look around Truitt's legs to the guards. One has a shield and a stick and another man points a plastic toy-looking gun at Truitt. The one who scares me the most points a similar gun at me. I slide up the wall behind Truitt and he angles himself between me and the toy gun pointing at me.

"Don't move or you'll get tazed!"

Truitt does move a little though, he smashes me against the wall behind him. He's so big he completely shields me. I pull my throbbing, limp arm as close as I can and put my head down by his shoulder and close my eyes. God, make it stop!

"Put your hands up."

"Step away from the girl."

"We're civilians."

"Down on your knees."

"We're here for a Bible study."

"Now!"

"Last chance!"

I can't believe Truitt still refuses, what does he think? He's going to protect me from the guards? I step from behind him and lower to my knees with my left hand lifting my right as high as I can. Rational thought starts to reenter Truitt's face and he also lowers to his knees in conformity.

Once he complies it doesn't take long to figure out that we are the missing Bible study leaders. We're escorted through a strangely quiet prison to the main office area where we originally checked in.

More paperwork waits for us. I don't want to sign anything—even to get x-rays for my arm. I just want to go home and pretend like none of this ever happened.

"Truitt, I think you're going to have to drive." He has a similar look of pale and about to pass out as he did when Cori said her "all who kill..." speech.

Seriously, where did she get that? If there's no forgiveness in this world or in the one to come—what's the point?

"No." His whole body is carved out of the stubborn tree.

"Why? If I can't drive and you won't...I'll have to call my parents." Does he not understand the trouble I'll be in?

"It's not like you can hide what happened." He points to the ace bandage on my wrist.

How irritating that he sees right through me. I pull out my cell phone, now that I have my purse back from the front desk, and try to see my mouth in the reflective back cover. Strange that it doesn't hurt more—my lip is a little swollen.

"Don't you have a license?"

He takes his sweet time answering. "Yes."

Ignoring the missed calls notification, I slip my phone back into my purse and my fingers slide across the coolness of the YWAM paper. I open my purse and the yellow blazes against the natural, unbleached cotton of my crocheted bag. Adventure? No thanks, God. I rip the paper in half and glance around for a trash.

"What I still don't understand," the office lady, Mrs. Almeida, says as she returns, "is how you got as far as you did."

Truitt looks to me and waits. He still looks sick from when I asked him to drive. "We followed someone who works here," I say.

She sighs, drops her head a little and uses her left thumb and forefinger to smooth down her eyebrows—but it is more of a massaging action than grooming. "Good. Wouldn't wanna think the doors malfunctioned during a crisis." Her round cheeks are smooth but the wrinkles in her forehead have only increased since we first came out. "Can you describe the person?"

"She had a long braid."

"How long and what hair color?"

"Brown and very long, to her waist." I remember the feeling that I wanted to follow her more than I remember her appearance.

"Ethnicity?"

Mrs. Almeida's eyebrows constrict and her head leans slightly forward as if she can't hear me well. "I'm not sure," I say. "Probably not white. Her skin was kind of darker."

"A probably not Caucasian woman with a braid?" I stand insulted — she stands smiling.

"And you just walked right past a group of men with riot shields and they didn't stop you."

"We stepped aside and let them pass," Truitt answers. "Almost like they didn't see us."

She sighs again. "What was the woman wearing?" She directs to him.

"I didn't see anyone. I wondered where Leah was going the whole time."

My head autonomously jerks to look up at Truitt and a bit of dizziness results. I touch my face with a wince.

"Let me get you another icepack, I think it's been off twenty minutes." Mrs. Almeida turns to a coworker guy behind the counter. The last icepack ended up on my swollen wrist.

"You didn't see her?" I study his face for truth.

"Un-uh," he replies.

"Are you kidding? No wonder you grabbed me back. She walked across the room."

"She was there before the riot?" he asks.

"Yes, just before. About when Cori started talking about murder and killing."

Mrs. Almeida crimps the instant cold pack in her hands. "Just activating it. Here you go. What about you? What kind of clothes?"

"A straight dark skirt and Mary Jane shoes."

"Are those with the strappy...?" Truitt chimes in.

"Yeah," I hold up my hands, "About this much heel. They were dark gray." I move the icepack to my wrist; it hurts far worse than my face.

"Well, good thing you noticed the shoes on the probably not Caucasian woman with a braid." Her eyes scrutinize the wall behind me and it looks like her tongue explores her mouth.

"You don't believe me."

"No sweetie, I just doubt that you have your details right. We aren't allowed to wear heels to work—and I don't know anyone with long hair here." She turns around and approaches the counter again, mumbling to her coworker.

"Are you sure she was wearing those kind of shoes?" Truitt asks quietly.

"I never lie." Hide maybe. Misdirect. Avoid disclosure. But not lie.

"I believe you." Every tension in me deflates. Good. We share a smile, a secret experience. "Thank God, you're all right. Except for this." Truitt reaches out and pats my hand and leaves it on top of the icepack.

I slip my hand out from under his and touch my lip. "Thank you, too, Truitt." We both giggle and lean toward each other, the anxiety and fear has left us drained, and almost serene if not giddy. "Sorry about your guitar."

"It wasn't mine. I borrowed it from a friend."

We both find this hysterical.

"I couldn't believe you were just running through the prison like that," he says.

"I saw someone—"

"I don't doubt that." He looks up at the florescent bars humming on the ceiling then back to me. His green eyes glow like they absorbed some of the electricity. "Think it was an angel?"

The overwhelming idea that God was in that place with us fills me with relief.

"Are you guys anxious to get out of here? We're almost done—but I think you need to get an X-Ray. You probably shouldn't drive."

I look to Truitt, his face like a graffiti hand impression in cement saying, "Halt. You shall not pass."

Fine. "I'll call my parents."

***

My mom's hesitant hug is emotional overreaction.

"I'm not going to break."

My father seethes, but when he pulls me into his arms I think he might cry as well, so tenderly does he hold me out and inspect my face. "My delicate Leah."

The office gave me a brace for my wrist. Mom touches it with one hand on each side of it. I hear her praying.

"I don't want X-rays."

My parents answer me with skeptical "hmms", "mmms" and shrugs.

"Let's just wait twenty-four hours and see if it still hurts."

They agree. Dad presses his palm to the top of my head and trails down like a brush several times. I let him pull me into another hug. We leave the building in the silence of a funeral procession. It looks different outside in the dark. I barely remember coming here this afternoon.

Mom'll drive me and my car. Good luck with dad, Truitt. Shortly, I bet he'll wish he'd driven. Dad can make the loudest silence in the world.

Mom doesn't have to adjust my seat or mirrors at all and we pull out behind my dad.

"Why do you think he doesn't own a cell phone?" Mom starts in right away. "Is it because his credit is so bad no one will offer a contract? Or maybe he can't even afford a pay by the month."

I know what she's doing. This is the Socratic method of questioning but it's displaced because she thinks I was interested in Truitt to follow him here. To the gates of hell.

"Why do you think he has such trouble with his weight?" Mom's coercion is always more direct than dad's. Which is funny, because she thinks it's more subtle.

She doesn't wait long. "I'm glad he doesn't know how to drive. I don't know if I'd feel safe with him in charge of your life. It's good we had to come get you."

"I think he knows how, Mom."

"Then I wonder why he wouldn't."

Ugh. It's working.

She doesn't stop. "Why do you think he volunteers at the church? Can't he get a job?"

"A few months ago Dad couldn't say enough good about what was going on in the youth group." I lean my chair back hoping she'll have compassion — I'm tired.

"Truitt was a better alternative than Hayden at the time."

"I thought you loved Hayden." Like I did. Enough to break one of the fundamental rules of letting your parents choose your mate, and care deeply for someone before engagement. Even if it was just one date to a charity function.

"Leah, we still love him. But he was led astray by his passions."

Hayden will always be known as the guy who married a stripper.

"Mom, I don't care for Truitt in that way."

"Good."

How could I care for someone like Truitt? He's funny, but he's weak. Like Mom said, he doesn't have a job. He's kind, and seems to inspire sincere friendship in everyone. But what are his goals, ambitions? He isn't driven and motivated like my dad.

He is godly, but...I don't know. There's something wrong. Something he's hiding.

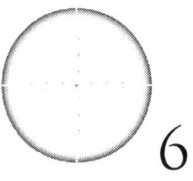6

If she can't ride her Harley, Mom always unwinds in the bath. The first thing she does whenever there's stress is hop on the bike or into the giant jet tub. She'll make it so hot she stumbles to bed dizzy—so I know I won't see her again tonight. A bath would cause more stress than relief for me. Why would I want to soak in a container of my own filth?

I want to get into some pajamas and look through my telescope, but Dad is staying up late. If I could encourage him to go to bed I'd be able to check if Lucas still has company or if his parents have returned home.

I stretch out onto my covers. Metal scraping. Shoes clacking. People striking. No way I will sleep tonight. Adventure? Again, no thanks, God. I wanted something fun—not something scary. Even if that was an angel in there, I'll stick with the coffee ministry.

I pull the torn YWAM paper from my purse

and lay it flat, both pieces next to each other before I go see what dad is up to.

The continual clicking of a computer mouse erupts when I enter my dad's office. His back is to the far wall and I only see the cords and vents on the backside of his monitor and CPU. He turned his computer because he doesn't like being "sneaked up on." When I step into the dark room a little farther, I see his face. He's shadowed in insipid light.

"Hi, sweetheart." Click, click, click. His eyes move rapidly while he apparently closes out several windows and logs off. "You're up late."

He doesn't know I haven't even tried to lie down before one in the morning in years. "Yeah, a little keyed up."

"Your lip hurt?" His chair whines as he shifts to face me.

I shake my head no and slide my brace behind my back.

"Why would you cast your pearls before swine, beloved?"

"Swine?"

"Yeah, the precious jewels of God trampled by people who will not respect it. What good would it do to go sing to the Lord in a place like that? They obviously aren't interested. That's why they're there."

"I thought…" Well, I knew it wouldn't be his chosen ministry for me. Apparently no one told God I was to be a wife and a mother! I breathe in for courage. "I wanted to fill in for Hayden while he—" my voice cracks "—honeymooned."

I wish he would ask me about Hayden. I wish I could talk about it with someone. Dad clears his throat. He won't ask because he already knows. Just like when I asked about college, about YWAM. The disapproval drapes me like twelve yards of crushed velvet.

He turns off his monitor and rises. "It's late and I want you to come to work with me tomorrow."

"Oh?" I don't want to spend a day wandering around church. "I planned to add a new page to Mr. Cunningham's site." I scrounge for a reason. "Tips on Lawn Care."

"You can do it from the office. Mom is visiting Aunt Margaret and you don't need to be here all day." I force myself not to blink as he studies my eyes. "Alone."

Of course. It will take time to earn his trust again. "Yes, sir."

I receive a kiss on my forehead and walk myself to bed, but I wait at the door until he heads downstairs to the master bedroom. He opens the door to the garage, probably checking on the Harleys and the lock. I feel so safe with him always making sure everything is locked up tight.

I meander inside my room. No hurry, the show won't start for awhile. The weight of a rock lands in my stomach as I lock my door and turn. This morning when I ran out in a hurry, I left my telescope set up, pointed and focused directly into Lucas's mom's house. Reaching for the light, I wipe the switch down quickly. Settle, Leah. It isn't spying. I'm not looking at anything they aren't showing. If they wanted privacy, they'd draw the curtains.

Where did Lucas's mom and stepdad go to be gone so long? Not that it matters. His activities are much more interesting than theirs are. Lucas is dancing with a girl; this one has long dark hair. I might assume his girl from this morning got a new hair style, but you can't grow ten inches in a day. Two different girls in one day? Their dancing gets handsy. He pushes her back toward his parent's table and she pulls her top off before she slides backward on to it.

I jump back. Oh my. It's time to go brush my teeth.

When I return, I'm curious to see if they are done, but I don't chance it. I turn the telescope to the east to see if the waiter is home. I don't have the ease of dexterity with the wrist brace so I remove it and massage my hand, arm and wrist. It barely hurts anymore. My eyes cross in fatigue as I try to refocus the telescope. I wish I could sleep instead.

The waiter's home. He and his wife are arguing again. At least I've always assumed he's a waiter because he wears black pants and a white shirt with a tie every night. The wife walks out of the kitchen and he puts away dishes. It looks like he's slamming cupboards, but I can't hear anything.

She returns with a basket of laundry and shakes a piece at him before she leaves again. I'm probably the only one on this street with my window cracked, but if they opened their window I could hear why she's so upset.

The waiter plops down at the table and puts his head in his hands.

Weird. When I see them on the street, taking walks, they look so happy.

***

"Another meeting?" I try not to stare at the tiny, pulsating vein under Dad's right eye. What does he have to be stressed about? I'm the one who had to get up early on a Monday to wander around the church while he works.

His eyes blink rapidly and every time he opens them he's looking somewhere else. I glance behind me but no one is around. "Sorry, honey," he says. "I'm just really busy, I can't...I can't babysit you."

"Pffft."

"Oh, you know what I mean." He dismisses me without words as Mr. Blake enters the church foyer. "Erik." Dad walks past me and greets him.

They don't shake hands. Mr. Blake is worked up as usual. His russet coloring doesn't stop at his hair line. They turn and walk toward the boardroom side by side and almost try to walk through at the same time. Mr. Blake relents and lets my dad walk through first. Oh, to be invisible for a minute and slip in behind them.

I remember the spanking.

They shut the door to the boardroom, so I shuffle along toward the nursery and listen to my feet scrape the faded low-pile industrial carpet. The teething toys are gathered in a laundry basket so I scoop them up and head down the hall to the kitchen.

"Ow!" Toys fly into the air. A full body slam from Truitt, lumbering out of the kitchen, knocks me flat on my back.

"Timber!" He calls as his mass topples toward me. Arms flailing and torso arching, he manages to land next to me instead of on me. "Oh my gosh." He bursts out laughing. "I'm glad I didn't kill you!"

I'm about to say something non-committal but his big belly is exposed. Pale skin, covered in dark hair and stretch marks. He sees me looking. We make eye contact and slowly, dramatically he pulls his shirt back down with school-teacher disapproval. This makes me fall back laughing and I can't lift my head up.

We're still giggling as we crawl on hands and knees to gather the toys and teething rings back into the basket. Truitt sighs and leans back against the wall, not bothering to stand. I arrange my skirtlot and sit facing him. He raises one eyebrow as I push the skirtlot back below my knees.

"You make your own clothes, Leah?"

"Sometimes." My mom made this for me

though.

"Smashing style." He winks. "Have you heard of the latest invention? It's called a bicycle."

I try not to smile so big and chuck a red teething ring at him. "Shut up." It feels good to use harsh language, especially because he obeys. He keeps grinning though.

After a minute, he says, "I'm really sorry I didn't drive you home last night." His smile is gone and there's a pucker in his chin as he works his lower lip around his teeth. I want to give him the opportunity to speak what he wants to say, so I wait.

The obscured echo of arguing flickers into our quiet. Someone's leaving the meeting.

"What do you think is God's will?" Barkley King's hot chocolate voice flows from around the corner. Truitt stands, quietly, and looks toward the voices, then into the kitchen. I close my eyes to focus on listening.

"It wouldn't be like this." Not sure who said that.

"Then we do it right, godly." Dad.

"Come back inside." King.

The meeting room door latches and I open my eyes to see Truitt already looking at me.

"Your wrist is feeling better?" Truitt holds his hand out and I place mine in his. He puts his other hand under my elbow as he hoists me up with a ridiculous grunt. "Sheesh. What do you weigh? A hundred and ten pounds?"

He's off by twenty. "Shut up." I like saying this.

"You keep using that word. I do not think it means what you think it means."

"Princess Bride!" Did he seriously just quote my favorite movie?

"Inconceivable," he replies.

I look down at my hand, still in his. Truitt's eyebrows, shoulders and lips all seem to sink slightly and he drops away from me. He turns and picks up the laundry basket. "Do these go in the dishwasher?"

"Yeah." I wait a second and watch him carry the toys into the kitchen before I follow. His shoulders sag.

"I brought this for you." He sets the basket on the counter and slides a brochure from his back pocket.

"YWAM School of Evangelism." When I touch the acronym *SOE* with my finger, a tear pools. I wipe it with my knuckle and then pretend like my face itches in several other places to hide the action.

Truitt opens the dishwasher and flips the basket upside-down. Most of the toys tumble into the bottom rack, a few fall onto the floor. He lifts the door and tries to close it but a plastic giraffe sticks half in and half out.

Bang. Squeak.

Bang. Squeak.

Each time he shuts the door, the toy complains.

Truitt moves up and down, grabbing toys and throwing them inside the dishwasher. He throws a strawberry so hard it bounces back out. I dive for it and pounce like a cat. He holds the door and I toss. It bounces off the back wall again. Truitt squats and presses his back to the door with his arms spread. He jerks forward like the toys are trying to break down the door. "Don't let it get away!" He points to the strawberry.

I trip on my skirtlot and fall, smashing the strawberry under my stomach. It isn't that squishy and I grunt from the impact.

"That's it!" Truitt cheers. "Way to sacrifice yourself!"

I roll onto my side and reach for the strawberry. When I feel it, I roll again, squeeze it for the noise and fling. While it floats through the air Truitt opens the door to receive it. He slams it shut as soon as the strawberry hits the inside.

"We did it." He stands and leans over the sink, wiping at a pretend tear. "It was touch and go there for a while."

"Truitt?" I try to express terror in my eyes. "What about soap?" His look of horror is my undoing and we laugh until I am sore in the middle.

With the ancient dishwasher groaning and filling up behind us, we head out of the kitchen.

"You can't do this!"

"You're a volunteer board member. We don't need you."

The cuss word that follows makes me feel

like I am going to throw up. But it is as much from the animosity as the word. Someone strides down the hall toward the kitchen. I turn to Truitt, my breath trapped in my stomach.

More cussing!

Just as the foul mouthed man is about to reach the kitchen, Truitt grabs me and pulls me down behind the island. The dishwasher swishes and moans next to us so I don't hear much else. I'm glad because what follows is vehement yelling and arguing. Truitt strains to hear with his eyes comically wide, but I don't laugh. I'm as uncomfortable with his proximity—squatting close enough to smell his breath—as I am at the thought of an elder walking in and finding us eavesdropping. And hiding.

My heart pounds with the thrill.

"You can't fire a man while he's on vacation."

It's my dad who says "F-you," this time. "We're not firing Damon while he's on vacation. We're voting while he's on vacation and we'll fire him when he gets back."

At the sound of his voice my suspicions are confirmed: who we are is not the same as who we say we are.

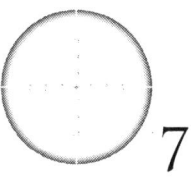

7

When the hall quiets down, Truitt and I stand. We smile at each other like someone just passed wind and we don't know who did it. I leave the kitchen first. Truitt doesn't follow me. I shuffle alone into the sanctuary and align a few of the padded chairs. My deep-breath-sigh reverberates in the room so I take another, louder.

I stretch out on the chairs. I'll need to nap for a bit since I had to get up so early with Dad. One of the byproducts of an insomniac, you do what you can to get through the day.

I can see the stage from where I lie. An overwhelming sense of ugliness surrounds me.

Who we are is not who we say we are.

Am I successfully hiding how much I hate worship? How will it look if I'm discovered for the fraud I am? I'm so messed up, it feels like God is looking down at me now—not even present in the sanctuary. He's supposed to be everywhere, but it feels like he's far away. Just watching me from his telescope. It makes me want to weep. I don't, and this proves, again, how impervious I am to connecting with him.

"Yes, sir." I wake to Pastor King's voice and then my dad's chuckle.

"Truitt normally leads the college group but he said he'd love to have you as a guest speaker tonight, and eventually I'd like to see you..."

Obviously, they haven't seen me. I stay still across the chairs in the middle of the sanctuary and rub crusty sleep from my eyes.

"I'm honored."

"Er, well—" my dad normally never stumbles over his words. "My Leah attends."

Pastor King does not respond right away. "I look forward to getting to know her better." His voice is like a rare winter sun streaming through the window.

"Yes. I hoped you would." After my dad says this I hear their hands clasp, and something like a shoulder pat.

I lie still for a long while and stare at the arched ceiling. I'd had a weird dream of being naked and reach down for reassurance. I finger the coarse, practical fabric my mom sewed into a heavy, modest...Truitt made fun of my clothes. Who does he think he is? Another one of the kids in the college group?

So my dad hopes the new pastor will get to know me better. It makes sense; when my parents discouraged me from YWAM, I didn't have direction, so they suggested an online graphic design school. I didn't have a client; they found a few for me. I don't have a husband, maybe this is just one more provision.

"There you are." Truitt leans over a chair.

As my dream comes back to me, I sit quickly for modesty's sake.

"Want to help me lead worship tonight for group?"

I feel a closed-mouth, snarl-smile attempt to stretch my lips. I'm usually more adept at pretending—but I'm tired.

"You don't want to?"

"No, I..."

He plops on the row behind me and folds his hands over the chair in front of him.

"I thought we did really well yesterday together, before..."

"Are you kidding, Truitt? We caused a riot." We both laugh with levity and I feel safer. "I don't really like worship." I meant to say singing—not worship. I look around quickly to make sure no one else could have heard.

He waits and seems to mull something over a while. "Did you know—"

"Truitt, I was raised here in church." I arc my hand across the room. "It's been a long time since I heard somethin' I didn't know."

There's a long pause but I'm still glad I said it.

"Fair enough." Truitt leans back and crosses

an ankle over his knee. His arms stretch across the chairs on either side of him. He's not cocky, or smirking, he just studies me with innocence and concern.

I relax and try again. "What I meant is: I know worship is about God and not about me. I know worship is a sacrifice. I know our songs are sweet incense to him…"

"Well, a worship leader," he emphasizes the last word, "walks a precarious road." His foot begins to jiggle.

I wait. I heard once that when Satan was cast from heaven, he landed in the music ministry. If Truitt says that, so help me, I will scream.

"It's almost as if your job," he takes a breath, "Is not about God. Your job is about people. Drawing people into worship."

I nod. It feels like it's about people—and not God.

"If you get too into it," he makes finger quotes, "praising God, free-styling the words so no one can follow you—it just becomes a concert. You have to sing in such a way that people can follow. You have to try to please everyone, from the hymns-only crowd to the ones who fall asleep if it isn't a rock show."

"And worship is the first thing that turns people away when they try a new church." I laugh and we gain momentum.

"Worship carries the responsibility of preparing hearts to receive the Word," he says.

"People will be your friend only because they think you can talk your dad into letting them sing on stage."

"No," he says this like a balloon losing its last bit of air.

"Yep. Happened to my mom, too." That was so painful for her because she rarely makes connections in church anyway. Pastor's wives have to 'be ye separate,' and 'above reproach.' Everyone is a potential gossip and pastor's wives can never confide in prayer groups. I feel heavy remorse when I realize my mom has less friends, more burdens, and has to look even more perfect than me. At least she has Dad.

Does she?

God? Is that why she's at Aunt Margaret's today?

Truitt shakes his head slowly. "And if all goes well, you have to balance the adoration—which should be for God—when it is easy to think you were responsible for a particularly engaging service."

"So what's the point?" I pull my shoeless feet onto the chair and sit cross-legged.

"Of what?" Truitt scratches at his teeth with his fingernail.

"Worship." I feel the nakedness of my dream.

"There was an evangelist in the eighteen-hundreds, kind of the same caliber as Billy Graham, named Rueben Torrey. He talked about worship." Truitt cracks his knuckles and wiggles his fingers.

"He said worship of God is the soul bowing down in complete, no, absorbed contemplation of him."

"Contemplation. Just thinking about him?"

"Yeah, he also said or quoted something like: prayer is occupied with our needs, thankfulness with blessings, but worship…worship is being occupied with God alone."

I turn and stare at the front of the sanctuary. The ancient sound equipment Dad always complains about is pressed up against the wall and a dull gray vacuum sits in its place. I've had to vacuum this room with that thing, many times. It takes forever. A perfumed carpet powder barely hides the moldy smell. "Just think about God?"

"Yeah, don't even think about how much you love him, what you want to do or don't do for him. Dwell only on getting to know him. What are his characteristics? What defines 'God Most High'?"

"Just think about God."

"Leah, there you are." My dad's entrance ruptures my line of thought.

I stand and walk toward him but not before I catch a glimpse of Truitt, his hands are folded and his face is so relaxed I know instantly—he is just thinking about God.

"Hi, Daddy."

We meet halfway across the room. His forehead shines and the extra skin between his eyebrows creases into three deep gullies. "I'm sorry, sweetie. I can't take you out for lunch."

His pale lips press into taut, lean strips. I'll

not add to his stress by showing how upset I am. "That's fine, I think there might be a cup of noodles in the kitchen."

"Sir." Truitt stands and pulls his shirt down to the height of his jeans but it triangles over his stomach like a tent. "I can take Leah with me when I grab some lunch. Would you like me to bring something back for you?"

Dad's whole body shifts as he looks from Truitt to me in an almost confused state. "Uh..."

"Bryan. Thompson's back." Marta's father, Mr. Miller, stands in the doorway with stiff-straight arms and a crouched back, almost like he is about to sprint off.

Our pastor has returned to get fired.

"How'd he get here so fast?" Dad strides toward Mr. Miller and I can see back muscles flexed and rippling through his 'Faith Church' polo. "Truitt." He turns back toward us. "That would be great. You two kids get out of here for a bit and take your time. I'd love a sandwich or something." He smiles.

My dad, Mr. False.

"Yes, sir," Truitt says to dad's departing back. He stretches his arms and rolls his head in circles. The popping of cracking joints echo in the empty room and I can't help but smile at all of Truitt's gross body noises.

"So you're taking me, huh?" I fold my arms. "Does that mean I drive, pick the place and pay?"

"No." he says. "I pick." He grins and looks

downright ornery. "But I'll let you drive and pay."

"Not happening, Truitt."

He starts walking toward the door. Even thought it feels lighthearted—we don't laugh.

"Have you ever been to Deux Gros Nez?" He holds the sanctuary door open.

"Two big...noses?" One side of his mouth crowds his cheek but I don't question my four years of online French, only his pronunciation.

"It's so good."

"I'll be driving then?" It's a question only by technicality. I already know.

"I'll pay," Truitt says under his breath but I still hear the subtle truce offered. I want to insist that someday he's going to tell me why he won't drive. When we get out into the hall, my dad is entering the boardroom.

"Truitt, do you ever wish you could bug someone's house or tap their phone line?"

He halts his awkward gait and plants his hands on his sides. Several men down the hall round toward the conference room without notice of us. One of them is Pastor Thompson.

Truitt looks at me with unguarded frustration. "Right now I do."

I believe him because of the way we hid in the kitchen.

Two days in a row I leave church with my youth pastor. But right now, he feels more like a friend.

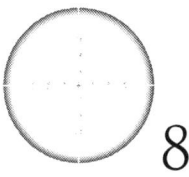8

"Let's get one thing straight," I say. Truitt stops fidgeting and pointing to my seat belt. He nods before I continue. "I have a license—not a permit." His sheepish grin is pretty funny and it hugely bolsters my confidence. "I will not tolerate your backseat suggestions, sir."

"How will you know where we're going?"

"I'll take directions." I hold up a 'just a minute' finger. "But you will either trust me or follow on your bike." I point that finger to the door.

"Yes, ma'am," he says with Southern respect.

Truitt navigates us left and right, then to the freeway. He is a horrible directions-guy. "Oh hey—turn here."

I whip the wheel and the back right tire climbs over the curb. There's a 'thunk' as his right hand hits the door and his left grasps the handle in front of him. "Sorry," I say as I pull to the side of the road.

The only sound above Truitt's breath is my

blinker click-ing, click-ing, click-ing. His skin color has faded to the shade of the pages in my dad's antique hymnal.

"No, I told you to." He opens his eyes and resumes telling navigations. I never come down to this part of Reno. Of course, I don't really go anywhere but home and church.

"Park here," he says.

My face feels tight from the huge smile that splits across my face. On the corner of the first floor is a big red sign that says "Spy Guy." There is a magnifying glass illustration on the sign.

"The restaurant's upstairs." Truitt hops out of the car before I have the key out. He stretches and walks over to my side of the car. My eyes are on the sign and I start to cross the street. Truitt grabs me, one arm around my back, grasping my right arm and one hand circling my left arm's inner elbow. "Whoa, tiger."

A car, I don't even notice the color, speeds down the street.

"Do you *want* to be a pancake?"

I laugh and lean into him and then pull toward the Spy Guy shop. "You want to go in there first?"

He doesn't let go and guides me across the street. We are both laughing as he tries to maneuver the door with elbow and feet because his hands are still holding on to me.

An Asian woman and a teen boy watch us as our laughter interrupts their browsing. But they quickly return to the teddy bear cameras with creepy eyes. She wears tight jeans with sparkly stitching across her bum and purple leopard heels that seem almost as long as her tiny legs. I smooth out my skirtlot and pull my braid to the front of my shoulder.

"Good afternoon." Someone behind the counter speaks. "Are you looking for anything in particular?"

Truitt answers. "Nope, just here for fun."

"Welcome, let me know if you have any questions."

They banter a bit more but I keep staring at the woman and her son. She places a hand with shiny black and silver print nails on his shoulder and he laughs like they're sharing an inside joke. They don't look like Christians. But then I wonder why I think that. The nail polish? The sparkly seat?

What surprises me the most is that I might find a good family out here — in the world.

"Actually, we want to know how to bug a house and tap a phone line."

I turn at Truitt's words. He's grinning at me with a sneaky smile and we share our own private joke.

*** 

The music gets louder every step up the narrow stairway leading to Deux Gros Nez. Half way up, a curvy girl with a tiny waist maneuvers past us. Her hands are full of a tray. I try to get a look to identify the delicious smells, but all I see is some chunky ice cream thing in a mason jar.

We enter the dining area and someone from behind the counter yells over the music. Cycling shirts and bike décor cover the walls. Most seats are full and the conversation level rivals the base guitar coming over the speakers. This is not the kind of restaurant my dad would ever go to. Maybe I'll bring mom here sometime.

"You have to either get the almond butter milk shake or the grape juice float."

"How come you get to pick what I order?"

"I'm trying to save myself from ordering two ice cream drinks. But they're both coming to this table."

I smirk and set my menu down with a shrug. "Okay."

I avoid all nuts since I'm allergic to walnuts, and ice cream and juice simply don't appeal. I pretend interest in the bike and cycling paraphernalia while Truitt orders pesto pasta. I get humus and veggies. Of course! Truitt rides his bike everywhere. His love for cycling still doesn't explain his aversion to driving though. I try to orient myself to this street, California Street… and the spy shop is just around the corner on Virginia. I could find my way back. And I simply have to get back to that store.

"I'm surprised you didn't get anything at the Spy Guy ."

"Why is that?" I readjust in my seat. Was my face that obvious?

"I don't know. You seemed like...you were pretty into that stuff. Are you sure you want to go to YWAM and not the FBI?"

I laugh. Maybe a little too readily but I think it covers. "It's just for fun."

"Well, I agree that it would be nice to know what is going on in the boardroom today."

"Why aren't you there, Truitt? You're technically the youth pastor."

"Not just technically. You were right, I am." He slouches.

"Here's your drinks." A blonde guy with bony wrists covered in homemade twine bracelets sets two mason jars down in front of us. He isn't our waiter. He smiles through his floppy hair but when he sees me he sort of blinks. At the second take he looks me up and down. I look down at the jar. It's the almond butter shake but I think the grape juice float will be less disgusting.

"Thanks, dude," Truitt says and grabs a long, skinny spoon and plunges it into the grape juice, halving a clump of creamy looking vanilla ice cream. I take a sip of water.

"I'm sorry," Truitt turns his spoon upside down in his mouth to clean it a second time. Noise echoes around us and I'm not sure it'd be any different on some crowded foreign street. Today feels like the furthest I've ever been from home. I could almost pretend I'm in Europe.

"I should have asked which one you wanted. I just took the one in front of me. I haven't double-dipped yet." He slides the Mason jar toward me and starts to grab the almond butter milk shake.

"Nah." I wrap my hands around it. "You probably reached for the one you wanted most."

"Actually, they're both phenomenal." Truitt sets his licked-clean spoon on the table. "I don't care at all."

"I'll just drink this one." I take my spoon and skid it across the brown and white speckled cream. When it hits my mouth I can't hold back a little "hmmm."

"Good, huh?" Truitt beams like he created it. "Now try this." He slides the grape juice jar forward.

"Without getting a new spoon?" Gross.

"Your germs won't bug me. I'd slurp this stuff off the table."

I plummet my licked-off spoon into the juice and try to scrape up a little ice cream when I pull it out. I was hungrier than I thought. "Oh my, Truitt. Refreshing. Divine."

He winks. "Such harsh words, Leah?"

"Fine." I grab both jars and pull them toward me. "I'll drink them both. You can have my hummus."

Before I can get both jars sheltered on my end of the table, he's reached across with his spoon and stolen a bite from the almond butter. With his gross double-dipped spoon.

"You understand this is war, right?" I hold the grape float closer and release the almond butter.

He looks behind me with eyes twice the size of normal. I can see white on all sides of the iris and several tiny red lines. I turn to see what had his attention and when I look back there is a drip line of ice cream across the table and on his chin. He stole from the grape juice float.

"Seriously? That's gross. Now you've double-dipped in both."

"You're the one who wants to be a missionary. You don't think someday you're going to be served dog? You have to eat what's put before you with thanksgiving." He grins. "And right now this is what I am offering you."

"Double-dipped ice cream?"

He chuckles and reaches across the table to tug my braid.

Fine. I take a bite. He's my youth pastor. I probably won't get a cold, mono, herpes...

"Seriously, Leah, I thought you were going to have a seizure in the spy shop. Why didn't you get anything?"

Now I feign interest in a yellow jersey. Nothing is said for what seems like long enough but when I turn back Truitt is still waiting for an answer. He even ceased to wolf down his shake.

"One humus-veggie and one pesto."

I raise my hand and a reedy brunette with facial piercings hands me the pasta. She sets my sandwich down in front of Truitt.

"Don't tell me we have to share our lunches, too." I laugh, but Truitt looks at me like I'm wearing an "On Sale" price tag that is twice the original. Okay, no veggie for Truitt.

I lift and scoot my chair closer, then spend several seconds getting my bulky skirtlot to lay right. "I'll pray. Thank you for this day, thank you for your provision, please put a hedge of protection around us. Bless this food to our bodies."

"Leah." His voice is gentle, reaching to me like a scented candle. "What are you hiding?"

It may be my imagination, but the din takes a collective breath and then turns to a charged hum. I feel tingles on my skin.

"Sometimes I watch my neighbors." I murmur faintly, he nods. "I…" Inexplicably, I'm overheated and suddenly understand what a menopause hot flash must feel like. Truitt takes my hand and squeezes. He's not getting any more than that.

He bows his head, still holding my hand. "Dear Father. Thank you for this friendship, for Leah's trust and this food. Please guide us."

No admonition? Counsel? Rebuke?

He switches plates and stabs his green-speckled pasta with a fork, twirling like a hurricane in an ocean of seaweed. He tears into it like he hasn't eaten in years.

"Truitt." I can't even think about eating anymore. "Sometimes I feel like you are hiding something too."

He swallows his bite even though he barely put it in his mouth and hasn't chewed at all. I can see how slowly it moves down his throat.

"Something to do with driving," I press.

Truitt pushes his plate forward and sets down his fork. "There's nothing."

I wait, but he won't look in my eyes. I end up studying my hands. "Promise?" I ask quietly.

Our original waitress finally stops by. "Is everything all right today?

"Everything is great." Truitt looks at his watch. "But we need to order one more thing to go. Could you bring a menu?"

"Of course." She turns.

"And a few to-go boxes." He calls after her.

"Leah, would you pick something out for your dad? I need to use the restroom."

He bumps the table when he leaves.

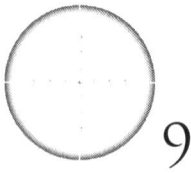9

The drive back to the church feels like unspoken promises and betrayal. Truitt holds a plastic bag filled with the Styrofoam containers of our uneaten meal.

He doesn't give a single direction once we reach highway 395. When we pull into the Faith Church parking lot, I have an upset stomach.

"Truitt?" I say after I pull the key from the ignition.

"Yes, Leah?" He stares at the bag of food.

"Is there some secret…burden you carry?"

He looks up with an impish grin. "There's nothing, Leah."

He uses his elbow to poke me but it doesn't hurt like the stab inside. Was I just imagining he had something so I didn't feel like the only one in the world with a secret sin? Am I the only one who is dirtier on the inside?

"Are you still helping me with worship tonight?"

"Will you…" I will not cry. The resolution means it takes a second before I can finish. "…tell anyone?"

"You mean about watching your neighbors?" He answers quickly. "I don't really think watching people is a sin, per say. But you are feeling guilty, that much is obvious. So the Holy Spirit might be convicting you."

But he doesn't know how I watch them.

He continues. "If you do something and it takes you away from God—makes you want to hide from him, then it is definitely something you want to remove from your life as quick as possible."

I think of the verse that talks about plucking out your eye or cutting off your hand if either causes you to sin. He's right of course. There shouldn't be anything between me and God. But it is "that nothing" that's between me and God. A vast nothing surrounding me. Hiding him. Stasis.

"Let me get this into my dad while it's still hot."

"Thank you for coming, Leah. I had fun."

I breathe in deep, suddenly aware of how shallow my breaths have been and how my lungs crave refreshment. "Thank you, Truitt." His green eyes are so bright I think of his unfinished pesto. "For lunch, for listening, for your friendship."

His mouth scrunches up into his nose and he flicks his hand, "Forgetaboutit."

I laugh, but when I look back into his eyes, he is staring at my lips. My heart picks a new pace and

I think I gasp a little.

"Race you—" He leaps from my Jeep and slams the door, "inside!" The last word is muffled because he is halfway there.

No way. I bolt and make a valiant effort. You'd think I could beat a guy carrying that much extra weight and three to-go boxes, but he is laughing and toying with me. I start to gain and then he sprints, only to slow and make me think I can catch him again. Obviously, riding your bike everywhere improves the strength and stamina of your legs.

We burst into the foyer and my dad stands sentinel with arms crossed and a stern mouth.

"Hi, Daddy." I try to regain breath and slow my hammering heart.

"Children…" He cracks a grin. His face is flushed and he has his keys in his hand.

"Did you go get lunch somewhere?" I ask.

"No." Dad looks down at his keys and then back at me. "Oh, yeah. I ran an errand."

"Here you are, sir." Truitt takes one container out and checks it. It's the pesto pasta. He hands the bag of my untouched lunch and dad's chicken sandwich to him.

"What do I owe you?"

"Nothing." Truitt turns and smiles at me. "Enjoy lunch with your daughter."

Dad takes a long, deep breath and visibly relaxes. "That sounds nice. But I only have about twenty minutes." Dad's hands are shaking and he seems out of breath.

Truitt waves and I follow Dad into his office. His eyebrows look cemented together. I fake a yawn surreptitiously. Normally I can do this and get him to yawn. This time it doesn't work.

"This is great." He mumbles into his sandwich. He's eating and we haven't even prayed. I pray in my mind. *Thank you for this day, thank you for your provision, please put a hedge of protection around me. Bless this food to my body.*

Dad's hands are smooth, his nails trimmed and clean. His shirt is pressed and tucked neatly — though I do see perspiration stains in his armpits. Even the way he sits in his chair is refined compared to Truitt. Dad doesn't look at me; he just focuses on the chicken, avocado and focaccia. He used to smile so much. His mouth is creased with the proof, but I can't remember the last time his face spilt into a genuine full-faced smile.

"I'd like to help Truitt lead worship for the college class tonight," I say as Dad finishes his last bit. "If it's all right with you." I set my unopened Styrofoam container aside and pull my braid apart, finger comb it and begin to plait it together again.

"I think that would be lovely." Dad pulls a wet wipe from his top drawer and begins to clean each hand from thumb to pinky.

"We should head up to Mount Rose and ski this weekend," I say — even though there won't be enough snow since winter has been pathetic.

Dad sits back in his chair and the smile I was

looking for reaches his eyes. "We haven't done that in awhile."

"Why didn't we get passes this year, like normal?" It was a standard Christmas stocking stuffer for years.

Dad stands and places his container carefully into the plastic bag, meticulous to not re-dirty his hands. "Honey." He said he had twenty minutes but it has been less than ten. "I don't want you to concern yourself with the things adults worry about, but things have been a little tight."

Adults? I look away even though I risk irking him by not making eye contact.

"Work…" He takes a breath like the word is medicine his taste buds reject. "Work's been hectic."

He doesn't make me look at him, he doesn't wait for me to eat, he doesn't even say good bye. He just walks out of his office and closes the door between us.

Next to dad's monitor is a framed close up of my face on the ski lift. Brilliant snow drapes the trees behind me. I always loved the pink in my cheeks and brightness of my eyes in this picture, I look like the picture of health—or like I have makeup on.

Other pictures show dad holding my nieces and nephews, hiking when we were younger, playing at the ocean. A silver frame with ornately woven edges holds one from my parents' twenty-fifth wedding anniversary when they upgraded their motorcycles to Harleys.

I go to my dad's desktop and slide into the tall leather chair. Ahh. I could sleep right here. I move his mouse and type in the password he shared so I could play solitaire.

I check Caps Lock and try again. Access still denied. I sit straight and type each keystroke purposefully, then hit backspace until I clear it and try once more just to be sure.

I'm locked out. I haven't hung out with him at work for a while, so he could have just routinely changed it—and not had a reason to tell me. How long has it been since I spent the whole day here? I focus on my parents beaming next to their "hogs."

How long has it been since everything wasn't the strained silence of my mom glaring at her painting and my dad hiding in his office?

No solitaire if I can't log in. I could sleep I guess. I'd rather install one of those gadgets from the Spy Guy...I reach behind dad's computer. The tower has a USB port in the back—so it might work to plug in the USB keystroke recorder I saw and I'd know every key he presses. I could know every password, every website, every email...

Instead, I shuffle down the hall listening to the sound of each shoe sliding across the faded, gray-blue low pile. I need to stay busy or I really will go to the spy shop and dip into the five thousand I'd saved for YWAM.

What's the point of saving it? In case I catch a husband, I can buy a couch?

I hear voices from the meeting room.

Happening by the room, tying my shoe or picking up a dropped stack of papers would offer legitimate reasons to linger. I look around for something to drop nearby.

Pastor Thompson exits his office down the hall like a he's lost, or at least bewildered.

He glances down at me, his eyes are faded like the carpet.

What has happened? I try to ask with my expression.

He says nothing and strides away holding a box and a plant. It is muffled, but the words "Dear Heavenly Father," filter from the meeting room down the hall in the other direction.

I watch the dark, vacant hall as the men who fired our pastor pray. Guitar strains drift and ebb, cascading like a gentle shoreline—it pulls me from where I stand—the rocky edge. It is Truitt I find in the college room. His eyes are closed and he hugs his guitar, unaware of a spectator.

"I don't want the world to see me, 'cause I don't think they'd understand."

I slide into a chair while he serenades what he thinks is an empty room. The earnest voice combines with the hungry lyrics and it nearly brings me to my knees. This isn't a song to God, I think this is secular music, but it is a heart crying to reach him nonetheless.

"How long have you been here?" His voice is still husky like when he sang.

"Forever." Not time-wise, but I heard that in

the lyrics down the hall.

He smiles, but there is resignation — not joy.

"What was the song called?"

"Iris." He starts strumming again. "Goo Goo Dolls. I was twelve the year this came out."

I walk over and pick up the homeless guitar which hangs out in here. I want to play too, but it's never in tune. I start to remedy that.

"It was really..." I want to say passionate, but the words drift off.

"Did you like it?"

"Was it a Christian — worship song?" I know it wasn't because of some of the lyrics.

"Don't you think any song could be switched? I mean you can worship other things than God and still sing 'I worship you.'" His voice lilts and he trails off playing for a minute. "And the very best songs could be said to a lover, or to God."

I stop tuning and stare at his hands. The few times I've turned on the radio I was disgusted by how much they sang about the sex act. I haven't heard a "very best love-song" before.

"Are you going to sing with me?" He changes from pleasant strumming to chords. "Do you know 'Yellow,' by Coldplay? Another popular one from good ol' Jr. High School era."

I don't and he smiles, happy to introduce us I guess. In a minute, everything is yellow. Not just because he keeps saying it, but because all I see is my YWAM paper. He couldn't have any idea of what it would mean to me. There has been a shift somehow. Truitt is not the dorky leader no one knows well anymore.

His humor is still here, his confidence—but now there is intensity. My yellow paper is still torn and unfolded on my desk. I haven't thrown it away. As Truitt's smile energizes me, I can't help but respond in kind. I don't break eye contact even though I feel heat creep up my neck.

My adventure, God? You haven't forgotten me.

Just please, not the scary kind.

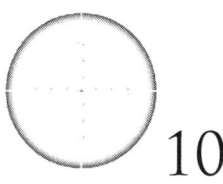

10

In twenty years my parents have taught me everything I cared to absorb about piano, guitar, backup singing, rhythm, scales...the art of swaying but not using my hips. My life's been as filled with music as the downstairs den is filled with instruments. So why does it suddenly feel like I've never heard it before?

"Close your eyes, Leah." There is light and humor in the green of his eyes.

"You sure are bossy. Stand. Sit over there. Slow down, close your eyes."

He leans over and bumps my shoulder with his. "You're starting to zone in again. Relax. Stop focusing and trying so hard. 'The people honor me with their lips but their hearts are far from me.' Don't do that, Leah."

I close my eyes.

"Let your heart be drawn."

The tempo increases but it doesn't throw me.

"Let it rest, Leah."

We're still in sync. He doesn't always lead, he lets me improvise. We sing the song "Yellow" a dozen times. I start by singing it to my yellow YWAM application, and in the end I sing it to God. Relaxed, I open my eyes.

Truitt looks like he may be singing it to me.

"Your hands are pretty."

The sound of my hand smacking the hollow wood halts the play. My hands are ugly. Big for a girl, with short, wide utilitarian nails. I hold them up and inspect. No. They're still ugly. He matches my hand in the air, barely touching.

But I still feel it.

Okay. Awkward.

I lean back and he starts playing again. His fingers slide up and down the strings and I can't help but start watching his hands. His eyes aren't closed, but he doesn't seem to be looking anywhere specifically. His light brown lashes are short, but full. That earnest, hungry sincerity I first heard when he sang the song by the Goo Goo Dolls and I came down the hall to find him returns.

He sings, "Holy, Holy, Holy" and looks upward. My arms feel weightless. The ground feels holy—I slip from my chair to sit on the floor. God is always near, but right now I want to be lower, like he is nearer than normal.

Inhibitions slip away, but I don't feel the embarrassing nakedness I felt in my dream. The harmony, the unity, my own voice: it's all noticeable, but background. God is present in a way

I've never experienced. Even while I watch others, he has been watching me. I see myself from his eyes. I am a spying sneak. But he loves me.

"Beautiful." My dad stands in the doorway and I realize I've been crying. I wipe my face with my hand and get off the floor. He walks in and gives me a kiss on my forehead. "Are you going to help Truitt lead worship tonight?"

"I asked her to." Truitt sets his guitar down and stands, like us.

"Perfect," says dad.

"Will you?" Truitt smiles at me. I cross my arms. It was nothing out of the ordinary for Dad to answer for me. But at Truitt's question I realize it was my choice. Not Dad's.

I nod and return Truitt's smile. Even though I'm returning Truitt's gaze, in my peripheral I see Dad's head shift slightly, like he is inspecting us. Truitt gives me a half wink and I know two things at once. Dad didn't see the wink, and I am blushing.

"Come on, Leah," Dad says and he steps toward Truitt to put his arm on my shoulder and guide me. Truitt has to step backward out of his way.

I spend the next hour folding bulletins in Dad's office. My foot keeps jiggling. Normally I'd take another nap right now, but I'm not tired at all. Group is about to start, I hear kids arriving, but dad hasn't released me. I hurry to finish in case finishing the bulletins is what he's waiting for.

"You sure are humming a lot." Dad has an

edge to his voice.

His irritation strikes me as funny and I smile at him.

"Finish up and you can go. Take a second to freshen up if you want." He pauses awkwardly. "Fix your hair, powder your nose." He smiles, but the attempt at humor is forced. He doesn't want me to wear make-up.

I don't mind. My fingers press creases and move in competition to the jiggle in my leg. The bulletins…they are all yellow.

***

When I return to the college room for worship, several girls await—no Truitt to be found. I know them by name only: Rachel Morgan, Kaitlin Speers, Hailey Burks or Bucks and Madison (something).

Three are whispering with wide eyes and stricken faces while Madison sits off to the side watching and occasionally leaning forward trying to get involved in the conversation. Whatever it is, it must be good.

"I think we need to pray." Hailey stands and attempts to adjust her extremely tight jeans. Rachel and Kaitlin stand immediately with murmurs of agreement. The threesome waltz away and Madison makes obvious effort not to watch them leave.

A private prayer group. Funny they couldn't pray in here. I pick up my guitar, ignoring the desire to ask Madison what the gossip was.

Liam enters. It's one of the only times I've seen him without Marta since they became a couple last fall. If he and Marta start making fun of Truitt like yesterday...

Liam stretches and roars an overly dramatic yawn. He directs his intensity at Madison like I'm not in the room. "I need coffee." His shirt pulls up during his stretch, yet he stands like an exhibitionist with low waist jeans displaying the rim of his underwear. "Madi, wanna grab some?" His auburn hair, less reddish than his dad's, flops when he tosses his head. I've never seen a girl resist Liam yet.

She glances at me and hesitates, but only for the slightest second. "Yeah." Madi grabs her purse and jumps up. She's out the door before he is. That's why I'm alone when my dad escorts Pastor King into the room.

"Leah is always where she is supposed to be."

Yeah, except yesterday when I went to the prison. My hand reaches for my wrist reflexively.

"Lovely to see you again, Leah." Pastor King rolls my name out as two words and when we shake hands he holds my fingers gently and cups my elbow. His eyes are alight with unshielded interest; his teeth are smooth and clean. I feel singled-out, honored, respected.

Truitt walks into the room blowing his nose and all attention is directed toward the noise.

"Hey." He nods and shoves a pink napkin from some past baby shower into his pocket. He sticks out his hand, changes his mind and wipes it on his jeans, then offers it again.

Pastor King takes it graciously. My dad kisses me and shakes with the pastor, prattling on about leaving the group in his capable hands. I haven't seen Dad act like this since my last nephew was born. Dad starts to leave, but steps aside to make way for Marta Miller to enter first.

Her long, dark lashes clump and frame red-rimmed eyes. She walks with her usual arched-back, head-up-grace and breezes through the room. When she lowers herself to the chair her lip quivers but she covers it with a joke. "I thought I was late but I forgot about Faith Church time."

Pastor King walks over to her and just before he bows slightly, his heels tap a tiny noise that silences the handful of additional people walking in. Marta stays seated while he takes her hand, and when he turns to greet the next person her eyes follow him continually. It's almost like I can see his charisma sweep through the room as people trickle in. The private prayer group comes back. They're carrying sodas from the soda machine.

Pastor King speaks about our effect on the community, whether or not we are reaching the lost sheep who are looking for a shepherd. When his voice softens, the group leans in. We laugh, we are subdued, we feel collective remorse—it is an emotional night for the college group.

Afterward, everyone lingers to shake Pastor King's hand—yet he takes time with each person. There is no rush for me. My dad has to lock the building so I will be last anyway. When it is only Truitt and me with the Pastor, Truitt says to him, "I'd like to speak with you."

"Very well." Pastor King answers and Truitt turns to pack up his guitar. "Do you mind, Leah?"

"Of course not." I stand, but before I turn to go, Pastor King pulls a small rectangle from his pocket. He escorts me to the door like he is the host of a dinner party and when I turn to leave he bows slightly and holds the envelope out.

"I'm glad you were here tonight." His eyes are so earnest and sincere I look back just as directly.

"Thank you." Finally, I take the envelope and turn to go.

The paper is thick and soft, almost like cotton. I roll it around in my hand, savoring the anticipation. An invitation? A personal note?

The hall goes dark. "Will you be ready soon?" My dad calls from the opposite end, his hand on the light switch.

"Yes, sir." I answer quickly, sliding the note into my Bible—right on top of the YWAM brochure Truitt gave me this afternoon.

"Take those bulletins you finished folding into the office."

"Yes, sir." I hurry to his office. Rather than finding a box, I make several trips back and forth, each time I pass the college room I glance at the light from under the door. Truitt's and the pastor's voices emanate louder on my last trip by, and as the door handle to the college room turns, I step back into the darkness of my dad's office.

Peering around the door jamb, I hold my breath. Truitt looks like he has rubbed sandpaper across his face and then splashed water on his cheeks. He wipes at a tear and they shake hands. Pastor King pats his shoulder and they walk away together.

So he does have a secret.

My dad and Pastor King say their goodbyes while I continue to hide. Now the note rests in my pocket and I turn it over, touching each corner. At last it is just Dad and me. I carry the remaining stack of bulletins to the office and hurry to the women's restroom. I can't wait any longer, but I won't risk opening the note when my dad is in the room.

My heart speeds as I flip it over. Both sides are blank. I slid my finger under the flap and remorsefully tear open the envelope. The paper is as cottony as the envelope and an embossed BK adorns the top of the note card.

*Leah,*

*Your father has expressed intent that I pursue you for courtship. His heart is good — he cares for you.*

*However, I did not want you to be caught unaware and I would like your blessing first. I have been invited to your house for dinner on Friday. If you would*

*consider getting to know me better, please wear green or*
*blue and I will see it as a signal.*
    *Yours Truly,*
    *BK*

Dad is quiet in the car, which is fine with me. I slide my fingers up and down the note card in my pocket. It was agreed that my parents would help guide me when they found someone acceptable for me to court. Maybe it took this long because it just wasn't time yet.

What do you have to say, God?

I slide the note back into my Bible next to the brochure that made me tear up when Truitt handed it to me.

I feel strangely detached from the situation. This is the way it is supposed to be, I know. No emotions getting involved. I'm glad for that. And I am pleased that Pastor—Barkley, I mean, sought my approval.

Maybe the question now: is God guiding me through my parents?

And another: if God's plan actually is marriage—will my desire for YWAM fade?

Dad pulls into the garage, gets out and approaches the door to the house before I'm all the way out of the car. Mom stands in the doorway to the house with her shoulders slumped and arms crossed. She looks very small. My temples and the back of my neck begin to tingle when I see her widened, childlike eyes—but not as much as when she speaks.

"We've been robbed."

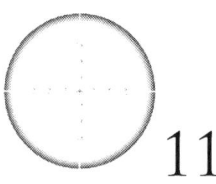

11

"What makes you say that?" Dad steps around her, watching where he places his feet. He walks through the entry way and sets down his leather satchel by the hall tree bench. Dad unbuttons his collar and raises one eyebrow at Mom. "Any there signs of forced entry?"

This thought seems to only now occur to Mom and she darts past Dad to their bedroom. "I didn't even look." She calls on her way.

I peer around the corner to see Mom lifting the curtains to check the French doors.

"We haven't been robbed." Dad slips each foot from a shoe and sits in the glider in the corner of their room. He rubs each foot and lays his head back.

"My grandmother's ring…" Mom is crying as she lifts the lid to her jewelry box, "…and the rubies you gave me for our twentieth."

Dad sits upright. "Did you check the dish by the sink?"

"You know I don't wear either of those things around the house. They're only for special occasions—when I'm not going to be doing dishes!"

"We'll replace them."

"Are you kidding?" Mom checks the French doors one more time. "First off, heirlooms are not replaceable. Second, we don't have money lately to go out somewhere nice enough for me to wear them. How are we going to replace them?"

I glide out of their bedroom and head upstairs to the main living area, bedrooms and office. The table is set and a ceramic dish of tuna casserole sits on a trivet in the center. Cold.

While my parents yell at each other, I systematically walk through the house checking windows and the glass slider on the upstairs deck. Fortunately, the deck does not have stairs leading to the ground or I wouldn't sleep up here alone. Opening and closing blinds leads to opening and closing cupboards. When I find myself in front of Mom's glass display cabinet I feel as though I am guided to look. I put everything away last Thanksgiving when my sisters and brother and all their families ate here. Since I'm unmarried, I'm the only "child" left; the grandkids are too small, so I polished the silverware alone.

Before I open the cabinet door I sense they're missing and I'm correct. In place of the silver flatware box is a stack of hand towels which belong in the kitchen. I swallow to ease the sudden, dry-roughness in my throat.

My parents are still fighting. I don't feel in the mood for tuna casserole so I make myself a bowl of cereal for dinner. They aren't here to tell me what to eat — in fact I think I'll eat it on the couch, or maybe even in my bedroom.

I stretch out on my mattress and place the empty puffed cereal bowl on my nightstand. The yelling has subsided and I pull out my laptop. They'll be up for dinner soon so I can't get on the telescope. I lay back and open a browser.

I type: "home security spy camera."

Who knew there were so many ways to incorporate surveillance in the average American lifestyle?

Just as I am about to re-read the email from Ava, Dad fills the doorway. He wears his black leather vest and dark jeans. Good. They're done fighting. "Leah?"

"Yes, sir?"

"Your mom and I are going for a ride."

"Okay." I close the laptop and set it aside. "Dad, I…" His shoulders drop and his head looks too heavy for him to hold up. "What is it?"

If I mention the silver now… "Nothing. Well, I'll probably be asleep when you get back." This is a full blown lie but it's for his sake.

"Clean the kitchen for your mom first." He pulls at the vest to adjust it. He doesn't fill it out like he used to. "Your mom and I will probably grab In and Out."

Fast food? Mom must be really mad. I

definitely better not say anything about the silver.

"No problem." I rise from my bed to go put away the table. "Dad?"

He turns but doesn't answer.

"Lock the door behind you."

"You're safe here, Leah. No one's going to hurt you," he says this abruptly, with the dad-voice that bodes no argument.

"I know I am, Dad." Another lie.

I have the dishes put away by the time I hear a Harley fire up. Mom has her own, but only one leaves the garage. I wrap plastic over the uneaten casserole, put it in the fridge and walk directly to my telescope.

*** 

The waiter and his wife are fighting again. Every time she leaves a room, that I can see, he follows. They come back into the kitchen. She is crying and pointing. She pushes him and he slaps her face. They both stand staring at each other in bewilderment. I'm just as surprised, they've never fought physical before. Her hand cradles her left cheek but he just turns and walks away. She grabs a cup from the counter and hurls it across the room then slides down to cry with her face on her knees. After a time, she rises and closes all the blinds.

It hasn't felt like winter yet this year, but it is January and Mom and Dad have been gone for hours. I pace the house, checking locks and pulling curtains tight. I double check all the windows and my parent's French doors. My mom's jewelry box lid is still open and I poke around, looking at her treasures. A few times she let me play in this as a girl.

I start sliding drawers open and closed, glancing inside. My parents keep their drawers impeccably neat — just like everything else in their house. I wander through rooms looking in cupboards, wondering if anything else will be missing. I end up in Dad's office. He has the nicest leather office chair, and I sit down and listen. Only the hum of his computer interrupts the silence of the house. I never wander at night while I am awake because I am afraid the creak of walking above their bedroom will wake my parents.

Dad's computer has a pass lock now. I see why he might need one a work — but he never had one at home before. I push back from the chair and look around the desk for possible clues. The room seems different, off balance somehow.

Two of his drawers have new key locks. Maybe that's what's new. Very new, if the tiny pile of wood shaving dust on the floor is an indicator. The top drawer on the right does not have one so I open it looking for a password notebook, keys, anything.

The garage door hums about the time I realize there is nothing helpful in the drawer. I jump up and rearrange the chair and desk to look the same as when I arrived. There's a pile I didn't notice before. Two small boxes labeled "Chrome Door" and "Cabinet Keyed Lock" and an electric drill rest on the chair I used last night when he told me not to cast my pearls before swine.

And I thought he went to sleep after he sent me to bed.

I speed down the hall to my room so I won't have to see my parents. It isn't worth my bother because they make almost no noise and head straight for their bedroom. I get ready for bed and stretch across my duvet. My ceiling light is turned off but there is enough illumination from the closet to see. Before me I spread my Bible, the YWAM brochure from Truitt, the torn yellow application and Barkley's note card. With clear scotch tape I repair the application and lay them all across my duvet.

I read through each one hoping for some sign from God—some sensation or feeling.

"Thank you for this day, thank you for your provision, please put a hedge of protection around me. Please guide me."

After about thirty minutes of staring and praying, the downstairs shower kicks on. I stack the papers together and roll over. Maybe tonight I'll sleep.

Maybe not. I know better than to watch the clock so I don't know how much time has passed. I still hover awake between decisions, desires, demands: my life in perfect stagnation. Predictably, I go to the telescope and see if others are the same.

***

Mom sleeps later and later these days. I don't normally get going until ten or ten-thirty, but here I am showered, dressed, filled with a large omelet... Mom still isn't up and it's almost noon. I wander around the house. I'm bored, but glad I don't have to spend another day at the church—even if Truitt made it more fun than I can remember having there.

I return to my laptop and search spy gadgets and tricks. Mostly I find online stores hawking their wares, but I also find a television show about spies that interests me: *Burn Notice*.

Who knows how many more hours I'll have to occupy? I pull up Netflix and start the series. "My name is Michael Weston. I used to be a spy..."

And so progresses the week: sleepless nights, mom rising after noon and going to bed early, both of us napping all day, dad hiding in his office or the two of them fighting, and me alternately watching my neighbors or the spy TV series *Burn Notice* through the night.

Suddenly it's Friday.

"Would you like to go shopping today?" I pull down my earphones to see if I heard mom correctly.

"Shopping?" She has a little makeup on and looks very awake for eleven in the morning. I didn't even know she owned makeup. What would dad say?

"Yes, we have company coming for dinner and I wondered if you would like a new dress."

Pastor King: *Please wear green or blue and I will see it as a signal.*

Green, like Truitt's eyes.

I had several outfits planned ranging in color from blues and greens to reds and yellows. I still haven't decided.

"Yes, Mom. I'd like that." Last time we went shopping was for Easter dresses last year. Well, shopping from a catalog. "Let me shower."

"Hurry, because we need to get a few groceries and start the meal."

The department store is frustrating. We never bothered to look in the juniors' section—but even here in women's, why is it so difficult to find a dress that covers both shoulders and knees?

"What about this, Mom?" I wish we had ordered something. I'm not just tired of shopping—I'm just tired. My mom hasn't spent this much time awake in weeks. She's got to be exhausted.

"We can try it on, but I think the material will be too clingy like that other one."

That clingy one was surprisingly similar to pajamas—if it had been any color besides screaming look-at-me-red, I'd have wanted it. I hold up two similar versions of a dress. One is blue and one is yellow. The yellow one is a little short.

"Oh, those are nice."

Blue: heaven, twilight, sleep…Barkley.

Yellow: joy, sunshine, life…adventure.

"Try them both on, Leah."

"Yes, ma'am."

"You know, Leah…" She takes the dresses from my hands. "You don't have to say 'yes ma'am' when it's just the two of us." Her shoulders sag like the dresses are weighty.

"Yes, Mom." I smile and she nudges me with her elbow.

"This is fun," she says over her shoulder. I follow her to the dressing room. "I hope soon we can shop like this for your trousseau. When you get married—everything you wear should be new. Inside and out." Her cheeks turn a little pinker.

"That would be reason enough to get married."

She laughs and I'm so pleased she saw it for the joke I meant.

"There are other reasons." A loud beep signals that we have passed the threshold into the dressing rooms.

"Like what?" I ask, flushed. Embarrassed to be so near the topic of copulation. She hands me both dresses and studies my face.

"The Bible says it's not good for man to be alone," and then, just like she is used to listing the reasons for a Sunday school class, "to create a godly legacy…have children."

I'm biting my lip pretty hard. She sighs.

"Because there is nothing greater than having someone know you completely and love you anyway."

In my head I know God knows me completely and still loves me—but it would be nice if a human did.

I step back into the dressing room and lock the door. There are two hooks near each other and I hang the dresses side by side while I remove my boots and jean jumper. I lift a hanger and slide it out of the dress I really want.

"And it would be pretty miserable—" My mom's voice is quiet and not just because I'm pulling my clothes off and over my head. "To spend your whole life alone."

I sigh and pick up the blue dress instead.

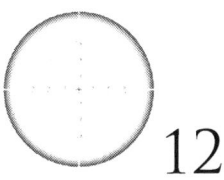

12

"I'm sorry sweetie. Do you have another credit card?"

My mom grimaces, she hates when strangers call her sweetie, darlin' or sugar. "Run it again." Mom holds her bag tightly.

"I ran it twice, honey. But okay." The thin thirty-something pushes a plastic coil bracelet with dangling keys up her pale, freckled arm. "Nope. Still rejected. I can't see why—just that it doesn't work."

"Here, Mom, I'll pay."

"No. I wanted to buy it." Mom takes the card back like it might be infected and hands the attendant her ATM.

It doesn't work either and I hand over my ATM card.

"Perfect, sweetie," the clerk chirps.

I wink at my mom and whisper for her alone, "Sure thing, snookums."

When the girl turns around with the slip for

my mom's signature I'm sure we have ridiculous grins on our faces, but we hold laughter until we are at least ten steps from the door.

We stop at the grocery store and I feel like I am ten years old and our homeschool field trip is grocery shopping. It hasn't just been months since my parents were happy—as I keep the grocery balance in my head and mom and I plan dinner, I realize—it's been years. It wasn't just because Ava left either. It was after that. Was it Anne-Marie's wedding? Could my parent's unhappiness be because I haven't yet found a husband?

At home, I make the crème brûlée first so it has time to chill in the fridge. Next, I knead a loaf of French bread while mom boils the conchiglioni shell pasta, browns the sausage for stuffing and roasts peppers for the sauce.

"How are you going to wear your hair?" Mom jerks her hand from the cast iron skillet handle and runs it under cold water.

"I guess I hadn't thought about it." I take over sautéing the roasted peppers, onions and garlic while she deals with her burn.

"I'll be fine—you go shower." Mom grabs the wooden spoon from my hands and tugs my braid. "Try wearing it down."

"It's just so frizzy."

"I have a bottle of mousse under my bathroom sink." She's acting overtly nonchalant. "Try putting a handful in your wet hair instead of brushing it."

I shrug and nod on my way out. "Are you sure?"

"Go. I can finish up dinner." She winks.

I start to leave but then turn and hug my mom. "Thank you." She probably thinks I mean for the shopping trip. Sometimes you don't realize someone has changed until you have a reminder of who they were.

I grab the hair mousse from downstairs and take the steps two at a time.

"The Visa." Mom sounds barely controlled speaking into the phone. "Of course I had them run it twice."

In her listening pause I shuffle to my room and shut the door. There's movement at Lucas' house and I set the mousse down on my way to inspect. It isn't quite as easy to see in the daylight as it is at night with interior lightning. Still, I can tell what's going on. Lucas is with someone again. Only, this time it is so shocking—I don't look away. I can't.

Shame pours over me. My mom yells into the phone from the kitchen. It's muffled through my closed door, but I hear the amount totals we spent today shouted like curses or indictments. With that as background noise I watch all the way to the end, until Lucas is finished. When I close my eyes, the sight of two men coupling stays imprinted in my mind.

I shower until my skin feels squeaky, dry, leached. What did I expect? I was looking into people's lives for secrets. I'm sorry, God. I cover myself with my robe and return to my room. With hair plastered to my face I spin the focuser dial on the telescope and lower the adjustable legs to collapse it down. I move the entire thing to my closet and close my blinds.

It isn't until I'm smearing mousse over my head in the mirror that I realize I'm crying. I won't do it again. I won't spy. I grab a dozen squirts of oatmeal lotion and start in on my hands and arms to ease the dryness of my skin. You'd think since I was born in Nevada and lived in zero to five-percent humidity my whole life, I'd be used to it. I lie down on top my bed with a cool, damp washcloth over my eyes, hoping it will reduce the swelling, and pray for forgiveness.

I wake to a hand on my shoulder and my mother's voice. "You fell asleep?"

I dreamed again that I was naked, just like I did at the church, but it is closer to the truth since I only wear a robe. It's dark in my room. The sun sets by five-thirty in February but the lack of light makes me disoriented.

"Did I miss dinner?"

"You're shivering." Mom folds the cloth I'd put on my face. "Did you have a headache?"

"I think I took too hot of a shower." Mom has never questioned my napping—since she normally sleeps more than me.

"Dad called, they're leaving the church now."

"Oh." I sit suddenly. "I'm sorry I didn't help with dinner."

"It's all under control." Mom places a hand on my forehead. "Are you sure you feel all right?"

"I'm fine." I scoot away from her and turn on the bedroom light. She looks all over the room but if she notices the missing telescope she doesn't say.

"Oh Leah, your hair is beautiful down." I turn into the bathroom and flip on the light. The curls are uniform and shiny even though I slept on them. I look like a different person than with the customary French braid pulled over my shoulder.

"Like a woman instead of a girl," Mom says as she stands in the bathroom doorway.

I do feel like a little of my innocence is gone, but not from my hairstyle. "Let me get ready, Mom."

She looks hurt but I don't care. I want to be alone. I hear my bedroom door latch and then put on a slip and nylons. My reflection isn't bad — though I am suddenly wishing my parents weren't so against makeup. A little blush or lip gloss would be nice. Trying to add pinkness, I bite my lips and pinch my cheeks then add a little more lotion to the dry spots all over. There's the front door — I can stall no longer. I pull the dress over my head, slip on some shoes and leave my bedroom.

Dad doesn't greet Mom at all. When they see each other she mumbles and turns to the kitchen.

"Leah!" he says. "You look beautiful in blue, and your hair..."

I start to say thanks, but my voice fails me when I see the appreciation in Pastor King's dark eyes. The warmth I feel shooting from my abdomen flares at my cheeks and temples. I guess it is a good thing I'm not wearing any unnatural blush.

"It is the most beautiful shade." His compliment bolsters me in a way I've never felt.

Smack. Dad's loud clap seems to wake us. "I'll see if your mom needs any help. Leah, will you give Pastor King a tour?"

"Of course." I open my arms. "This is our living room." He laughs like I am truly funny and not as idiotic as I feel. He follows me down the hall. "Here is the upstairs bathroom. Our guest room. My dad's office." I open the doors. "This is my room." I don't open the door. "You already saw the living room."

"Truly marvelous," he interrupts. Truitt would have burst out laughing after he said that, but Barkley used it seriously.

"The kitchen." I point where my parents are hiding as I head for the stairs. While reaching for the stair light my shoe catches the side of his. One arm slips around my waist and a hand cups my shoulder. He pulls me to his chest and I don't fall, but feeling the length of him pressed behind me makes me feel as though I am not touching the earth. I turn my head to the right and look up into his eyes. He trails a finger down the side of my face to move a curl. His left hand is still around my waist and I feel the heat of his skin through my pajama-like material. It makes me wonder if I am dreaming.

"I don't think I've seen a more beautiful color." His voice is so low and intimate it feels like it rumbles through me, inside my head and chest. When he steps away and offers his arm I hear my own breath begin to work as it should, automatically.

We walk down the stairs with my hand resting on his forearm and covered by his fingers. They are warm and smooth, darker than mine, and like him, beautiful.

I show him the garage and Harleys. He raises his eyebrows at the bikes but then mostly looks at me. I show him my parent's bedroom and the den downstairs which holds musical instruments. I show him my mother's painting.

"It's called 'Captivity.'" I wait for his reaction. "The artist who most influenced her was Jean Millet. It has the same delicate, hazy quality as his 'Walk to Work.' Are you familiar with…" When I turn to see if he is interested or I am just babbling, he has moved into my body space. One stair down from me, our faces are aligned. I feel the warmth of his pleasant breath. He has one hand on the railing and one on the wall. His pupils are so dark that I'm not sure — but it almost looks like they are dilated.

"Leah, you look so beautiful." He reaches out and puts his hands on my sides below my waist, pulling me back toward him. "I'm honored that you wore blue." No one has ever touched me like this — directed my hips to move my whole body. It fills me with both a surge of thrill and warning. It's ironic how trapped I feel, like the woman in the picture hanging above. I start to stumble backwards, up the stairs.

I push his hands back toward him. "Your note asked me to wear blue if I would consider getting to know you better." He turns his head to the side with a knowing smile. I continue. "We are not yet courting. All I've done is agree to consider it."

He bows his head in that regal way and when I turn to walk upstairs I have the most powerful sensation that I am naked to him. He doesn't begin to mount the stairs until I've reached the top. I do not wait for him.

He watched me the entire way.

***

"Dinner was delicious, my dears." Dad pats mother's hand and turns an approving look on me. Their affection and manners indicate they live in bliss. They're certainly pleased with me tonight. I don't feel like I've ever made them prouder. They've done nothing but wear delighted smiles and list my praise and accomplishments for over an hour. Mom didn't even notice I set the table with the regular silverware tonight.

Pastor King really seems like a king the way he sits tall, eats with perfection and offers benevolence and condescension with words.

Mom and I stand to clear the table. Dad brings his own plate while Pastor King stretches back and says, yet again, "What a fine meal."

When I enter the kitchen with mom and dad, he sets his plate on the counter and pulls her into a hug. I hear soft words of apology and forgiveness. They turn to me with shimmering, glowing visages.

In their eyes I am already married to the pastor, and their pride in me opens a gulf between us. I don't want to be approved for this—as much as I don't want to disappoint them.

"Time for the crowning jewel of the evening." Mom rinses her hands and walks to the fridge.

"Did Leah make dessert?" My dad places his hand on my shoulder.

Mom pauses as though she expects a drum roll. "Crème brûlée."

This was what I have always planned: to leave the covering of my father for the covering of a husband, to allow my parents—in their wisdom—the influence to guide me toward a godly man. To trust God with the details of my future.

Why do I feel like I ate bad shellfish?

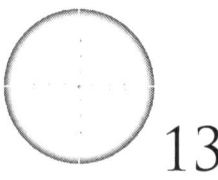

13

After Pastor King leaves, Mom and Dad go for another motorcycle ride. I think they're celebrating. They tell me not to worry about the kitchen, but I'm staying away from my bedroom. The Orion Space Probe feels like a tender pimple that isn't quite ready to surface. I want it out and cleaned but I'm afraid the infection will just make a mess.

After I check all the doors to make sure they're locked, I scrub every dish, preferring to hand wash rather than use the dishwasher. The counters are cleaned with antibacterial spray — I even used window cleaner on the appliances after I hand-dried and put away dishes. My blue dress is wet from the splashing suds and my hands are blotchy from the soap and chemicals.

I don't want to snoop through the house or my dad's office tonight. I don't want to find or see anything that isn't for me. I start to walk toward my room since I have nothing left to clean but myself.

My hand rests on the closed door and the images of loving and fighting come writhing back. If I go in there now — will I end up pulling out the telescope? I can watch more vivid escapades on cable — is it so wrong to peer into a real person's life?

What would Truitt say?

How strange it is that I wonder about his opinion: not my dad's, the pastor's...even Hayden's. Worshiping God with Truitt earlier this week — the pleasure lasted for days. When I compare Hayden and Truitt I realize Truitt knows more about me than I ever shared with Hayden. In fact, I didn't really know anything about Hayden other than what I imagined.

Maybe my infatuation fermented into something more than it really was. All it needed was a little heat or light to turn my grape juice for Hayden into vinegar instead of wine.

My feelings for Truitt are anything but wine. He's just a friend.

"The people honor me with their lips, but their hearts are far from me." The longing to worship God like that again draws and soothes. In all these years of singing I never actually worshiped. I knew that though — the revelation is that I didn't really understand what worship was.

I head to the music room downstairs. I want to sing, but I also want to play my dad's Goodall guitar. I flip on the light. The room looks the same as when Pastor King glanced inside, feigning interest.

His attentions are a compliment. I might have seemed forward by wearing a solid blue dress. It was probably like screaming "yes" to him. Perhaps he was not inappropriate, just responding to my invitation. Hayden and I never actually courted or expressed intent, so I don't know what the rules are like when acted out.

My dad's guitar is not here. I picture the light cocoa color and the clear, woody sound. I want to play that instrument more than any other. My dress is still damp, my hands still chafed, and irritation niggles. Nothing else will do but that guitar.

The den doesn't have a closet so it takes almost no time at all to verify that it isn't here. In fifteen minutes I feel like I've exhausted every possibility in our house. It isn't at home, but I'm sure it isn't at the church either. My stomach hurts again. Dad has always been adamant, ridiculously obstinate—since cedar scars easily—that his "forty-five hundred dollar guitar" never leaves the house.

*** 

A few other things have turned up missing over the weekend. A few first-print hardback books I was never allowed to read when I was a child. Other things seem to be gone—but I'm not sure—like power tools. Maybe we got rid of more things than I remember when we downsized to this house after Anne-Marie married.

Fortunately, I was able to skip on first service

again. I could do no wrong since Friday's dinner with Barkley. The kitchen clock is thirteen minutes fast so I only have...I try to do the math—time, clock...

Suddenly I know what was off balance in my dad's office last week. I race into the room I've avoided for days. The glass wall-display cabinet holding my dad's Civil War pocket watch has been replaced with an ornate wood frame holding one of my mom's paintings. There is the slightest difference in the taupe paint since the frame does not cover as much space as the display box did.

I look around the room and study the neatness. The watch was worth less than a thousand dollars—but to my dad it represented the legacy of a family who knew God. Precious metal passed down, rewarded to the next generation each time one chose to follow the Lord.

How often he has compared his legacy to the one mom brought of brokenness in her "Captivity" painting. He would never part with his.

I sink into my dad's computer chair and stifle the urge to cry. It's so obvious now, a blight on the wall. I rest my head back on the smooth leather and the office chair eases back slightly. I want to look in his computer, search his files, pull out my telescope and learn why Lucas will have intimate relations with anything that moves.

If my dad doesn't know who took the stuff— then someone has been in our house. The realization speeds my pulse and now I can't get to church fast enough. I don't want to be alone here in case they come back.

I take a long route, drive by the Spy Shop and forget to watch the time. When I arrive, Sunday school has already started. In fact, it's nearly over. But I don't mind or rush, I like to walk the halls when they are empty more than when they are filled.

If Christ's church is the people, why do I prefer the vacant building?

In the foyer there is a four-foot by eight-foot board on a stand with a thermometer titled "building project." We're fundraising now?

I stop near the college room and listen to Pastor King's lyrical cadence. He's telling the story about how he used to stutter again. I don't think I'm being dramatic when I say I can sense the energy of the room from out here.

Rounding the corner I see Pastor Thompson as he disappears into the office. How weird that he would stay after the board let him go. The halls are otherwise strangely quiet, not that I am normally out here during Sunday school.

"I wondered if you were coming today." His voice is just like I remembered.

"Truitt." He gives me an awkwardly earnest side-hug.

"Are you skipping Sunday school?" His eyes are not as green as normal under the flickering fluorescents, unless something else is causing the dullness. I'm still standing close from the side hug and I smell a harsh combination of body odor and cologne. He's stressed.

"I didn't plan on skipping."

"I brought you something." He smiles and winks. I think it makes me blush again like when he did it in front of my dad.

"Lead away."

I follow him to the kitchen where two large, white cups with straws sit on the counter. The straws are in the cups but have the paper sleeve still covering the very tops.

"Almond butter." He extends an arm with the title then pulls back and holds out the other arm. "Grape float. You pick first. I didn't drink any."

My mouth waters at his words—I didn't have any breakfast. "You're going to make me fat." I reach out and take the almond butter milkshake and slip off the paper.

"Sorry." He looks down at his cup but doesn't drink.

He looks so sincere I take a dramatic drink. "Oh, this is good."

"We can go for a bike ride sometime to make up for it." He takes a drink now but studies me with his next words. "Hayden and I used to ride all the time."

I swallow my mouthful. "Truitt," I linger on his name for emphasis, "I'd really like that."

"Cool." He holds up his Styrofoam drink for a toast and I meet his with my own. "Ching." He sings out the word.

"So what's with the building project board?"
I ask. There's a little table in the kitchen and we sit
down across from each other.

"Pastor King is starting a bunch of new
things." Truitt's leg jumps up and down. He looks
away from me.

"This bugs you?" He doesn't answer right
away, so I reach across the table and bump his hand
with my fist lightly. Truitt glances up and I see
almost sadness in his green eyes. He nods. After a
pause I say, "Pastor Thompson's still here." It comes
out as a statement even though I meant to ask.

"Yeah." Truitt sips and turns to me. "He
thought that he should stay even though he is no
longer the pastor. He said it would be godly to keep
the unity and just be part of the church. Just a
member    as    the    church    comes    under    new
leadership."

"The old pastor stay? But not teach?"

"Well," Truitt scratches his chin and his
speech speeds. "He was going to teach Sunday
school like normal, but no one went into his class."
Truitt glances side to side and leans forward. "There
are these little pockets of people studying the Bible
on their own instead of going into his class—but
mostly, everyone went into the college room. Pastor
King's class is packed. People were sitting on the
floor."

"Pastor King's teaching your class now?"

Truitt interrupts a drink to answer me. "I
went to get chairs and when I came back, King had

already started." Truitt lifts his cup higher in salute. "Liam and Madison were sneaking off to get coffee, so I hitched a ride and talked them into Deux Gros Nez."

He took Liam and Madison to Deux Gros Nez. I look down at my hands so he won't see my face. I'd rather no one else knew about it but Truitt and me. As Liam cycles through the girls in group — they'll all know eventually.

"So, last I saw — Pastor Thompson was sharpening pencils and walking around the church. Basically, he was keeping busy and looking lost." Truitt takes his plastic lid off and tilts his head back, using his straw to shovel in a mouthful. "I'm not sure how I feel about..." Truitt trails off.

"Pastor Thompson staying?" I offer.

Truitt shakes his head no as he slurps the last of his drink. "In theory, that is good."

In theory.

"You know, most of the board has been holding their own Bible studies during the main service for weeks now."

"Even my dad?" I'm full so I pass my cup to Truitt.

"Are you sure you're done?" He takes my milkshake and switches straws.

"Was my dad holding private Bible studies instead of attending Pastor Thompson's Sunday school?"

"Yeah." Truitt looks away. "I actually saw this coming. There's a business meeting today after church, for the whole congregation."

"What are they going to announce? That they fired the pastor?"

Truitt pushes my cup away like he's had enough, too. "They want to announce that Pastor Thompson is living in sin. Unfit to shepherd." Our voices have hushed even more and I scoot closer. Truitt's breath is warm. Which is good because the shake — or something — has given me the chills.

"Announce it? What's Pastor Thompson doing?" I picture myself standing in the middle of the college room. The idea is more than just something similar to the dream I've had twice now. It's the worst thing I could imagine — I'm wearing a lovely gown but when I look down I see that it is completely transparent. I am naked in front of everyone.

"Bethany is pregnant," Truitt says quietly.

His daughter? "She's away at UNLV." Pastor Thompson was so sad when his only child chose Las Vegas for school instead of remaining here in Reno. I would have jumped at the chance to go to college anywhere. A charged silence surges.

"They want me to bring the accusation."

"You?" I look around the kitchen. It's still empty.

"Me." He lifts his hands with a little laugh.

"You can't do that." If Truitt stands pointing at the Pastor — will he turn on me next? Good thing I was vague when I told him I "watch" my neighbors, that I never mentioned the telescope.

"I don't want to do it. They're using the verse: If a man cannot manage his own family, how can he lead the church?"

"Who are 'they'?"

Truitt wets his lips with his tongue. "She's an adult, you know. At what point is she responsible for her own actions? She hasn't lived at home for four and a half years. That's the 'vacation' he took. He and Laura went to go see her."

"Truitt, who are 'they'?" I repeat.

His chin dimples with a pressed frown. "Your dad."

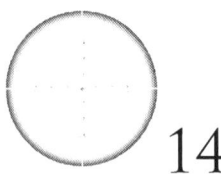 14

I'm shaking my head. "You...you can't do this."

Truitt looks pale, his eyes are still the dull green I noticed when I first saw him. "I don't want to."

"I mean it, Truitt. You have to say what you just said and stand up for him. Take Pastor Thompson and Laura's side. Be their advocate instead of their accuser."

"The whole board is in on it. They've already cast the vote, Leah—now it's just time to inform the church."

"But why do you have to make the accusation?"

"I'm the only part of the leadership who didn't vote. They want the leadership to be unanimous. They want us all in this together."

"What are you two doing in here alone?" My dad's arms cross over his chest, his legs are planted a shoulder's width apart and he looks at our table over the bridge of his nose.

I jump up, guilty for being alone in a room with someone I'm not married to. Good thing the door was open. Truitt stands respectfully, albeit a little bewildered. He takes both cups and starts toward the trash. "We were just drinking shakes and getting ready for the service," Truitt says.

"Well, it's time to go. Come on." My dad turns and leads, we follow.

"Don't do it," I mouth to Truitt as we follow my dad.

Truitt acknowledges my words with an eyebrow lift and tense lips instead of a reply.

In the sanctuary, the microphones—which normally grace the stage for the worship team—sit stacked at the side. The glass pulpit is also pushed to the side. Dad points to the first row and Truitt and I obediently sit.

"Be ready for your announcement." Dad indicates toward Truitt, and then leaves us. He marches to where Mr. Blake stands like a guard by the side door marked with a red exit sign. Then he heads toward the back. Hardly anyone is here yet.

"I never wanted to be a leader," Truitt says quietly. "I didn't want to be involved in this kind of thing." His breath is shallow.

"Maybe you were put in here for such a time as this." I quote the passage from Esther: the noble queen who had to trust in God and use her position to save a nation. I reach over and place my hand on his. He rolls his palm up and interlocks his fingers with mine. His hand is cold.

"Pray, Leah."

"I am."

The sanctuary fills.

The buzz of conversation ceases uncommonly quick as my dad and Pastor King walk down the aisle to the front. They mount the stairs and turn to the sanctuary. Truitt squeezes my hand tighter. My dad doesn't look at us but I hope he does—that he sees our hands interlaced and knows our allegiance. I feel almost strong enough to face my dad with Truitt beside me. I crane my neck looking for my mother. Where is she?

Pastor King reverently bows his head. My dad begins to speak. "We will not have regular service today. We have an announcement." There are a few murmurs, but as soon as Pastor King raises his hand, a hush falls. "Truitt, I believe you have something to say," Pastor says.

Truitt trembles, but he lets go of my hand and stands. "I do not."

My dad jerks his head back in surprise, but recovers so quickly, I wonder if he expected it. My dad makes the announcement then. "Damon and Laura Thompson are not fit to serve our body in a leadership capacity."

I turn with the whole church to where Pastor Thompson and his wife sit. She has her head in her hands, weeping. His jaw flexes like he's grinding his teeth.

"It's not going to go down like this. We were

supposed to wait for the business meeting. After."
Eric Blake yells from the side of the room. It is so
unusual to hear noise from this direction. Tears start
in my eyes at the discordance. I turn back to the
podium, thinking how the glass is see-through, like
my dress in my dream, so that anyone who stands
behind only has a semblance of covering.

Dad, don't trust it, we'll be exposed.

And then I see it. Something stands behind
the pulpit. Some ethereal figure. He isn't looking at
me, but I'm afraid to look away because he was not
there before. If I look away, will I lose track of him?
Will he show somewhere else? I feel like I've been
swaddled too tightly and am secured to my seat.

"You don't belong here." I don't think I say it
aloud but it squeaks from me nonetheless.

He turns his head to me and even though he
doesn't speak audibly or with a moving mouth I
hear the reply: "You don't think so?"

I feel embarrassed, not fearful — more like I'm
the one who doesn't belong.

"It is going down like this." The
congregation hushes at Pastor King's microphone-
augmented tone even though it doesn't really sound
like him. He steps directly in front of the pulpit and
I can no longer see the spirit. Even Mr. Blake
becomes subdued. King points to my dad to speak.

I like to think my dad is hesitant, but maybe
he just pauses for effect. "Damon Thompson cannot
manage his own family. He and Laura have just
returned from a trip to visit their daughter and

confirmed that Bethany is pregnant with an illegitimate child."

"You can't—" Mr. Blake begins to speak but Pastor King takes over.

"Neither can he manage this church, for he has hired both adulterers and murderers as his council."

"I have not." Pastor Thompson stands to speak. Several women are crying now.

"Erik Blake's computer is filled with pornography." Pastor King stands in front of the church with his arm extended toward Liam's dad. "Do you deny it?"

Mr. Blake leans back to the wall, his normal ruddy color fading into the eggshell paint.

"And Truitt Ridgemann killed a pregnant woman while she pushed a stroller."

The shock on Truitt's face proves the accusation. Through my tears I see so many shapes—I can't tell who are from the natural and who live in the spiritual realm in this chaos. I blink several times to meet Truitt's eyes—he cries too.

But he also nods.

*** 

"Mom, go lay down." She shuffles like her feet are too heavy to lift.

The phone rings. "Don't—"

"You don't want me to answer it?" I hold the door to the garage open as I ask.

"Just don't." Her arm sags like she can't drag her purse up to her shoulder. I take it from her and ignore the ringing.

"Here, Mom. Let's go in your room." She nods again, but there was never any question—since she became a jellyfish in the car—I needed to get her in her bed. "Why don't you lie down?"

The phone starts up again and she turns to me fearfully. "Please don't answer it."

"I won't, Mom. Don't worry." I put my hand on her shoulder and she feels smaller than I remember. Not just the weight she's lost—but even her shoulders seem less broad than mine. I unplug the phone from the jack and she melts into her bed like fondue.

I want to ask her to stand so I can pull covers up and tuck her in, but I think better of trying to move her. Instead, I pull the comforter from Dad's side over her.

The phone begins again, but it's muffled from upstairs. I check her French doors and close her bedroom door. She is already asleep.

I look out into the garage to make sure the automatic door went all of the way down and I lock the door to the garage. The trill of another call increases as I climb the stairs. I was the last one here this morning and I look around the living room to make sure nothing is different. While we are at church would be a perfect time for the person robbing us. I check the windows even though the house seems unmolested.

Quiet, phone! I'll not answer anyone's questions or feed their curiosity—and Mom is pretty much checked out. I unplug the phone upstairs, too.

Truitt a murderer? No chance.

A pregnant woman, though?

Why isn't he in jail?

I can't silence the spinning thoughts. I pull out my laptop, type, "Truitt + Ridgemann + killed + pregnant woman" and hit enter.

The first eight results are not for him as Google tries to spell Ridgemann as "Ridgeman" or "Ridgemont." There it is. Why hadn't I done this before? Searched him out?

Santa Rosa, California. Texting. Pedestrian. Pregnant. Negligent homicide. Community service. No jail time.

Two families forever changed in one moment of inattention.

Not just two families—a whole community, and everyone in our congregation impacted. Not the least of all, me.

I type in "Barkley King." After several pages I haven't found our Pastor King. He doesn't seem to exist online. The pain in my chest constricts tighter. I can't think. I try praying, *Thank you for this day, thank you for your provision. Please put a hedge of protection*— but my mind picks up speed again. There is only one thing I really want to do right now.

The Orion Space Probe has gained weight

since I put it in my closet three days ago. Maybe it is just the skipped breakfast and lunch that's zapped my strength. Who am I kidding? I'm weak because I can't stop picturing Truitt's face. Weeping. Nodding.

I turn the dial to refocus the telescope. I will intentionally fill my mind with images rather than relive this morning's church service.

My laptop beeps, signaling limited battery. I plug it in and readjust the telescope up on my table. There is a house I never tried to view before—but here in the daylight I can actually see them pretty well. My heart beats a little faster at the idea of getting to know a new family.

After it's focused I turn to my laptop and type: "Spy gadgets."

Thrill and excitement replace the pain and sadness. It was so easy to find Truitt's secret. If I had tried at all—we wouldn't have been blindsided.

I will never be caught unaware again.

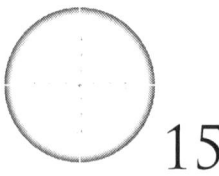

15

It's a bit chilly—but still not full-blown winter even though we are almost a week into February. Exhaust from my Jeep clouds the cold air around the Spy Guy shop. I won't turn off the motor until they open the front door.

Two minutes before nine o'clock, a man approaches the front door with a mug in his hand. He looks at me for a moment before he opens the door and waves me in. Removing the key, I leave the warmth of my car and run to the shop. He holds the door open and when I walk past him I smell scents of morning: coffee, bacon and Irish Spring soap.

"Howdy," he says. But I don't think he wants a reply since he raises the sage green mug to his mouth and turns away. His graying hair is military short and he has the look of one who once filled a doorway, but whose height and bulk have diminished with age.

First off, I pick up a USB keystroke recorder.

It only costs 19.95. Maybe I won't have to clean out my savings.

"What you got in mind?" His words are elongated like his face.

"Nothing." I smile too cheerily, covering nervousness with giggles. I hope he doesn't see it as friendliness.

He does. "Not that it's my business." He walks over and the smell of his coffee breath moves into my sphere. "But this says exactly what it is right on it." He reaches out to the package in my hand and before I can move away he takes it and holds it up. "See?" His hands shake. "Keystroke recorder. Do you need it to be discreet?"

I didn't think of that. "Probably a little more discreet."

"This one here is my favorite." He reaches up and pulls another one down. "Is it your computer or someone else's?"

He holds it out and I take it just so I don't have to watch his hands tremble. "Not mine." I feel my forehead pinching and I try to relax by turning over the package and pretending to read.

"Well, all you do is plug it in a USB port. Most people wouldn't notice it. It holds about two months of data and even if there's a power outage it'll still work because it uses flash memory. The best part is you can unplug it and look at the info from another computer."

"Oh." I point to the first one. "You have to use that on the same computer you were recording?"

"Affirmative." He draws out his affirmative longer than his already stretched out speech. "And you add a password to it so only you can see what was recorded." He drains his cup and looks over the rim at me. "In case it's discovered and someone else tries to access it."

I press the eighty-five dollar price tag down and bite the inside of my cheek. "I'll take three. Now, what do you suggest for bugging rooms or listening to phone calls? Oh yeah, and picking locks?"

***

Returning home, I find the house still asleep. The blinds and curtains are closed, preventing whatever shy winter sun might try to glow. I secure the door after I walk through it and listen near my mother's door. She doesn't snore—so there is as much chance that she lays half awake as half asleep. What does she do in her room all day?

The heater kicks on and the restrained blow fills the house with as much noise as there ever is here anymore. I spent most of the night working up the courage to follow through with my plans. Why do I feel so hesitant now? I start to open the package of one of the USB keystroke recorders. It hadn't occurred to me before I spent all this money—why not just ask him?

It shouldn't be too hard to convince Dad that

I need his computer, not my laptop, for an afternoon. I pull out my cell and press the shortcut.

"What's up, Leah?"

"Hi, Dad. Am I interrupting lunch?" I glance at the time trying to orient myself. It's only 10:30. "Oh, I mean, are you busy?"

"Nope. I always have time for you."

"I want to use your...has your password changed? I need your computer."

A very long pause is the only reply. I better come up with something better. "My neck is a little sore from looking down at my laptop and I wanted to work on..." My brain can't conjure a single client.

"Why don't you just rest today?" Parents are good at phrasing commands so that they seem like questions or options.

"I rest every day, Dad." I can't help it, but bitterness creeps up and I think of the things I have asked to pursue. College. YWAM. Getting a job outside the home. Since I stopped doing homeschool it has been one long string of sleepless nights, lazy days and volunteering at the church.

"Then come down here today."

"I don't...no, Dad, please." Why didn't I see this coming?

"You'll be coming for college group tonight, anyway."

"I thought since Truitt—there'd be no more group."

"Of course not, Leah. In fact, it is even more important that the leadership put up a strong front so the sheep don't go astray thinking they don't have a shepherd. You need to be part of the group more now than ever. The wolves will creep in again if we aren't vigilant."

Truitt was not a wolf — but Dad takes my thoughtful silence as acquiescence. "Great. Be here in time for lunch."

I try one last grasp: "Can I get on your computer before I come?"

"No. You can do your little projects here."

Little projects? He admits my life's purpose is insignificant. "On your desktop?"

"Ahh, no. I think I'll be needing it today."

"Dad, your computer is the only one with CS3 installed."

"Leah—" I can tell I'm trying his patience. "We'll install your design software on the secretary's computer."

Then I'd have to share a computer with Betty? "We only have one license."

"Daughter," he says the one word sentence as a warning.

"Yes, sir?"

"Be here by lunch." And he hangs up.

After I wash the tears off my face, I brush my hair until it frizzes. No need to shower — I opt for zero lotion and pull my hair back into the tightest braid I can manage. It's almost severe enough to pull the skin from my face and slant my eyes. My head already hurts and I like it.

I un-wrap the keystroke recorder and plug it

into my laptop. It doesn't take long to configure it so I do the other two as well. My linen skirt does not have any pockets so I slip two of the devices into my brassiere. It feels racy, adventurous. The sleepy haze, the living in stasis is gone—I feel alive with the thought of using these.

There is no guilt when I plug the gadget into my dad's rear USB port, but I try not to analyze that. He has two ports in the front of his computer tower and four in the back. Only three are used in the back. One for his printer, one for the mouse and one for the microphone headset. It is exposed and free of dust. If I add a plant, it will be a beacon to inspect the area. No, I'll have to assume that adding a small black rectangle will not get noticed. I move the printer cable to the top so it drapes over the keystroke recorder.

All four ports in the back are used now. I'm not sure if there is a chance the printer will give a notification when he re-boots since I moved the cable. I'll just have to risk it. Likely, if he ever uses a thumb drive or something—he plugs it in the front because that is the closest to where he works.

It's hard to decide if I want to show up just past noon to be rebellious or leave now and get started on planting and installing all my new gadgets. Eventually I decide to arrive at exactly lunch time so I need to waste an hour. Instead of looking into other's homes, I reread the news stories on Truitt. The pain that rises up in me, for him, chokes my breath. He never wanted to lead. I type part of his email address in the search bar of Outlook Express. It begins to list his college group mailings. I open the last one, sent a week ago as encouragement to attend the Monday night group and the verse of the week he wanted everyone to memorize. As far as I know, no one has ever bothered.

I hit reply then type a salutation. My finger hovers over backspace. Never mind, just go for it.

*It all makes sense now. Why you won't drive. Why you freaked out when I tried to use my phone while driving. The burden you obviously hid. Why you were so affected in the prison riot after they talked about murder.*

I want to tell him I'm sorry, that I forgive him. But who am I to forgive?

I end simply with:

*Call me, please.*

Obviously he doesn't have a cell phone, but I type my number anyway.

As my laptop powers down, I pull my knees to my chest.

Dad isn't even around when I arrive on time. I should be glad that he trusts me to obey, but instead I'm pricked that it's always been a given. God, this attitude can't be from you, right? Shouldn't I feel like I am honoring you when I obey them?

This would be more fun with Truitt. He turns washing nursery toys into an event.

The obnoxious poster board with our current fundraising goal of two million dollars is hardly noticeable beside a new rack of clothing. The rack is situated like a metal barricade and decorating it are T-shirts with "Flourishing Faith Fellowship" written in trendy, grunge font. Apparently "church" is no longer part of our name.

A UPS man enters and smiles. His dark hair is cut too short to be curly and his eyebrows are so thick they will grow to be one before he has gray hair.

"Afternoon." He smiles and there is a missing tooth in his lower jaw.

"Do you need a signature?" I take the box, surprised at its heft after the casual way the UPS guy carried it.

"Nope, you're good." He turns and leaves the building in the hurried "paid by the mile efficiency" of the delivery profession.

"Oh, fantastic. That's probably our postcard campaign," Pastor King says behind me.

I turn, relieved to hand over the weight. Did his hand really slide across mine like that? He sets down the box and pulls a box knife from his form-fitting dress slacks. His back muscles ripple through his smooth-as-silk polo as he bends and cuts the seal.

"What do you think?" Pastor King stands and holds out a postcard.

A smiling family stares back. If not for the words "Does your faith need flourishing?" it could as easily be a dentist advertisement as one for our church. "It's very—"

He moves on with dynamic excitement, "And these shirts: they have a huge margin of profit. Here, Leah. I want you to be the first one to wear one." He pulls out a twenty from his wallet, uses his key chain to open a money box and then hands me a hot pink T-shirt. "You should see the plans your dad and I have come up with for the remodel. There will be a gym so we can congregate for sports, a professional kitchen on the side—big enough to start a soup ministry…"

I find myself swept up in his excitement and vision. I look over at the frayed, dull blue carpet by the entry doors. More than thread-bare, there are strings we always have to cut so no one trips. I know the roof leak in the children's wing has created a mold problem and the playground still has a merry-go-round—the old fashioned kind that most parks have replaced because of injury. This is long overdue.

I take the T-shirt from his hands. "Thanks."

"Make sure you wear it soon. You're a leader, Leah. Kids look up to you." His smile illuminates his entire face and he takes a breath like he is about to say something else—something significant.

I don't give him the chance. "Is my dad around?"

His smile cocks to the side and his expression turns impudent. "Yeah, he's in his office."

"Thanks for the shirt." I wave it as I head toward my dad's office like nothing unusual happened at yesterday's service.

My dad's office computer doesn't hide under a desk either. This one sits on the floor next to his workstation instead of on the top. The back of it is only slightly obscured by a trash can. I certainly won't plug it into the front where he could notice the USB ports. I pull the device from my bra with a smile and insert it to my dad's computer. Hopefully it will be hidden enough in the back.

I plug it in the lowest port and move the trash can. When he empties it—that will be a problem. And it looks like it has long needed to be emptied. That's easily remedied. I go to the kitchen for a trash bag.

There are three empty kitchen trash bag boxes in the drawer next to the dishwasher. Under the kitchen sink I find a box of lawn and leaf bags. Perfect. I throw away the empty trash liner boxes and look for a shopping list—how long as it been since someone restocked supplies? The list is full. Sure enough, kitchen trash bags are written several times.

Where should I put my last keystroke gadget? Trash cans everywhere are full. Ugh, even the nursery trash is full as the potent smell proves when I walk in. Why didn't they use the smell-proof hamper? Oh, it's full too.

The maintenance needs of this place are ridiculous. Since really only my dad and Pastor King are here now, I guess I already know where my last gadget will go. I turn the corner to Pastor

Thompson's old office.

"There you are, Leah," Pastor King says. I didn't know I was lost. The confidence and ownership in Pastor King's eyes brings heat to my cheeks—I feel it. But it isn't for the same reason my dad is obviously assuming. "What are you doing? You should not lower yourself to taking out the trash."

"It's fine."

"No, sweetheart. He's right. You don't need to be doing that. We hired a mentally disabled guy who should arrive..." Dad looks down at his watch.

"In an hour." Both my dad and the pastor speak at the same time and then chuckle with the easy communion of fraternity. They've been spending a lot of time together.

Pastor King takes the black plastic bag from my hands. "You should be doing something more important than trash. Any retar..." I can't tell if he caught his own words or if he is responding to my gaping mouth. He recovers so quick I'm not confident he was about to say what I thought. "Leah—your dad has told me about some of your skills. Flourishing Faith Fellowship could really benefit from having you here full-time, as secretary."

So they are removing the word "church."

Dad would let me work outside the home? Tears almost prick at the joy—secretary? "What happened to Betty?"

"She decided to step down. She's leaving the

church, actually." My dad is appropriately sad. Betty is as old as the facility—I think she came with the building when they bought it, attended as a child when it was a Methodist church.

"Retiring? We should have a going away party! Who in this whole church hasn't had her as a Sunday school teacher or suffered through her direction of the Christmas play?" Betty: the on-staff grandma.

"It's not that kind of leaving." My dad's lips pinch like when I experimented with a Greek lemon broth for dinner one night.

Oh. That kind of leaving. "So you just need help for a little while?"

"No, Leah." Pastor King's voice rumbles with intimacy like we are the only two in the room. "We're changing the face of Flourishing Faith Fellowship with the name. We need someone relevant to today's culture." We all look down at my bulky jean jacket, ankle-length linen skirt and "Simple" brand clogs.

"Relevant?" I ask.

"We need someone young and beautiful." He corrects himself.

Not exactly a compliment—I'm not sure what expectation there is for my reply. Pastor King tosses the black trash bag to a pile by the door which contains a dusty CPU and an old monitor as deep as it is wide.

I guess I won't be putting the recorder in Pastor's office today. "Rearranging?"

"Remodeling." Dad claps his hands together and they both start to move again.

"We're going to get rid of that." Pastor King points to the window.

"Really?" Since I was a child I always loved the stained glass of Jesus on a cloud.

"Oh?" Dad looks surprised.

"It might be worth something, so we'll remove it of course." Pastor almost looks like he is joking—or doesn't believe it has worth at all. It isn't old enough to be antique, not even old enough to be retro. Just outdated maybe.

Still, I can't imagine the room without it. There were whole summers Bethany, Anne-Marie and I lay in the sun stream, reading below the rainbow light. Every time I saw it—I'd be reminded he'll return the same way. "What else are you doing?" I look my dad instead.

"New furniture arrives today," Dad says, still staring at the picture of ascension.

"The new face of Flourishing Faith Fellowship." This is obviously Pastor's mantra.

And so that's how I find myself working outside the home, at a building which no longer claims the word church.

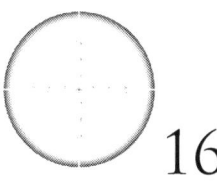

16

Once the postcards are taken care of, the Sunday school class registration cards will be the next thing I organize. No, maybe I will get the list of volunteers in a mail merge, send out letters, emails or phone calls and verify that they still want to volunteer. This whole operation could stand to be updated and cleaned. One thing about Betty is she liked to print every email as though the ones in the computer might disappear. Where will I store the boxes of random correspondence—should I just throw them away?

"Are you coming to group tonight?" Marta blinks her intriguingly long lashes. Her pink lips rival the iridescent black pupils in shine. She looks lovelier and shinier than normal.

"I...yeah." The monitor is covered with floating bubbles so I tap the keyboard to remove the screensaver. Monday, February 6, 5:49 p.m. "I guess I got wrapped up in working."

"You're working here, now?" She smiles so

sweetly I almost forget her dad was trying to get the church to hire her a few months ago.

"Just helping in the office." I stand and stretch the stiffness from my lower back and neck. "There's been some changes."

"I'll say." She crosses her arms and shakes her head slowly. "Liam's dad. Such a shame."

I'm not sure if she means the porn or him getting fired. Would she have brought this up if she and Liam were still dating?

"And Truitt! Can you believe all along how we trusted him?"

Trust. I almost trust him more now than before I knew what he was hiding. "It might not be what you think, he might not…"

"Are you kidding? Murder?" Her face is covered in delight, except the mouth which pinches in containment.

Rachel and Hailey walk straight over to us.

"Did you guys hear about Bethany? We really need to pray for her. She's pregnant."

"Yeah, she used to babysit me."

"I totally looked up to her."

Rachel buzzes with so much energy I feel drained. I wonder if my dad still has a box of granola bars in his office.

"Hi, Marta." Rachel smirks in Marta's direction but doesn't actually look at her. "I'm so sorry about you and Liam."

Marta looks down, her excitement about Truitt gone in the reminder of her own life.

"Bethany needs our prayers." Hailey emphasizes it in case I didn't quite understand.

"Let's go pray for her, she's not married." Rachel tugs on Hailey as Kaitlin enters the foyer. Kaitlin sees us through the window and waves. Rachel and Hailey speed walk out of the office calling to her.

"Did you get my texts? We need to pray for Bethany…"

Marta and I are left staring at them. As beautiful as Marta looks, there is a new sadness in her. She lost something to Liam—I see it in her reaction to Rachel and Hailey's comments about Bethany. I see it in her posture. It is so similar to Truitt's mannerisms in the prison after they yelled the word "murder."

I wish I had an appropriate word in my vocabulary for Liam.

"Time for group," I say and Marta tries a fake smile out.

The room hushes when Marta and I enter. This will be the second room I bug, the conference boardroom being the first. All eyes move in sync from Marta to Liam's new conquest, Madison. Madison is keying in her phone and doesn't notice the attention. Marta lifts her chin, grabs my hand like I'm her new best friend and sits. She angles her back to Madison. There is a subtle shift as Kaitlin, who was sitting in the chair next to where Marta plopped, jumps up, grabs a Bible and moves across the room.

So whoever Liam discards is the new pariah. Well, they'll all take a turn then.

King walks in and several people jump to greet him. Marta reaches him first and hugs him, her sadness completely gone. So do several other girls, but Marta stays near, continually touching his arm and fluttering those long lashes at him.

"No pictures." Pastor's hand is in "halt" position, covering the business end of Hailey's camera phone. "Turn off your phones completely. No texting. No interruptions."

Hailey giggles and blushes a little. Everyone pulls out their phone to turn it off. Truitt never got that response. Of course, he never said it so severely.

After about fifteen minutes, Pastor King speaks to me. "Leah, would you like to lead worship again?"

He means like last Monday—with Truitt.

"I'll help." Rachel rests her hand on Pastor's forearm when she offers. Even though she used to sing solos every year for the Christmas play, she's never helped with worship.

Worship time pretty much ends up being another concert. Rachel closes her eyes in dramatic earnestness and proves her extensive range and talent. Some of the kids whisper but most listen inattentively. I accompany her on guitar, without singing.

"Beautiful. Thank you, girls." Pastor King launches into a sermon. Actually, a pep talk.

Platitudes and motivational one-liners delivered so skillfully I feel out of place as the only one not drinking in his speech, or with a Bible.

We take prayer requests for about twenty minutes and when Pastor notices the time he bows his head and says a quick prayer for "all the things that were mentioned."

I miss Truitt.

As soon his honey-voice announces, "Amen," I slip from the room. I have my own car. Dad and Pastor can lock the building without me. I'll text Dad that I'll meet him at home.

Without bothering to put my car in the garage, I enter through the front door. I'm tired, hungry and weary of heart. If there is any day I could use my mother — it's today. It would be so nice if she were up making dinner...available to talk about yesterday. I turn the deadbolt...crying?

"Mother?" Yes, another whimper. "Are you all right?" I stumble over a pair of shoes where we are supposed to leave them, turn towards the master bedroom and enter the lightless room. "Mom?"

"I'm okay."

Yeah, right. I left her in bed this morning near noon. Seven thirty at night and she's still in bed. I sit on the edge of her mattress. She curls a little tighter under the covers. My eyes are starting to adjust. She's left several piles of clothes scattered around the room and on top of the glider rocker. "Are you upset about what happened at church yesterday?"

Her guffaw turns into a full blown crying jag and I reach out to touch her foot. When she's finally reduced to sniffles I pat her foot and stand to leave. It's okay that she didn't make dinner — I'm not hungry for food anymore.

In my room, I'm alone with my telescope. It's a long time before I tire of watching the new family even though nothing interesting happens. They watch television. They read a book to the two little kids. They leave and come back without the kids and watch more television.

Funny thought — what if they are watching a reality show while I watch them?

After, I read through the digital recorder manual I bought for the conference room. Finally, I stretch out in the dark, hoping to sleep a few hours uninterrupted.

I wake to arguing. In the dimly lit room my Space Probe hunkers by the window like a giant, long-legged bug. My curiosity satisfied, I stare at the telescope with feelings of remorse and disgust. Glaring doesn't help. God, help me stop.

Their words crescendo in bitterness and diminuendo in defeat. God, where is the harmony that should be in a house full of your worshipers? I put in my earbuds to block my parent's dissonant life and watch a few episodes of Burn Notice.

Both my laptop and I rouse from sleep mode tangled in power cords. Big thrill, another day... before I roll over to sleep some more, I remember working at the church. The mission of dressing and leaving the house propels me from my horizontal position. First, I check my email though. No response from Truitt.

After I dress in a calf-length denim skirt, tall boots, the too-snug pink tee from Barkley and a cardigan to hide the definition, I check again—just in case. But Truitt hasn't emailed me back. Back when he was the youth leader, he used to email within twenty four hours. Sick of my curly hair—I run a brush through it. Runaway strands form crepuscular rays around my face. Wishing I'd left it alone, I pull the entire mess back into a bun and wash my face.

Then I check my email again.

I pack a bag with the audio recorders, lock picks and keystroke recorder to take with me.

A furniture rental truck is leaving the Flourishing Faith Fellowship parking lot when I pull in. Inside, Dad smiles cryptically at me.

"Morning," I say, afraid to add the "good" in case he slept like me.

"You wore the T-shirt." Pastor King enters the secretary's office—my office now—with the same dramatic flair his voices commandeers when he prays. He wears a blue shirt under his suit jacket and a shiny blue tie that compliments. I look down at my beige cable-knit bubble and when I look up a woman stands next to Pastor. She's several inches shorter than me and very slight in frame, with pale—almost sepia—skin and hair the unnatural color of cayenne. Her hair is parted on the side and cascades over her shoulders with large smooth curls. How does she get her hair to obey? She wears a coal skirt and matching jacket with four buttons on the front. Dad and I look like displaced hillbillies at their power lunch.

They are waiting for something. "Hmm?" I look to dad.

"Take off the sweater and show him the shirt."

"No, I…" I know my mouth is probably hanging open. Take off my sweater?

"Model the shirt, Leah. You are the first person to wear it—the new face of Flourishing Faith." Pastor King holds his hands clapped in front of his chin.

"No. I'm not going to do that." I turn and grab a stack of papers, tapping them lightly on their side to straighten them.

"Leah," Dad says as though I am seven and forgot the proper way to interrupt an adult conversation. "Show us the T-shirt." There is the voice he used when I spied on that counseling session and received the stick of correction.

Everyone is expectant, but the woman's brows lift over her almond eyes with an almost imperceptible attempt to hide her humor.

My chest is more than adequate for my frame. Normally I do a good job hiding the fact, but this shirt is a size too small. I start to slide the cardigan down my arms. The words are stretched across the front of me—and now everyone's eyes are, too.

Dad coughs and turns away, but not before I see his cheeks redden. Pastor does not turn away.

I pull the sweater back up, and look down at my buttons as though I need to see to fix them.

The woman fills the awkward with an introduction. "My name is Selena Chan." She steps forward and offers her hand.

I take the cold fingers and look directly into her eyes with fake confidence. "Nice to meet you, Selena."

"Miss Chan is a consultant here to help us grow the membership and plan for the fund drive."

"We're very lucky to have her experience," Dad adds with the kind of pride he normally reserves for his grandkids.

"Nice to meet you, Miss Chan," I say to correct my error, but no one notices.

They generate a momentum, the three of them. Plans and ideas tossed between each other like a tempest. They head out to lunch—now that I am here to watch the building. When they leave, I feel like a reed—thankful their winds have subsided and I can sit still.

I open the "TO DO" folder dad left. Number one: no pictures, text bio only, update the church's website with Pastor King's profile.

There is only one who is both pastor and king.

But first, I will not waste this opportunity of

being alone in the building. I walk down the hall with a more powerful heartbeat and excitement than when it gets really interesting at Lucas' house. Pastor's office surprises me. In so little time, he has completely remodeled. Of course, the furniture truck.

There is a mocha leather couch and loveseat with peach and tan accent pillows. An enormous, empty bookshelf covers the right side of the office. An accent palm-type plant sits in front of the stained glass window he plans to remove, next to the shelf. The new desk is larger than our kitchen table and I can somewhat see my reflection in the surface. It goes all the way to the floor—a solid piece of furniture where no one could see your feet. Touching it anywhere would leave a fingerprint, I'm sure.

I text Dad: Let me know when you are on your way home. I might be hungry. Thnx

He isn't fond of texting, but I know he'll appreciate that I didn't interrupt them in a restaurant. And I'll appreciate a warning when they're on their way home.

I move closer to the desk, but my throat tightens like there is less oxygen. Why do I feel so afraid? Somehow I know if I bug this office—Pastor will know. Even if I put it back perfectly…

In convincing myself not to put the keystroke recorder on his computer, I've walked out of the office. Standing in the hall makes me doubt myself. I breathe easy and feel silly. What would be my punishment? I picture my dad insisting I show everyone my T-shirt. He thinks of me as a child. He won't spank me—but I am willing to risk being grounded. It isn't like I go anywhere, or that I would mind not being allowed to attend college group.

Now that Truitt's gone.

I need to use the restroom—but I want to do this first. It will only take a second. I step back in the room and immediately the air catches in my throat like too much starch in my esophagus. God, why do I feel this fear? I want to pray—but will God help me spy on my pastor?

I think I'll have to do this alone. I hate to admit it, but I proceed because I know God will forgive me in the end. Sin all the more that grace may abound? May it never be!

But sometimes it is.

Mentally coaching myself helps each foot find a spot on the floor as I progress toward the Pastor's new computer. It's perfectly organized underneath. Of course no dust—it's all new. The cables are professionally bound with black rubber ties. There's almost enough light emanating from the CPU to illuminate the USB ports in back, but I end up needing to use my phone's backlight to add visibility.

A text is waiting from Dad.

"Still here—forgot something."

I have time to hit "silent mode," turn off the screen and stand up before there's a shuffling noise at the door. Oh, dear! I jump behind the palm beside the bookshelf. My right hand, holding the phone, rests against Jesus' cloud in the stained glass. I punch a wad of my skirt between my legs so it doesn't flair out beyond the shelf and I press my back against the wood.

I know I said I'd have to do this alone, but I cry out to God anyway. No eloquence — just emotion, devoid of words, flung vertically. What am I doing? I could explain standing in here easier than hiding! What tangled webs…

"Did you find it?" My dad calls from down the hall. A muffled response reverberates from somewhere else in the building, but whoever is at the door of the office does not move. My dad must be near the front door and foyer based on how far away his voice sounds.

Waiting is easy even though blood courses almost audibly through my veins. My hands are warm and puffy. My eyes see more clearly and oxygen feels more satisfying. I feel focused and alive.

It could have been seconds or minutes that passed since that focus waned. Whoever came is gone and I start to step away from my hiding spot. Only, my body doesn't work. My foot won't lift. Shifting weight, I try the other. It won't work either. My head is stuck the same — but instead of panic I sense a large hand pressing me down. Fingers over my face, the palm at my knees. Gentle and firm.

"Yes." Pastor's voice has inspired attention,

adoration and generosity the last two weeks. Now it stimulates fear. Sinking deeper into the wood, even if only in my mind, I welcome the hand that holds me. Cover me God. Cover me.

"Of course." Nonsensical platitudes and quips jut into the $CO_2$ between us and when he leaves, Pastor King shuts the door.

Instead of moving, I glance at my phone.

Leaving. Where are you?

I reply: sorry dad. bowel issue.

And from the deal going on in my stomach— it isn't that big of a lie.

My screen lights again: Sorry honey. If there is soup, I'll bring some. Don't hesitate to go home. Driving away.

Fifteen minutes of stale air trickle from my mouth. I'm careful not to bump the plant or disturb anything. Pastor, Dad and 'the Miss Chan' have left, but I don't think I'm alone anymore. I never was alone, only now I acknowledge it. The Mary Jane shoes at the jail, the being who spoke during the service, the hand which pressed—there is more than Dad, Pastor, Truitt and me happening in this church.

I insert the key recorder and scoot in his chair. Was the chair in or out before I got here? Now I really need to use the bathroom.

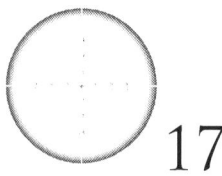

17

When I leave the restroom, I'm still stressed about the chair in Pastor's office. Is that why he waited? Did he see something amiss? Was it pushed in or out?

I go to my dad's office where he keeps his stash of treats. He hates prepackaged foods for the most part, but Mom found several brands of organic, date-sweetened granola and cereal bars.

My handwriting is nowhere as cultured as Pastor's, so I have to rewrite my note three times. Barkley expressed interest by letter first, and it is perfectly acceptable to allow written communication. But no matter how I tell myself that my parents would like this—I can't stand the thought of written intimacy with him, even to create a plausible reason for me to have been in his office. I would look ridiculous as his wife. I think I'd need to get manicures and go to the spa—Marta would fit him better. She sure seemed up for the prospect.

I finally settle on "Thank you for the job." I

give a little flourish to the "y" and draw the tail across the bottom of the sentence. It doesn't look half bad. I take it and a granola bar into Pastor's office and leave it on the desk as a gift. Now he will have plausible cause if he notices his chair is moved. The question is: Were I not paying attention, would I leave the door open or closed after I found it closed?

No, the real question is: in which rooms do I leave the audio recorders?

With the extra external battery, I get thirty hours of voice-activated recording. If I replace them every day — I could come in early or stay late to charge them. His office makes the most sense — I turn to take in the new luxury, including an enormous oil painting of a triple fountainhead water garden in the Holy Land. Water flows evenly from three separate founts into the basin, surrounded by lush Israeli scenery.

It is so precise and vibrant it looks like a caricature compared to my mother's dreamy painting style.

The black rectangle fits in my hand, but it's obviously a recording device — and with the external-extended battery it will be anything but inconspicuous. I would have liked the one half the size of my finger, but four of these cost the same as one of those. At least I bought one pen recorder.

The one-hundred-and-fifty dollar model will have to do, and I do need to leave one in here. I can't remember how far away it will record, but I don't really want to put it near the desk. Empty bookshelf, palm tree, couch…the picture. The lip on the picture's ornate frame extends almost three inches. Balancing on a chair, I place the recorder on top of the picture frame. I don't even need to secure it. Unless there is an earthquake it should stay. Even then, if the triple-fountainhead stays, so will the recorder.

I stumble from the chair and it bangs the table under the painting so I'm unable to identify the sound I hear in the front of the church. A moan? A hello? Or was it the sound of a child?

I return Pastor's chair to his desk, wiping imaginary shoe prints, and tiptoe out of his office. I've never minded being alone before, especially at church—but I feel differently about this place since Sunday. Since Truitt.

Since the spirit.

No one is in the foyer or my office. I want to look in the sanctuary for the noise, but, well—that thing talked back to me last time and I don't ever want to face it again. Shouldn't it be that nothing like that could ever come into God's house? Why couldn't I make it leave? What does that mean about spirits? About me?

The kitchen is also empty, so I return to planting the recorders. The conference room is next. Board meetings, counseling, all the decisions are made there. Maybe that's the problem; they should move those decisions to the sanctuary and place them at the foot of the cross. I'm a little smug in my cleverness until guilt settles on my shoulders.

Who am I to judge?

I don't care that they are wrong and I am wrong—I care about not being duped, shocked, lied to. I care about truth. I care about everything my parents never told me.

There isn't any kind of decoration or fruit basket to hold or hide the recorder. I could add a jar of pens, maybe, but that would probably draw attention. And if one device is found—who knows—they might start checking everywhere for more. I'm just going to have to tape it under a table and hope no one looks. Moving to my knees, I reach up toward the underside of a table.

"Are you playing?" The man's words are slow, drawn out, and lack enunciation.

My squeal makes him jump back with an equal-in-volume yell. I turn so I'm sitting and no longer on my knees crawling up under a table. The recorder hangs by a piece of duct tape only fastened on one end. He wags a finger at me, "Don't you, don't you, don't do that."

"You scared me," I say to his navy, Velcro sneakers. Besides those, he wears dirty acid wash jeans and a pink and white striped polo with a green alligator symbol. His lips are crusty and slightly slack, like his head which hangs submissively to the side. He looks about fifty years old, but his hair is still brown, no hints of gray. He holds one bent hand near his mouth and shifts from foot to foot without making eye contact.

"Are you here for the food bank?" I use the table to stand up and press the tape down as inconspicuously as possible.

"I take out the trash."

"Oh, that's nice." I stand and face him.

"The trash," he insists.

"Randall?" A woman's impatient Jamaican lilt finds us. "Randall." She halts and drops her hands to her hips. "Why didn't you wait for me?"

"She's playing. On the floor." He points to me with his crooked hand and smiles, but still does not make eye contact.

I laugh but can't think of a lie quick enough so awkward silence follows my non-explanation. I stand.

"Let's go to the office and find the people in charge now, Randall." She rolls his name, especially, like a song.

"I was picking up trash." After I blurt this I wish I'd thought a little longer. Her head leans back and she regards me through sparkly painted, half-closed eyes. I don't have any trash in my hand to prove it. "I was looking for trash." Oh Leah, shut up.

"I take trash." Randall mumbles with a huge secret smile.

"Yow. Is the office open now?" The heavyset woman wears black fleece sweat pants, lime and gray sneakers and a tight lime sweatshirt. Her skinny, umber spirals are cut short enough to touch, but not rest on her shoulders.

"Yes, the office is open."

Randall squats and starts to crawl his way over to where I placed the recorder.

"Give a listen," the woman says to Randall. When he doesn't respond she puts her hands on her hips. "Get up man." But she doesn't exert any unnecessary movement. She just smiles at him with large pink lips and her leaning-back, skeptical expression. "Come now," she insists with both hands at once. Her fingers are painted lime green as well. She laughs and so does Randall. He stays on his knees and looks at her like an ornery child.

"You won't get to work today if you don't listen to me."

"Why?" He stands, agitated, and I pray he doesn't throw a fit.

"You got to listen is why." Her green-tipped fingers move rapidly as she speaks. So does her head. Randall shifts feet for a second of indecision and then goes to her obediently.

"I'm the secretary. May I help you?" I want to lead her to my office but she blocks the doorway.

"We're looking for a Bryan Jones."

"Oh, that's my dad. He didn't say anyone was coming." I speak to the woman but Randall holds my attention. He laughs softly at some private joke and his lips move as though he is in a conversation even though I barely hear his whisper. "I'm Leah."

"Your girl Alvita here." She sticks out her hand and I take it. She is soft and warm, and smells like tacos.

"What time were you supposed to meet with my dad?" If they have a counseling session or something I should leave them here. Only, I'm afraid Randall will get bored and look under the table. "Why don't you come up front and I'll see if the coffee is fresh. May dad should be back soon."

"Randall." Alvita calls. "You want coffee?"

"No. No. No."

Randall still shakes his head when Alvita speaks to me. "Well, I drink coffee."

I smile and point to the doorway she blocks. Alvita taps Randall on the shoulder and steps out of my way. They follow me down the hall sharing words I can't quite hear or understand.

We have two coffee machines. One industrial sized, used only on Sunday, and one regular. The regular carafe on the burner is half full, and probably burned. I don't drink coffee, but I know how my dad likes it since I fix it for him. He wouldn't drink this.

Randall doesn't want to enter the kitchen and it takes some coaxing from Alvita. He probably won't wait for a new pot—I better just serve this. "My dad takes his with honey and half-and-half. How do you drink yours?" I pull a mug down from the cupboard.

"Black, but I'll drink it the same as you." She moves her hands and the whole top half of her body when she speaks. The combination of her cadence and rhythm makes me think she's a barely-controlled song and dance waiting to happen.

"Trash," Randall says, and scrunches up his face to laugh at the hilarity of my lying attempt.

Reaching for the cupboard with a shaky hand, I take a second cup down. Don't speak Leah; you'll only make it worse. If I have to choke down coffee to keep them in here, it's a small sacrifice.

After I remove the cream from the fridge, I pull down the honey bear and pour both mugs, but mine only a quarter full.

"So, your dad is the pastor?" Alvita doesn't wait for an answer. "Sit down Randall. My father was a preacher." She slips in and out of accent-free English to me and the Jamaican English for Randall.

He keeps saying "No" and shaking his head. Alvita turns the chair backward, Randall smiles and straddles it. Her patience makes me think of a mom I once knew whose son had Down's syndrome.

"Your dad was a preacher? Where did you grow up?"

"St. Andrew. Close to Kingston."

That must be in Jamaica, but I only think that because the sound of her accent. I'm afraid to show my ignorance. "How long have you been here?"

"In America? Eight years."

I meant Reno. "Why did you come?" We don't have many refugees. At least, I don't think we do. "Religious persecution?"

She smiles and shakes her head, but doesn't answer right away. "There are many Christians in Jamaica."

I was right. Jamaica.

Alvita continues, "So many that it is easy to say you know God, but not ever do a thing to show it." She looks right at me while she brings the cup to her lips.

She could be talking about my church. I take a sip of my coffee-flavored, honey cream. It's nice. Cold, but nice.

"So many that pretty much everyone has heard about Jesus, and knows at least one hypocrite to give them an excuse to not go to church."

So exactly like here. We sip in silence. Halfway through my cup, I contemplate getting more. Instead, I glance at my phone to see if Truitt has emailed.

"Checking up on Facebook?" Alvita places a hand on Randall's shoulder and he stops squirming so much.

"No, I... I'm waiting for a friend's email. My dad says social media is like toothpaste. Once it's out there, you can never cram it back into the tube."

My dad also said Marta's and Liam's moms spend more time on Facebook than any kid could — making sure everyone's pictures and comments are "above reproach." My mom didn't think I saw her roll her eyes when Dad trumpeted their protection of the youth.

"Hmm." Alvita drains her cup and I'm not sure if the sound is conversational or coffee enjoyment. Voices trickle down the hall.

"Sounds like my dad is back." I stand and

Alvita follows. She puts her cup in the sink and pats my shoulder like she does for Randall.

"Don't mind the self-appointed toothpaste-police. The religious are the only ones Jesus ever cussed at."

"Cussed at?" Jesus wouldn't cuss.

She laughs and wrinkles her nose. "Vipers. Probably the worst thing he could have said. A vile, unclean serpent. Plus, Satan disguised himself as a snake. It was like he was calling them filthy, evil-incarnate devils."

I bite my nail instead of answer. Jesus wouldn't have cussed. Ever.

"And raised in the church—you have a greater chance of being a religious snake than sincere. Thank you for the coffee. Is that your dad? Come on Randall."

Still standing by the sink, I finally meet her eyes. How rude. She doesn't know me at all. "I'm not religious." Why would she insult me like that?

"Child, my dad was a preacher." She steps out into the hall and waits for me. I set down my empty cup and we walk together toward the foyer.

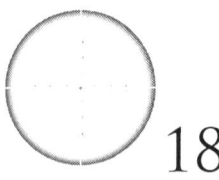

18

"How is your stomach?" Dad asks in front of everyone. I know by Alvita's compassion and Selena's patronizing eyes that I look as sick as I suddenly feel.

"I'm fine. This is Alvita, Dad. She has an appointment?" I pat the buttons on my cardigan — I never thought dad would share what I texted about having diarrhea...does everyone need to know my business?

Maybe it's worth it — two recorders are in place.

Interesting that both what offends me about my dad's question and what I'm planning to steal with those recorders, is privacy.

"Thanks, Leah," Dad says. "Randall is actually the newest helper around here." I'm not the only surprised person staring at my dad.

"I take trash." Randall answers without any coaching. He scratches his scalp with both hands and tiny flakes sprinkle his shoulders.

Duh! He wasn't saying that because of my lie—Randall is the mentally challenged guy they hired to do maintenance.

"Is that really necessary?" Barkley looks at Randall when he says the word "that."

Miss Chan nods. "It seems you could have found a volunteer to do the janitorial work."

"Yow. We are volunteers," Alvita pipes up. "Randall has an uncle here."

"George Bloomberg."

"Yes." Alvita nods at Dad. "George Bloomberg."

"We're helping him out as much as he's helping us." My dad purses his lips in a patient smile as Randall shifts from foot to foot and grins like it's a private joke. A gob of snot starts to drip from Randall's nose. "You might want to..." Dad indicates to Alvita.

Both Barkley and Miss Chan step backward. Miss Chan visibly recoils.

Alvita wipes Randall's nose with a few whispers I don't understand and Randall presents his face to her for a final inspection.

"And where do you come in the picture?" Barkley asks Alvita.

"I'm with Randy here." She crosses her arms and Barkley asks no more questions.

Miss Chan turns to my dad and puts her hand on his arm, "Are you ready to tackle the afternoon?" I find myself fixated on her hand and then her expressive face. I try not to glare. Some people are just flirty; it doesn't mean she likes my dad.

"Give me an hour or two, Selena. You and Barkley get started without me. I'm going to show Randall here all the chores he's going to do for us. Come on, the biggest is the kitchen trash." Dad heads back down the hall where I just spent the last half hour with Randall and Alvita.

Selena and Barkley both look mildly irritated. But then Miss Chan looks like she took a swig of olive juice when Barkley says, "I'm sorry you weren't feeling well, Leah," and puts his hand on my shoulder. He guides me in the opposite direction — toward my office. "They didn't have any soup that your dad thought you'd like."

"Mr. King," Miss Chan says. "I need to see you in your office."

"Do you feel up to working today at all?" His kindness reaches his whole face until he looks sideways at Miss Chan. "Just a moment, Selena."

"Yes." I wave him away. "I'm fine, really."

He glances back at her, then me, and finally follows her down the hall.

My office still has a reminiscent smell of Betty. It's an odd combination of an Avon perfume that smells like baby powder and some sort of topical, pain ointment. It lingers even though I tossed the partially used containers when I was cleaning out the drawers.

How many years did she sit in this spot? Will I grow old in this chair? I lower into the chair, spin quickly, and then allow my foot to drag me to a stop. I spin again.

Barkley leans on the door frame holding the granola bar. He has a confident half-grin dancing at the corner of his mouth. He takes a deep breath, but it seems more for effect than courage. "I love these." He salutes with the snack and walks into my space. "It's wonderful having you around the office."

"Thanks." I slide both hands, palms down, under my thighs and sit straight. He steps over to the desk and sort of sits by leaning against it. He crosses one leg over the other at the ankle—just like a catalog ad for slacks.

"We're going to remodel your office next."

"Oh, I don't need—"

"But the church needs it. The community needs it."

The dented, beige metal desk has a chipped faux-wood surface. I keep it clean though, and I already took down the faded cutesy emails Betty loved to tape up for wall decorations. Of course, I need to dust the walls now.

"This office is the first stop—the front lines really. It matters how we greet them. Are we inviting or not?" He leans toward me. "Are you inviting or not?"

I scan the room—since I grew up here I never really noticed how it would look to a stranger, someone who saw it for the first time.

"I'm thinking yellow walls…"

He trails off with other words about colors

and textures. I only hear Truitt singing the Cold Play song, "Yellow." I only see my YWAM application. This life cannot be the adventure God has for me. I'm not even sure I want to be here, with what I saw on Sunday. Who I saw on Sunday.

"I can tell you see it too—you can catch a vision." Barkley is so confident in his charisma I let him believe I was dreaming about the new office. "I like a woman who can envision the possibilities of something." His body language speaks in double entendre. "As to the possibilities of a courtship—"

"I've changed my mind." I hadn't known myself until the words came out.

"I knew you would. You'll love having a brand new office. Selena is amazing, she'll—"

"I mean about a courtship." I've never rejected a man before so I'm not sure how he should act, but the narrowed eyes and haughty smirk don't look appropriate.

"You know, Leah. I didn't want to tell you this. There's talk in the college group about whether or not you like men at all."

All the sudden I see myself standing before the church, as I have in dreams. Naked, or feeling naked behind clothing I didn't know was sheer.

Or a glass pulpit.

This situation could easily be twisted—just because I don't want Barkley, it would seem that I don't want men. My parents would be eternally shamed before I could prove them wrong.

"Your dad would lose his job." Barkley is as

he was on Sunday, the accuser. He waits long enough for that to sink in and leans forward. "You may not feel attracted to me now, but give me time. Let me prove my devotion."

My accuser becomes my redeemer? I've been sitting on my hands all this time, but suddenly I feel cold. Rubbing my arms for circulation, I avoid his face. He kneels before me and places one hand on my knee and with the other, he pushes hair from my eyes forcing me to see my reflection in his irises.

Iris was the name of that other song I sang with Truitt. It fits: I really don't want the world to see me.

"God told me that we were to be together."

Barkley doesn't know that this was a joke with Truitt before he came.

He continues, "Your parents want it for us, for you."

Barkley has no idea how my parents live at home. At one time, their desires would have been enough. But aren't their desires—for me or anything—only as pure as their devotion to God?

"The entire church wants it." Barkley is well aware of the girls' attention in youth group so this is a conscious lie. "And I want it more than you can imagine."

It feels surreal how slow he moves in. He plans to kiss me? I will not have my first kiss stolen, sour like vinegar. I am willing to wait for wine.

"I don't." I lean back. He ignores me and keeps coming. I put my hand over my mouth and he touches my fingers with his lips. He pulls back in surprise.

"I don't want it."

Barkley's face shows defeat and vulnerability. "But will you consider praying about it? In light of all that I have said?"

The only thing I remember is that he threatened my dad's job. It takes a minute for my voice to return. "Yes." I nod. He looks the proverbial happiest man on earth.

But I already know my answer.

By three in the afternoon the letters on my screen are melding before my eyes. I'm not hungry, but the coffee with honey cream sounds nice again. If it helps me stay awake, all the better. The vacuum drones in a back room, proof that Randall, or Alvita maybe, is getting along fine. Fresh coffee waits, I'm not surprised. It is the only unhealthy thing my dad will allow. Coffee is the only God-ordained drug.

A small black rectangle sits on the counter in the kitchen. It's the same size as — not just the same size — it's the same device! Right in the middle of the counter waits one of the audio recorders I hid earlier today. Instead of following my first desire to grab it back and run to my office. I casually reach for a mug and take it to the doorway to see if anyone is outside watching or knows I'm in here.

I dress the cup like I did a few hours ago with mostly half and half, but I microwave it a minute so the honey liquefies. The minute takes too long and I can no longer wait. I pick up the recorder to see if it has any remnants of duct tape indicating it's the one Randall saw me messing with. Or if it is the one I put on the picture frame in Pastor's office.

Smooth as new.

"Hi, sweetheart." My dad's greeting is punctuated by the microwave signal. "Why so jumpy?"

I do my best not to look at or draw attention to the black rectangle in my hand. "I didn't rest well last night." I pull a cup down and close the cupboard without looking at him. "Falling asleep at the counter, I guess." I hand him the cup.

Dad pours coffee into it and before he's finished, I pull mine from the microwave. Keeping the hand holding the recorder draped loose at my side, I hold out my cup for a fill. He hesitates with one brow raised. "You're drinking coffee?" I feel something almost like adrenalin at his question. I am twenty after all. I hold the cup a little closer to him and wait.

"Sorry, darlin'." Dad's words trickle like the tiny stream of bitterness flowing into my mug. "Did we keep you up last night?"

He doesn't fill my mug very full. Counting the earlier cup, I'll probably only drink a total two or three ounces of caffeine today. He sets the pot back on the burner and when he does I take it and top off my cup. I have to use the hand holding the recorder. This is almost like direct disobedience, filling my cup after he measured an amount for me. My hands shake as I tip it and this causes me to over pour.

"A good measure," Dad lifts his cup in a toast, "pressed down, shaken together and running over."

Even though I'm tempted to sip a little first because of the mess, I hoist my cup and say, "Poured into my lap." Dad grins and we drink our family toast.

"What's that in your hand?" Dad points with his cup after a long draw from it.

I can't remember ever successfully lying to him, except about the bowel issue earlier. And that was texting so he couldn't see my face.

One possible explanation for him is it is a case of some sort. With my luck he'll ask what kind and then want to see it. I could tell him it holds feminine products or something. He won't ask more.

Telling him the truth would be a relief. Maybe he would even figure out about the other spying and he could help me stop. It would be nice to have someone in on this, so I wouldn't have to feel so trapped.

I don't know if I'm more frightened of getting caught spying or finding out something with the devices—seeing something horrible again.

Maybe the scariest thing is that I'll never stop and it will just get worse and worse—that someday I'll be a creepy old woman who never got married and watches everyone with one beady little eye from my smelly church secretary's office.

"I better get back to work." Dad's shoulders sag as he leaves.

I swallow my confession with another sip and return to my desk.

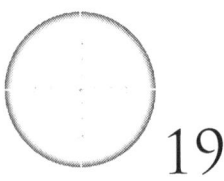

19

"Now?" I don't fully look up at my dad in the doorway. "I planned to stay late tonight." I made sure I would be in the middle of the web redesign when dad usually takes off. He's such an early riser I'll never beat him to work. It seems reasonable that I could stay after.

"You can't stay late." He wiggles his hands in his pocket and keys "ching" against change. "Barkley and Selena are coming to dinner."

"Dinner?" How will I check which recorder is missing, recharge and re-hide the remaining one? When will I hide the other two?

"You don't want them to come? You normally love company..." Dad takes a big knowing sigh. "Are you uncomfortable having Selena come over? Because Barkley isn't interested in her at all. I thought so too, at first. But I know it's you he wants to pursue."

Lucky me. "Dad, I..." He stops jiggling his change finally. "I'm not sure Barkley, er, Pastor

King is someone I could be interested in."

Dad starts jiggling again. "He's a fine man. He'd make a great husband. You'd be very lucky to catch him."

"Dad—"

"Look, Leah. Your mom and I can't take care of you forever."

"I could take care of myself." Dad just looks confused when I say this. "Not everyone is 'called' to marriage. Paul said 'I wish you could all be as I.'" Truitt's reminder, not mine.

"But that's not what he has for you." Dad speaks as judge and jury. "For you he has Barkley." And executioner.

I'm not sure when he stopped playing with his change, but the silence swells—and grows between us.

"Are you not walking with the Lord right now? Is that why you can't see what he has for you? Is there something in your life preventing you from hearing God?"

Glancing down at my hands, I realize they are pink and blotchy. A drop lands on one. I turn it over slowly and wipe the tear on my skirt. Dad's right.

"Sweetheart. Allow your mother and me to see things you cannot see. Let us help you." He pauses and tries again with a softer tone. "Will you consider praying about it?"

It is the same question Barkley posed. "Yes, Dad." This time I am not as sure what my answer will be. Maybe I should pray first.

He kisses the top of my head. "That's a good girl. Now hurry home and see if your mother needs any last minute help with dinner or straightening. Everything is locked. Leave through the front door and pull it tight behind you."

I reach for my purse and keys with my left hand and begin shutting down the computer with my right.

"I'm going to stop at the store and pick up a couple bottles of that sparkling apple cider you and your mom love so much. Barkley and Selena will meet us there." Dad means the cider as a gift—the closest thing he'll allow to soda—but it feels like the expectation of a celebration.

He leaves after I nod. When he does, I turn off the light in my office and try to pray with a longing to be close, to find God. *Dear God, thank you for this day, thank you for your provision, please put a hedge…*I like the pinch of squeezing my keys in my hand. It keeps me alert and dulls the feeling of lonesomeness. Why can't the feeling of God's presence be as real? Isn't he here?

The audio recorder power button is in the off position. Pressing rewind causes my heart to race slightly. Will there be some clue as to who found it and how it ended up in the kitchen?

I don't wait for it to rewind far before I press play. "I don't think you need to dust up there, Randall." Alvita's voice. "Come down and be careful. Follow me, we need to take this trash bag into the kitchen."

Absolute relaxing peace pours into my limbs as I lift my purse and walk down the hall. I slide the recorder into my purse with the other two. Dad, Pastor and Miss Chan don't know. I can just stick it in a new spot. I turn left and start to enter the sanctuary. Should I just leave it in here?

It's dark and cold. Maybe this is my chance to quit. No one really knows, no harm has been done. I ccould remove the one duct taped in the conference room then forget everything I've seen and heard and imagined.

Imagined? Staring at the pulpit from the doorway, I search for the shape which stood behind Barkley when the accusations flew. It answered me back. It did not flee my rebuke. I didn't imagine it. I'm still trapped. Neither God, nor Dad, Barkley, not even demons will listen to me.

There's no turning back. I'll never forget everything. And I can't leave this place fast enough.

At home, the house is dark and smells stale — not like dinner being prepared for guests. "Mom?" I kick off my shoes and head toward her room, but I already know. She never got up today. She never prepared dinner for Dad's guests. She still weeps on her bed.

They don't think I know about the money issues. But I hear amounts named during their arguments. If Barkley catches wind that Dad cannot manage his house either — where will that leave us? Without income at all, and humiliated like Pastor

Thompson. Think Leah.

I race up the stairs and flip open the phone book to order pizza. There's a gourmet shop that delivers whole wheat crusts and specialty toppings like goat cheese, spinach and heirloom tomatoes. I order three of their house specials, give my debit card number and promise a big tip if they hurry. Next, I pull out fixings for salad. I'm half-way through before I realize I haven't even washed my hands.

Sounds drift from the front door. A key, shoes on tile, Barkley's then Dad's voices, mingled with appropriately mild laughter from Selena.

Appropriately mild...what bugs me about her? Her beauty and class? The superiority? It isn't like dad said—that I see her as a threat to my connection with Barkley. In fact, I'd like to see him pursue her. They'd fit great. Sometimes they even move like they are comfortable with each other's bodies. Like Liam and Marta moved. Like Lucas and...whoever he's with.

"Have a seat, make yourselves at home while I get something to drink." Dad enters the kitchen with deep gullies of skin rolled between his eyebrows. "Where is your mother?"

"She didn't ever..." I start to shake my head.

He looks from side to side and even though there are plates stacked, cups pulled down and I am whisking a miso-soy dressing, obviously, no dinner waits. Dad's chest swells with a slow meditating breath—but it never deflates. He is taut and puffed like a max-inflated helium balloon.

"Salad is almost finished and I ordered three pizzas from Viego's." I spoon the last of the dressing into a pretty bowl, scraping out as many toasted sesame seeds as I can. He does not answer me. I want to appease him, but trying too hard will only make it worse.

"I need to serve some drinks." He pulls the fridge door open with more force than necessary and a few jars of olives and other condiments clink. I picture Miss Chan's sour face and pinch an errant smile. Olives would be a great appetizer for her. Dad stands in a daze searching the mostly empty fridge. Good thing he stopped for sparkling cider, otherwise, all we'd have to drink is water.

"Do you need ice?" I ask him. He mumbles a reply, but I know if I speak again his aggression toward Mom will be redirected at me. I pull out a block of Romano, cut off the hardened edges and hint of blue, and slice it. The slices, olives and a few pickles serve as an antipasto plate and I start taking things into the dining room.

Dad clanks around in the kitchen even though I already pulled glasses down. I finish the salad and leave him to his temper. Miss Chan stands awkwardly in the middle of the living room. "I have some appetizers," I say.

"Hmm." She smiles with only her lips. I turn but do not see Barkley right away. He stands on the stairs studying our family's pictures. Before Anne-Marie, Ava-Nicole and Bradley left home, we were very active. Shooting guns, camping, fly fishing, homeschool — we did everything together as a unit.

"You look like you must have had a happy childhood," Barkley says without turning to look at me.

"Yes."

"How nice for you." He turns to come up the stairs and I remember being alone on these stairs with him last time he came over. I step-hop out of his way but he doesn't acknowledge me as he passes.

When Truitt came over once, he asked me to point myself out in every single shot.

Barkley whispers something to Miss Chan, who still stands awkwardly in the middle of the room like she is afraid to get dirty. When he steps away, her countenance has morphed into agave nectar. "Bryan, it is so good of you to have us for dinner." She walks to the table and pops in an olive.

Yep, her expression didn't change with the sour flavor.

"Unfortunately, my wife is ill. So it's pizza after all." Dad walks into the room with three flutes of cider. Dad hands one to Miss Chan, one to Barkley and holds his up. I walk into the room and watch them toast. I guess I can drink water.

The doorbell rings, yet Dad does not move. Miss Chan leans in and he laughs, never taking his eyes off her. She touches him frequently. I run down the stairs and since I gave my ATM card over the phone, I sign the slip. The delivery guy looks so tired. He's at least ten years older than me and carries a hefty waistline. Not as big as Truitt though. I make good on my promise of a tip but he takes the receipt without thanks or even looking at the total. Heat seeps through the cardboard as I carry the stack up the stairs. No one glances up when I announce dinner's arrival—as though it isn't obvious by the delicious smells. Not sure if I should wait for prayer or help myself, I try again. "Pizza's here."

Without verbal acknowledgement, the three of them rise and circle the table. I step away from Barkley in case dad decides everyone should grasp hands.

"Pastor King," Dad says his name like the title it is. "Will you do the honors?"

"Sir," he smiles confidently. "It's your home."

"I insist."

"Very well. Dear gracious, loving, heavenly father..."

Barkley's face shows rapture and peace. He has a slight contented smile. Miss Chan is equally tranquil. When my gaze reaches dad, I jump. He stares at me with such intense animosity I jerk involuntarily. What have I done?

"...in the precious name." Barkley finishes without saying Jesus and reaches for a plate.

"There's three different kinds." Dad announces, but narrows his eyes at me and steps forward. I back up like I'm caught in his laser beam and shuffle to the kitchen. "You didn't close your eyes during prayer," he says when we are alone.

I don't bother hiding my surprise. "How do you know?"

"Because I had my eyes open." His nose and upper lip curl together. "And it's not your business what I do during prayer. I'm the father. You're supposed to be seeking God right now."

I lower my head and look at my hands. "Sorry."

He turns and leaves me. Unable to move, I continue to stare at my feet. Food is the last thing I could choke down. I'm still trying to chew on the reason my parents want Barkley for me.

"Leah, you forgot napkins." My dad's voice startles me. I didn't forget them, we're out. I go to the cabinet with the missing silver and pull out the linens. "Grab that other bottle of cider, too." I slip in and out, straightening, wiping, refilling. After they eat, I clean up the mess alone, and slip into my bedroom while the three of them discuss the future of our church — I mean fellowship — with fervor.

Shutting the bedroom door, I lock it against their conversation. No one noticed that I didn't eat a bite.

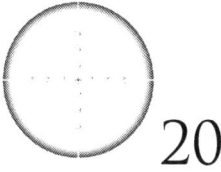

20

Last night was the last time I'll use my telescope. This time I'm sure. Lucas is no longer at his parents, so there isn't much to see. The hours I spent hoping—dreading for something to happen while excitement built to a nearly uncontrollable kind of craving—exhausted me. Somewhere in the middle of the night, the fatigue culminated into an ocean of need then dropped like the continental shelf into uncharitable depths of guilt.

The cycle of anticlimactic anticipation.

The strained blow of our heater is my only accompaniment in the predawn light of a disorganized room, a disassembled life. I check my cell phone again. Saturday: day six without an answer from Truitt. It's safe to say he will never respond. Pain simmers in my chest—the loss of a friend, especially when I need him. It feels like treachery. "There is a friend who stays closer than a brother," I know. "But you always feel so far away, God."

Even though I keep skipping meals or quitting after a few bites, I don't feel hungry. I like the emptiness inside. The gnawing is more like tightness than pain and I feel sharper, more alert. Anyway, there is almost nothing left in the house to eat. Mom wouldn't notice because she never gets up, and Dad wouldn't notice because he eats out with Barkley and Miss Chan every night.

From under the covers I stare at the ugly green of my telescope. Cleaning and shopping is something I can do. First, I put my room under control. I'm too comfortable in my jammies to bother changing before I head out to the living room. It's not like my manners are slipping—I won't wear them into town or anything.

The house doesn't need organization—no one is really living in it with dad and me gone most of last week. It is actual cleaning, bleach in the corners that it needs.

I pull out the spray cleaner and attack the counters, the cupboards, the appliance faces. Basically every surface. I use the vacuum hose on the corners and end up scrubbing the baseboards before my parents emerge.

"You're making a lot of racket up here," Dad says and glances at his watch. Mom's navy slacks hang loosely on her hips. But she is dressed, and even wears shoes. He puts a hand on her shoulder and continues, "I thought you two girls should go get another new outfit for church tomorrow."

Last time my mom took me shopping I ended

up paying. Since they support me I'll never mention it, but I'll also never wear it again because of what it represented. I should have bought the yellow one.

Maybe I can rectify that.

"Actually, I wouldn't mind making an exchange." I've only had that dress for a week, and I only wore it a few hours. Remembering Barkley's attention, I shiver in my thin pajamas. Come to think of it, I can't wait to get rid of that dress. I can't wait to wear yellow to church tomorrow. "And then I'd like to do some grocery shopping."

"Sounds great." Dad is overly enthusiastic as if to compensate for my mom's lackluster countenance. He looks at his watch. "It's nine o'clock. You should go out to breakfast first."

My mom nods and glances at me. She looks so pathetic.

"Why don't you two go?" I ask. When was the last time they had a date or spent time alone? "Take the motorcycles?"

Mom smiles and a barely perceptible flush returns to the apples of her cheeks. When she looks at my dad, her shoulders pull back a little.

He huffs and glances down at his watch again. "I don't have time for screwing off."

I'm so shocked at his harshness I can't even address his language.

"Look around, there's nothing in this house. You need your daughter to pull your weight. She's cleaning on a Saturday, planning grocery shopping and running the house. When I think of what Pastor

King would say if he knew how you mope around. Leah came to the rescue last week when I brought him here..."

The last thing I want to dwell on is what the pastor would have to say about our family—especially in front of the church. So I duck into my bedroom and change quickly. Mom and I had so much fun last time when we shopped together. I can cheer her again. A good meal will help her too.

"I'm ready Mom!" I call from my room, hoping to distract my dad without being obvious about interrupting his rant.

"Are you sure you don't want to join us?" I ask one last time as Mom follows me down the stairs, head drooping. I grab my keys and purse.

"No. You girls need to spend time together." He pretty much shuts the door on us, but not before he checks his watch a third time.

I unlock the passenger side of my jeep and she climbs up.

Mom says she doesn't care where we eat so I choose a sort of expensive breakfast diner that has unique variations of eggs Benedict.

"We haven't been here in a long time, not since Anne-Marie and Ava..." Mom trails off with my sister's names. The four of us had a mom and daughters' brunch about a week before Ava left. I've always wanted to come back.

We're seated quickly and I feel my appetite tickled with scents of sweet, fried breads and savory meats. Mom picks up the drink menu, spending an inordinate amount of time studying the Mimosas and Bloody Marys.

"Are you zoning out, Mom? Or actually reading that?" Peering over my menu I see a tiny smile spread up into her eyes.

"You were aptly named, my rock. My steady girl." Mom sets the menu down and reaches for the breakfast menu. "I shouldn't tell you—but Dad didn't want the name Petra." Her smile is much bigger now, and a little mischievous.

"What?" In my twenty years I thought I'd heard every story they had to tell.

"He wanted Leah Patrice. I wanted Petra Lee."

"That's kind of funny." The waitress stops and makes eye contact. I shake my head and say, "Not yet." Then to my mom, "My initials would have been P.J." Like I was predestined to have a love affair with pajamas.

"We never did agree on your name. He wasn't in the room when I started filling out the birth certificate." She giggles. "I had more spunk back then."

An argument with her husband is spunk?

"Don't make that face. I gave you the name he wanted, I just added Petra. Marriage is all about compromise. Peter, Petra—Rock. I still need something firm to hold on to." Mom focuses on her menu but her eyes are scanning far too fast to be actually reading it.

"I wish I was more like Peter." I tap her

hand—wanting badly to clasp it. To feel connected to her, pull her from wherever she's been. "He wasn't afraid of adventure. Jumping out of the boat when Christ walked on water. Unafraid to speak his mind. Running straight into the tomb without stopping to think."

"Me, too." She smiles hesitantly, sad.

"Oh, I forgot the dress."

"What dress?"

If she finds out the real reason, will she make me keep it? Okay, Leah—Petra, live a little. Blurt it out like your namesake. "I don't want that blue dress we bought because Barkley asked me to wear blue if I was interested in courting, and now I know I'm not interested."

"Are you ladies ready?" Of course the waitress picks this very moment.

Without giving my mom a chance, I turn the menu and say, "Yes. I'd like to try that." I'm not really sure what it was, but it said "House Specialty" next to it.

"I want your coconut funnel cake French toast. Please bring both powdered sugar and maple syrup."

When the waitress leaves we both burst out laughing. If dad knew how much sugar she was eating! The giddiness lingers and after several minutes Mom dabs her eyes with a napkin. Her humor seems a little inflated for the situation but it's good to see her happy.

"I can't say I blame you about Barkley."

Mom looks at her hands.

Wow. I took a risk, and it was worth it.

"I think, as parents..." She waits like she is still working out her opinion. "You sort of feel like your job isn't done until your kids are married." The waitress brings a little dish of maple syrup. "Even if you were living on your own, I wouldn't feel like you were settled until you had a husband."

"So it's more about you and your obligation to pass me off, than me and my purpose?" Whoa, 'Petra.' Shut up.

Mom doesn't react though. She just sits and thinks. Finally she dips her finger in the syrup and sticks it in her mouth. "You might be right," she says without a smile. "We'll go home and get the dress after we eat."

We don't laugh again during the meal.

At home, a burgundy Suburban and rusty blue and white trailer wait backed into our driveway. "I wonder who that is," I announce. But before I have my Jeep in park and the key turned, Mom has sprung from the front passenger seat.

"No!" She holds both hands at her sides, palms up, fingers flayed. A stranger walks her Harley up the trailer ramp. He looks as uncomfortable as she does horrified. "What are you doing with my bike?"

He stops half-way up the ramp and turns back pointing to another equally confused man. "Jeff?" The second guy steps away from my dad's bike and walks toward my mom, wiping his hands on his jeans.

"You say this is your bike?" He points to the door that leads inside. "I just bought them from Bryan. Ah, Bryan Jones."

As my dad's name is proclaimed he enters the garage holding a few papers. "Here's the..." He stops at the doorway and meets my mom's gaze, "...titles." His eyes drop at the corners and his chin grows when his bottom lip reaches up to cover his frown. It is resolution in his expression, then defeat—and then anger.

"It was a pleasure doing business with you, Jeff." Dad says forcefully, hands Jeff the papers and extends his own hand for a shake. The Jeff guy takes it, awkwardly, and with a sidelong glance at mom. He quickly looks down at the ground. They have both bikes loaded, secured with ropes and covered with the fleece-lined element shield before Mom has moved her hands from the "what is happening" position. When the two strange men hop into the driver's and front passenger seat, Mom finally sounds the pent up wail. She falls to her knees.

"Janet, not here." Dad starts to walk toward her, but she loses another mournful meow and doesn't look up. "Come inside and let's deal with this. Not outside." Dad looks from side to side but I don't think he sees me. He's worried about the neighbors. "Not in the front yard." He touches her shoulder tenderly and Mom leaps backward, shielding her face as though he was about to strike.

"Don't touch me!" Mom falls backward and

starts to crab walk away from him.

"Janet—" He reaches again.

"Don't you touch me!" I wouldn't have thought it possible but her volume actually increased.

"For God's sake, Janet."

"God's sake?" She stumbles upward to her feet, but precariously. "God's sake?" She starts to laugh, but it comes out as sobbing.

Dad's head drops to the side, part impatience, part patronization. He tries again to reach out to her.

I finally understand the expression "a blood curdling scream." For the noise that leaves Mom makes my heart stop and pump intensely at the same time. I don't know if I should run away or jump between her and Dad.

"You're making a scene." Dad raises his volume to meet her intensity. Leland steps out of his house onto his porch from across the street and leans on his cane. He looks at my dad with pursed lips as if to say, "There will be a witness."

"Try to touch me again and you'll see a scene." Mom stands and spreads her feet creating a blockade-style stance. She holds a hand up but it shakes violently. "I don't know who she is, but I hope she's worth it." Mom's hand curls into a fist except her pointer finger. Tears still stream and she licks her lips, drinking them in.

"What? No. I wouldn't, there's no—" Dad stammers.

Mom stops mid-sob. "Now you insult me with lies?" She walks toward my dad and says something I cannot hear.

I don't need to hear it though, because the venom on her face and the recoil from my dad is more than enough. She turns and walks toward the house, placing each foot as I imagine a drunk would — purposefully correcting the crooked steps, meticulously attempting a straight line.

Dad trudges to his Toyota. I walk backward into the shadow of the garage door. I don't need to hide though; he squeals away without looking back.

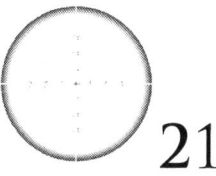

**21**

Unsure of what I want or expect to find, I end up in dad's home office.

Of the two lock pick sets I bought from the Spy Guy, one is for front doors and one is perfect for cabinets. I've brought the latter in my clammy hands. Sitting cross-legged, I balance the lock pick directions on my left knee and pick while I read them. I know I'll find something important behind this lock. What will there be? Love letters? A shirt with lipstick on the collar?

If there isn't evidence of cheating, I'll stop...No wait, I'll look at his computer next, just to be sure. Maybe the one at the church, too. Then I'll stop.

It takes longer than the directions said it would, plus, I both nick my finger and dent the key hole. But I have the drawer open. Unfortunately, the only thing in here is bills. Stacks and stacks of them. Unopened. Stacks and stacks of unopened bills. Slowly my mind takes in the information as if repetition is necessary for my addled brain. My finger slides under the seal of a random envelope, I tear it open.

*Circuit Court.*

*Summons.*

*To Defendant: Bryan Jones*

*20 Days.*

*Foreclosure.*

Our home address is listed under Dad's name. Twenty days? January. Last month.

"What are you doing in Dad's office?" Dark half-circles jut over sunken cheeks covered in blotches of raspberry. Her hair hangs in flaccid strings at her shoulders. She turns to the picture replacing my dad's beloved Civil War pocket watch display box. It's another she painted long ago. Everything was from long ago since she doesn't have time to paint anymore. "This is new." She crosses her arms and sneers at it in confusion, then wipes a finger at the discoloration in paint where the display box once covered.

I look down at my lap—the letters, the lock pick—why lie? "I was curious."

I lift my arm but the single letter weighs too much to actually offer it to her. She stoops to retrieve it. A soft moan comes out; it is the sound of loss. I leave her to the frantic opening of letters and go to the kitchen to make her tea. In five minutes I've nuked her favorite "Blessings" mug, steeped a tea bag of jasmine and returned. Dad's office floor now has envelopes laid out in some sort of organized fashion. When I offer the cup I turn the words away from her so she doesn't have to see them. The flowery scent lifts with the vapor.

"He's lost everything," Mom says to the floor. "We were going to be evicted any day—and I had no idea."

God can fix this. It will work out for good. I'll pray for you...quips rise like undigested dessert I didn't have room for—but ate anyway.

"What are we going to do?" Mom looks up at me. It's been more than thirty years since she did anything but volunteer. "Who do you think she is?" Mom's hands retract like cramped talons and she pulls them to embrace herself, still holding crumbled warnings from the bank. "Everything! He lost everything!" She shakes uncontrolled.

"You're going to go stay with Aunt Margaret." Although I might have to drive her to Carson. Even if Mom's car wasn't in the shop—if that is where it is—I wouldn't put her behind a wheel right now. She nods and looks up at me. I bend and lift her at her elbows, they are so thin. She stands with my help. The bills fall to the floor.

"Go see if you still have emergency cash in the safe, pack a bag, and call Aunt Margaret," I instruct. She nods, but her forehead is so wrinkled I wonder if I'm giving too many instructions. "Mom." I make sure she's looking. "Money." She nods at me. "Bag."

She doesn't nod this time but walks away like she understood. I use my cell to call Aunt

Margaret's home, then her cell. She doesn't answer either. I pace on top of the bills but get tired of the sound of paper under my feet, so I leave Dad's office. I'll need to look at his computer later.

You never really understand how small your network is until you need immediate help and have no one to call. This is life in the fishbowl. Everyone knows you but you don't know anyone. If only Truitt had a phone—I scroll through my contacts.

Hayden. He'll be home from his honeymoon by now. I've pressed "call" before I've fully decided whether or not I can speak to a man I thought I loved, a man who chose another.

"Leah." There is surprise and pleasure in his lilt.

"Hayden." I breathe out his name with a sigh of finally reaching a human.

"Are you doing okay?" he asks.

"Not really."

"It's going to be hard."

"You know?" I can't help the accusation in my tone.

"Truitt told me all about it." He means the church.

I want to be polite: ask him about Sparrow, the honeymoon, his health. "I can't reach Truitt." My voice cracks.

"Yeah," Hayden isn't surprised. "He's taking a hiatus this week."

I take a slow methodical breath so I don't sound whiney. "From life?"

He doesn't respond right away. "We've been fasting from food. Truitt is also fasting from all electronics. That's why you wouldn't be able to reach him. But tonight we're getting together to break it."

Fasting for six days?

"He felt like he needed a different kind of prayer before he decided his next step."

"I can't fault him that." The unwanted image of his face while Barkley called him a murderer rises. I see him standing alone at the end of a finger — with the entire congregation watching. "Some things are going on at home."

"Do you need me to go to his house and get him for you?"

Call-waiting beeps in the middle of his sentence. It's my aunt.

"No. I have to go."

"Will you come tonight? You can talk to him there. Sparrow would love to see you. We'll pick you up at six."

Call-waiting beeps again. "Okay," I answer quickly and switch calls.

"Hi Leah, I haven't heard from you in a little while."

"Can you come get mom?" I ask my aunt.

"We're in Vegas for Kristoff's birthday."

"Oh, no."

"Do you need me to fly home?"

"Yes. No. We might go to your house."

Aunt Margaret insists she can catch the next

plane to Reno.

"I have other options," I lie. "But I promise to call again if I need to."

I pace my bedroom, taking time to fold the taped YWAM application just for something to do and then slide it in between the pages of my Bible. I've awoken my laptop from sleep mode, so I pull up Outlook. The letter from Ava was marked unread so I open it again.

Call her.

She will come, I know instantly. And it isn't like I care so much anymore that dad forbade us to have contact with her.

"Hello?"

"Ava—" I choke on an explanation.

"Leah?"

"Yes. Oh gosh, I'm so sorry I haven't—"

Again she covers the silence. "I'm so glad you called."

"Can you come quickly? Mom is…well, she isn't…" Once I start, it's easier than I expected to tell someone our secrets. Strangely enough, Ava's nonplussed. She "um-hmms" like she expected our dad's betrayal and mom's breakdown.

A terrible smack echoes from downstairs. I manage a terse goodbye after I give her directions to our new house. Another sound of splintering wood and tearing fabric follows my mom's grunt and then a smack-smack-smack.

The base of the stairs is blocked by wood and pieces of black and red canvas. My mom calmly inspects a finger on her left hand while the right holds a tattered half of her oil painting "Captivity." She stops inspecting her finger and holds it up. "I got a splinter."

Mom moves a piece of hair behind her ears and meets my gaze with the no-nonsense eyes that used to make me squirm as a child. Her finger must bleed because she's smeared a streak of red across her forehead. What needs to be said? Asked?

"Ava-Nicole is on her way."

She just stands there. Inept and inert. At least she's consistent.

"Did you hear me, Mom?"

"My daughter's coming here?" She's roused, but I wouldn't give her keys to heavy machinery or anything. Another scream rents from her pale, slight body before she spends several minutes mutilating the rest of her painting.

The door handle jiggles. Mom drops the painting remnant and slowly turns around. She stares for a long time, when she opens it, no one is there. Ava bursts from the garage entrance. She opens her arms and Mom walks straight into them.

"Oh, my baby!"

Even at twenty-nine, Ava looks like the teenager who left. Her hair is just as long as dad made her keep it, but it is unnaturally straight and light. She wears make-up, heels, snug jeans and a drape cardigan the color of raspberry juice.

Mom pushes Ava back and cups her face. Ava laughs and touches mom with equal disbelief.

"Dad's gone?"

"He even took the emergency cash from the safe. Grandma's pearls, the silver…*my* heirlooms!"

Ava strokes Mom's hair and calls over her head. "Go pack a bag, Leah." I turn and walk to my room. My bag of spy-shop goodies is still emptied on the bed from when I pulled the lock pick. I maintained a surreal calm when it was just Mom and me, but now that Ava is here my hands tremble. I am again reduced to the nine-year old who watched her leave.

I return my gadgets to hiding and check my phone for email as I have done by rote for six days. Truitt hasn't disappeared and isn't hiding. I could see him tonight.

"Leah?" Ava sounds from somewhere on the stairs.

I run out to meet her. "I'm not coming with you just yet." I brace myself for the ensuing displeasure or maybe even argument.

"Sure." She turns to leave.

"You're not upset?"

"You have a license, right?"

"Of course."

"That's good at least. Do what you need to do—come when you want. Tonight, tomorrow."

 "Or in a few days?"

She turns back and looks at me quizzically, "You're an adult, whenever—whatever."

I'm an adult?

I am an adult.

My limbs are so tired now, they no longer shake. We tuck Mom into Ava's Subaru with a bag by her feet. A large suitcase fills the back seat. Mom has her elbow up on the window and the bridge of her nose pinched between her two fingers.

I don't want to disturb Mom, even to say goodbye. I walk to the front of the car and wave. Ava waves as she backs out and again before she pulls forward. Mom never looks up.

I call Hayden back to tell him I don't need a ride. He gives me directions to Truitt's house and tells me they'll be praying for me. I don't comment how much I need it. It makes sense to take off for Ava's right after I see Truitt, so I pack a bag large enough for several days. Turning slowly, I study my bedroom as if it is the last time I'll see it. Is there anything else I will miss if I leave here tonight and the house is reclaimed by the bank before I return? I stare at my telescope, the bag of spy gadgets, and finally my Bible with the slip of yellow still wedged inside.

I want none of those.

Now, to exchange that blue dress.

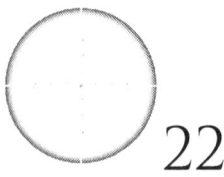

22

Sick of Meadowood Mall, I walk to my car with a yellow version similar to the dress I wore for Barkley—except this one is much shorter. It is satisfying to have the color I originally wanted. In the diminishing afternoon light I take peaks at the brightness, attempting to drive away the February gray. I climb into my Jeep and set the bag beside me with the mouth stretched so I can see color whenever I glance. If I leave for Truitt's now—I'll be an hour early.

It'd be better to wait a little to avoid being alone with him—assuming he lives by himself. So I decide to stop at the grocery store for a treat. He'll appreciate it if he's been fasting all week.

When I finally pull up to his house I'm glad light shines from the porches of several houses. I don't think I'd get out of my car in this neighborhood if it were completely dark. Since two cars are already parked in the driveway I have to park on the street, two houses down. I shove the dress and department store bag under my seat and throw a glance at my suitcase in the back. On second thought, I grab the dress bag and bring it with the bag of ice cream, grape juice and almond butter I bought. My suitcase is filled with denim and corduroy, handmade skirtlots and ankle-length dresses. I'm not worried about those; it would be a joke on the one who stole them.

Truitt poked fun of my clothes the other day. What will he think of my new dress? I look down and form a stubborn resolution—I'm warm in my flannel, plum-print dress. The skirt is the most A-line that I own but it still took five yards to make it. The weight seems to grow as I push toward Truitt's front door. What if he isn't as eager to see me as I am to see him?

I stand on a crumbling porch with laughter, music and light leaking from inside. It sounds like a party—like the kind I've never attended. I use my toe to knock but no one comes so I switch both bags to the same hand and ring the doorbell. Truitt opens it and simultaneously turns on the porch light. I squint from the shock of it so I don't see the screen door open out toward me in his exuberance. After the screen hits my forehead, I stumble back but the porch isn't as wide as it once was. The degenerating cement gives way like gravel under my feet and it is all I can do to try and stay vertical.

His arms reach around to my back at my rib cage and I no longer wonder what it would be like to be hugged by a bear. His scruffy face scratches against mine and his whole body presses firmly against me. Laughter jiggles from his rolling stomach to mine.

I don't recognize the dizzying sensation until my feet hit the ground again and it gives way to clear-headedness. When he caught me he'd completely lifted me up, not just given me a hug. My forehead smarts from the screen door.

"I'm so glad you came." He lifts the grocery bag from my hand. "Did you bring something to share?" He opens the bag and delight morphs into a thoughtful expression. "Milkshakes? This was the last thing I ate — we ate it together."

My eyes have adjusted to the flood lamp on his porch, but I turn and angle myself so it isn't directly behind him. The greenness of his eyes sparkle and we stare at each other for several seconds in question. We both seem to be asking the other — do you feel it too? Or more correctly: Where do we go from here?

Truitt hangs the bag over his right arm and offers me the elbow of his left. I slip my hand into it for the three steps back to the front door and we have to walk single file to cross inside. The house is small but well-lit.

Sparrow and Hayden sit in a corner sharing a faded, pink floral, overstuffed-chair. She sits slightly higher than him, sort of on his lap. Her long legs lay crossed like noodles and his hand rests on her knee. The other arm is around her. He looks less like a cop than he used to, with his mustache shaved off.

There is something on his upper lip that I'd never noticed before, a scar. Liam is in the kitchen pressing down a white mound of dough. He smiles and gives me a two-fingered salute tapping a drop of flour to his forehead. A man about two inches shorter than me walks forward and offers his hand. "Hi Leah, I'm Adrian. Truitt's neighbor." He points behind me. "I live next door."

Yeah, I got that from the neighbor part. His head is perfectly spherical with tiny black curls padding him from crown to chin. Through his beard, his grin grows insecurely and during the one, brief glance upward when he said his name, his eyes looked solid black like a bowl of soy sauce.

Truitt's face is flushed and blotchy and his voice chokes out slightly garbled. "I—I don't think you meant...I took the wrong bag." He holds out my Macy's bag with the ball of yellow crumbled at the bottom. I take it back quickly and look away.

"Leah, I'm so glad you're here." Sparrow approaches me. It looks like it takes her a minute to decide but she tentatively places a hand on my shoulder. I turn and glance at Hayden watching us and then reach up and hug her. Not the fake side-hug and faint air-smooch popular in group, but a two armed squeeze—albeit quick as possible. After, we both lower to the ripped-denim loveseat in the living room.

"Congratulations."

She smiles and glances at Hayden before answering. "Thanks." They have the softness of newlyweds. All glowing contentment and several extra pounds. "Oh, Leah—your forehead. It has a red lump." I touch the place the screen door smacked. "What happened?" she asks.

"Truitt. Well, and a screen door."

She grins and leans close. "He was really excited you were coming tonight. I've never seen him like that." She isn't grinning maliciously like I imagine any of the girls in youth group would if they were to tell me something similar. She actually has an almost warning or searching expression. As if to gauge whether I already knew and how I would react—but for Truitt's sake, not mine. "Truitt," she finally calls toward him. "Look what you did to Leah."

He's horrified when she explains. It's cute really. The jokes are merciless. He fumbles and mumbles away and returns with ice. "I'm sorry. So, so, sorry."

"No worries. I barely feel it." I hesitate to take the ice.

Sparrow whispers, "It's swelling."

I take the ice and paper towel hoping everyone will stop making a fuss. "So you went to the Midwest for your honeymoon?" I turn away from Truitt's attention and hold the ice against my pain.

"Oklahoma." Even under her exotic skin I see a slight flush. "We went to see my dad, but it was actually the road trip that was the honeymoon—not the destination."

She has a new confidence and peace present that she didn't have the night Hayden brought her to our house because she had nowhere else to go.

"How do you get this flat enough?" Liam holds up a lumpy, Frisbee-shaped piece of dough.

"You said it wasn't rocket science." Truitt is quick to answer. Hayden and Adrian laugh and walk to the kitchen to rib and coach a frustrated Liam.

Sparrow laughs at them and points to my bag. "Did you get something new?"

Since the guys are all in the kitchen I find the shoulders and lift the dress out of the bag partway. "Wow, Leah—that will look beautiful on you. The color—it's lovely."

Yes. Yellow: joy, sunshine, life and adventure. Something Petra would wear. Shorter than something Leah would own. I shove it back in the bag.

Sparrow pulls her waist-length, onyx hair from her back and lets it rest over her left shoulder. It takes two hands to move it all.

"How's married life?" I ask.

Her eyes are on the crowd in the kitchen when she blurts a long sigh. There is a hint of humor in it. "I'm not sure I get the whole submitting thing right." Sparrow bites her lip and looks at Hayden with an intimacy that confounds and intrigues me. "Learning to be patient with each other." She blinks her striking, almond eyes and looks at me. "Learning to give up control."

I lean back and picture myself trying to submit to a husband. I picture dad first—it's easy. I've submitted to him my whole life. Look what it got me. I've obeyed in almost everything and our church, our family: shambles.

I simultaneously see my parents driving away without looking back at me. No wonder they were so eager for me to get married. They wanted me out of the house.

This makes me picture myself submitting to Barkley. It gives me an odd sense of nausea and internal ridicule. That would be a joke of a marriage.

Sparrow looks over at her husband. They are silently communicating with their tender-but-flirty expressions. Yes, feelings for him were vinegar rather than wine. Potent and sharp, but not mature. Just a first experience of hope and affection—not love as I once thought. Not the aged and tried vintage they share.

Truitt walks toward us holding a bottle of wine and I burst out laughing. I can't divulge the inappropriate humor without sharing my previous thoughts. "What do you have in your hand?"

He looks at it in shock. "I don't know." He looks at me, then back to the bottle. "How'd this get here? What the heck?" He laughs at his own joke. Sparrow left the loveseat, but I didn't notice when. Truitt holds out his hand to me. I take it and rise.

"It's wine. We're breaking the fast with communion." He squeezes my hand and pulls me toward everyone in the kitchen. "I can't tell you what it means to have you here." His voice is low and earnest.

I squeeze his hand back and we take three steps toward the group before we let go. The lump of dough is now like a thick tortilla and smokes from a skillet on the electric range. Liam jerks the thin pan with a curse and the guys laugh and joke about his cooking ability. Everyone circles a ripped, vinyl-top, folding table in the middle of the cramped kitchen. Truitt puts a hand on my shoulder blade and guides me to the far side. I could stand at the table then turn around and use the sink without taking a step.

It looks like there's a casserole, salad and bread on the counter, but here on the card table sits the cursed, steaming flatbread and a large chalice cup. Hayden begins singing "Beautiful Things," while Truitt opens the wine. Sparrow joins her voice with Hayden's. Liam bows his head and mouths the words while Adrian begins to sing off-key to my right. Really off key, and Truitt's neighbor obviously doesn't know all the words because his are slightly out of sync.

Truitt sets the wine on the table next to the cup. He takes the bread and lifts it with one hand. "His body, broken." He tears it with the last word and for the first time the symbolism strikes me as literal. Literally broken. It hurt him to be crucified. Truitt tears a huge piece and hands one of the halves to me and the other to Hayden. Hayden tears a chunk and passes the rest.

The piece I take is tiny, like the cracker size at the monthly church communion. Everyone else took enough so that there is no bread left over. I hide my tiny piece in my hand, wishing I'd known how they planned to do it. Wishing for more.

Liam speaks and the singing quiets, "This bread is without yeast because Jesus said to beware the leaven of sin. A little leavens the whole batch." His hand quivers slightly. "So don't take this unworthily. Confess your sins."

Who is this Liam? The boy who's slept his way through our youth group speaks to me of sin? His father keeps porn on a church computer and now he makes our communion bread?

"I don't deserve this." Liam whispers it and even though his head is bowed I can tell he is crying. Everyone else is just as intent on their double-portions of bread. I look down at mine, it is smashed now—I didn't realize I was clenching my fist. There is an achingly long silence where I hold my unleavened bread and look at my shoes. This is all wrong. I've never been at a communion like this—can they even do this? Outside of church? Without someone who went through seminary? Is this legal?

Finally, Truitt speaks, "Christ said, 'This is my body, eat.'" Everyone brings their hands to their mouths and bites. But as I bring the bread to my mouth, something stops me.

Do not take this unworthily.

It is a warning. I can smell the simple richness of white flour and olive oil. My fingers slide over a few grains of salt on the seared skin of the bread. Everyone else is still chewing and biting and eating their huge portions, bite after bite. But I feel afraid to approach God, to confess, to give him everything. Afraid of his adventures.

There's a stack of paper napkins on the table and I pull one to discreetly place my bread inside. Everyone is so internally focused they do not look up as I fold it. I have no idea what I will do with it. I cannot take this unorthodox communion—but I can't throw it away. The singing begins again and then fades organically.

Hayden picks up the bottle and pours slowly, "Likewise, after the meal he took the cup and said 'This is my blood, poured out for you.'" Everyone focuses on the red stream—except me. I'm wondering if we are supposed to share a cup with strangers and drink real alcohol together in this run-down kitchen. My legs are tired of standing. Adrian's singing is really out of tune. What will I do when the cup comes to me?

Truitt drinks and dramatically turns the cup counterclockwise so Hayden can place his mouth on a clean spot. Hayden does the same for his wife. Then drinks Liam. When Adrian takes the cup he begins to shake. "Most of you know that Truitt told me about Jesus this week, and I still barely know what's going on." He holds the cup aloft. "His blood? This is a really strange ritual."

"Yeah." Hayden laughs quietly. So does Sparrow.

"But I want it. I want whatever is offered to clean me." He begins to cry. "I accepted Jesus Wednesday, but I still get loaded every day. I'm sick of weed. Sick of its control over me. I want this blood to wash me." He looks up. "Save me God." Adrian drinks and a sanguine trickle escapes the corner of his mouth.

Truitt steps forward to place a hand tenderly on his neighbor. I step back away from the table and look around at the ex-stripper and her husband, a drug addict, the youth-group gigolo and Truitt—a man who killed a pregnant woman.

And I am the one unworthy.

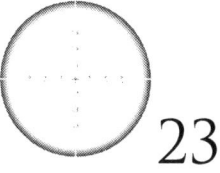23

The most inviting seat is the overstuffed floral that Hayden and Sparrow shared, but I feel weird heading toward it since they'd already claimed it earlier. I didn't think anyone noticed me leave communion but now I catch Truitt studying me. He smiles, inquisitive. I look away instead of trying to fake. My braid tugs, causing a mild headache. Actually—not that mild. Where did I set that ice? Is the lump still growing?

The group prays first for Adrian's drug addiction then specific requests for each other. The kind of specific requests only known through intimate camaraderie. I lean back into the denim loveseat and try not to wonder how many owners had it before Truitt rescued it from the side of a road somewhere. Finally, they pray for the meal and build their plates.

"Hope you're hungry." I open my eyes to a paper plate in Truitt's outstretched hand. I'd have to be hungry to eat the pile of casserole and salad heaped and barely balancing. I notice the thin paper looks wet underneath just before it wobbles — and folds down toward me.

Lettuce rains around my lap like glitter in the Kindergarten Sunday school class. The most surprising thing though, is the casserole's temperature. Still so hot after all that time on the counter. I feel it through my dress but also on my hands which rested palm up. Bits of lettuce hit my suede sneakers and stick to my tights. Truitt still holds the now-empty paper plate between two fingers. A dollop of ranch slides from the plate and he jerks his hand quickly away but this jettisons the dressing into the air toward me. In slow motion I see everyone's faces as the white goop travels toward my cheek. It lands.

Awkward silence reigns as the entire room watches Truitt drop to his knees and try to pick up each individual piece of lettuce, refilling the thin paper plate. "Sorry. I'm so sorry, I can't believe…" He looks up at me.

I shake my head slowly, trying desperately to ease his torment. I want to say: 'I'm not *that* hungry,' or 'I don't care for ranch.' I even try to muster 'I don't use plates at home either.'

But nothing will come out. The room's tension builds with the length of quiet until my day of loss bursts from me in sobbing gasps. I can't even cover my face in shame because my hands are full of cheesy noodles, broccoli bits and chunks of ham.

Truitt takes my messy hands in his own,

pulls me up and guides me to the kitchen. It's too late now — I lost my dignity and have nothing left to guard. Every time I try to smother the pain, it ruptures louder. Each time I do, it seems to cause Truitt as much discomfort as me and then that makes me feel even worse.

We walk right through the kitchen and down the hall to the bathroom. Chipped orange and yellow tile cover a backsplash and counter surrounding a dark, taupe porcelain sink. The toilet and tub match in age and chipped, dingy brownness. He guides me until I sit on the closed toilet. Next, he scrapes my handful of food into the trash then turns on the faucet and leaves. In a moment he's returned with a roll of paper towels and a folded bath towel. He closes the door behind us and we are alone with my ridiculous bawling.

I tear a paper towel and remove the ranch from my cheek. Then I fold it and start to wipe my hands, especially between my fingers. Apparently deciding the faucet temperature is good enough, Truitt takes a small cloth and holds it under the water. He opens the towel and sets it on my lap proceeding to wash my hands, one finger at a time with the warm soft cloth from the sink. He lowers to one knee before me and turns to rinse and wring the cloth every few seconds.

Watching his methodical and tender movements relaxes me and the ache inside starts to drain away as well.

"I'm sorry, Leah." His anguish brings more

guilt.

"Truitt," I shake my head. Where do I start? He thoroughly rinses the washcloth and hands it to me. I press my face into it and when I pull it down he is still close—picking remaining bits off my dress with a hand so light I cannot feel him. My head moves to his with a slow, almost magnetic, draw. He puts his arms around me, a strong, steady embrace. His cheek presses mine so that I hear and feel when he swallows.

I reach under his arms and hold him close so he can't move and see my face when I speak. "My mom and I came home today and my dad was selling the Harleys."

He adjusts his knees for balance. "Your mom's bike, too?"

"Yeah—she flipped. Dad drove away. Then she left with my sister."

"I thought she lived far away. In another state."

"A different sister." I don't want to speak anymore so I turn my face into his neck until my eyes are held closed over his collarbone and I can smell a mixture of his soap and deodorant. It's soothing.

He makes an appropriate sad sigh.

"The real problem is that he's been selling other things too. Like maybe heirlooms and other valuables. It's obviously been him all along, but he blamed it on a break-in." Actually, he never allowed that the break-in was legitimate. That was my mom's fear.

"Your dad's having money trouble," he says it as a statement.

"Well, I don't know, but the church sure seems to be rolling in it. Remodeling, advertising, decorating...hiring a consultant."

The hug seems to be over so I sit straighter, moving out of his arms. He doesn't move back as far as me though. "I needed you this week." I can't help the slight accusation in my voice.

"I'm sorry." He presses his lips together. No reasons or excuses and no reciprocation.

Who cares, I couldn't be more exposed or humiliated than I am right now. I want to be alone. "Will you go out to my Jeep and get my suitcase? I want to change."

He looks relieved, probably to have a task that will serve me, but I can't help but wonder if it is because all last week—he didn't need me.

After I have my food-streaked clothes tucked into a grocery bag and I've changed into a denim jumper from my suitcase, I feel a little more presentable. I take out my hair, brush away the few bits of grated carrot and cabbage and re-braid it. At very least I have to walk past everyone on my way to the car.

Adrian is serving himself seconds or thirds when I walk back through the kitchen. He has about a quarter inch stack of those generic white paper plates under his helpings. "Wanted to be safe." He holds his food up a little. I can appreciate that he wants to relieve the awkwardness but I don't answer him.

The living room lights are dimmed and the stereo is off. Truitt, Liam, Hayden and Sparrow are likewise subdued. A few tentative "Are you okay?" or similar questions come from the guys and I stiffen until Sparrow speaks.

"Come sit here," she says, and rises from her spot on the floor. I know instantly she won't make me confess that I'm all better just so she'll be released from fixing it or doing something. She will just let me be. It's the perfect seat too, I realize, as I lower onto the large, lumpy pillow. I'm below the illumination of the two lamps and beyond everyone's direct line of sight. The guys keep sneaking glances and I'm forced to smile and fake nonchalance. Sparrow leaves me be after one quick squeeze on my hand.

Hayden reaches for a guitar. So does Truitt. I close my eyes as they begin to strum and then I drop my forehead to my knees. Always with the worship—I can't get away from it. God? You've abandoned me. I can't sleep, and you promise sleep to those you love. I can't worship or rein in my mind and the only sacrifice you desire is one of praise. Am I even your child?

A humming grows in volume. I open my eyes to Hayden's hands cupped over his mouth. He wiggles one hand exposing a shiny silver harmonica. His guitar now sits beside him. The notes mirror my forlorn mood. Sparrow's arms move to raise a flute decorated with a leather strap of beads and feathers to her mouth. The three of them play around with an improvisational melody and then settle in on something familiar. Liam sings. Adrian eats. I wait.

I lower my head again and allow my mind to wander over the past week—the past few months. Mom and Dad. Barkley and Selena. Alvita and Randall. Hayden and Sparrow.

Truitt and me.

The worship grows in intensity so that even Adrian sets aside his plate. In between songs someone randomly prays or says a Bible verse. Most everyone has their eyes closed or lowered. I remember the peace I felt when I let go at church that day, worshiping with Truitt. He's leading on guitar now—why isn't it happening again?

It's almost like worship has more to do with me than my situation—or anything else external. Even more than God—since he isn't supposed to change. Externally and internally, I simultaneously hear, "The people honor me with their lips but their hearts are far from me." I shrink in my seat. Their passion increases. What will I do if they jump up and dance? Or start to speak in tongues? I want to leave.

If I'm honest, I want to leave because I'm afraid I won't feel the same compulsion.

During a lull in music, Adrian asks, "Do I need to be baptized?"

Truitt stops playing and when his hand

smacks his guitar I don't even try to disguise my
jaw dropping open. Nevertheless, only Truitt
notices.

"Do you want to get baptized now?" Hayden
asks.

"Should we go somewhere?"

"Use the bathtub?"

"No city pools are open. Sneak into a hot
tub?"

Everyone's excitement spirals into a vortex of
plans. Everyone except Truitt and me, who stare at
each other until I shift my focus to the guitar in his
hands. My dad's missing cedar-Goodall-acoustic-
forty-five-hundred-dollar guitar.

It's arranged then. They've found someone
who owns a hot tub and keeps it heated enough to
use in February. Liam's driving Adrian. Hayden
and Sparrow will follow. Truitt sets the guitar on a
stand and comes to the floor near me. He lowers
himself and sits cross-legged. "Will you come to the
baptism?"

"No." I pull my skirt tighter around my legs
but make no move to stand.

"I'm sorry. I didn't say anything. You're
right—your dad was selling things. I bought the
guitar. He offered me a Civil War era watch that I
think he ended up taking to a collector. He sold a
few things on Craigslist."

"I can't believe he did it in secret."

"Your dad is proud. You never saw any signs
of money trouble?"

"Well, yes. Maybe." I guess if the missing heirlooms didn't tip me off, the stress surrounding money issues and the declined credit cards should have.

"Are you coming with us or driving with Leah?" Hayden asks Truitt as he zips a shiny, fitted sweatshirt. He looks so excited—his face filled with rapture. Sparrow approaches him from behind for a hug, equally radiant.

"I'm not going." I rise and scan for my bag and yellow dress. I've never seen this much joy surrounding a baptism. Is it even a legal baptism? Out in the wilderness of the world? Without a pastor? Couldn't they just wait for a Sunday? Why are they so barbaric?

Truitt steps away and returns with my dress bag. "Leah." My name on Truitt's lips is pleading, coaxing.

"Don't call me that." He flinches so I continue softer. "I'm tired of being Leah. Tired of being..." Unloved—but I don't say that. "Weary." Leah was duped. I reach for my dress bag and zip it into my suitcase. Leah trusted her parents, their desires for a husband—Barkley. Their provision—foreclosure. Leah trusted God and her church—deception, guilt and the threat of exposure.

The party has bumbled outside and only Truitt and I are left. He looks at me in question, waiting for clarification. It's not time for us: Truitt and me. He has too many burdens of his own to work out. Neither of us are whole right now. But I can be strong.

"Call me Petra." Rock solid Petra.

He tries the name out and smiles like this is all for fun. After he studies my face a moment, his expression turns solemn. "Paul wanted to serve his countrymen—but Peter was the one called to minister to the religious."

"Goodbye, Truitt." I turn and walk to my car.

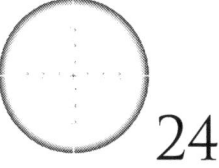 24

My phone sounds the "Burn Notice" theme song, but—since I found out about Truitt—I don't think I'll ever drive distracted again. Not even to see who is calling. I drive in silence down I-80 toward the address Ava gave me. When I approach the McCarran exit, my hands and feet move habitually with a flick to the blinker and deceleration. In my weariness I allow my Jeep to veer and drift toward the exit.

If dad has lost the house, I might as well see it one more time. The grumble of my phone vibrating indicates a text. Whoever it is really wants to get a hold of me—I start to reach for it, then grip the wheel tighter.

It's not worth involuntary manslaughter.

Most of the lights are green on my way home. Will I stay indefinitely with Ava or go to my aunt in Carson? Why, God, did you let my dad lose our house? I pull up the quiet street and wonder if anyone looks through their blinds at my arrival.

Their stories will continue even when I am not here to watch them. The dormant bushes and trees in our yard wait for spring with a promise—but I have no such hope.

The wrinkles on dad's face are scrunched up tighter and deeper than usual—making him look like he is older than when he left without looking back. He hugs me without words right there in the doorway where any neighbor could watch. I want to hug him back but I feel too tired.

"Let me set my bag down, Dad."

"I thought you left too." I don't like the weakness and vulnerability in his voice. He sounds like—just a regular man.

There are a few remnants of "Captivity" littering the entry way. I don't feel like sweeping, though. I want to keep the reminder and stay mad at dad. My parent's bedroom door is slightly cracked and across their bed lays my dad's shotgun. Without removing my shoes I take a step toward it, pointing. "Why is that out?"

He is quicker though, and pulls the door closed. "I was cleaning it." He picks up my suitcase and walks upstairs toward the main part of the house. "Mom got into my office? The drawer?"

"Yeah." I can't look at his face when I answer.

"Where did she go?"

"Aunt Margaret's." I stare at the closed bedroom door a second longer before I start to mount the stairs. "I'm heading there too." He doesn't need to know about Ava. And Aunt Margaret was our first choice after all.

When I reach the top of the stairs, dad sprints behind me. He grabs my keys from my hand. "No, Leah."

"What?" It comes out as a breathy laugh.

"There are things at stake you don't understand. Stay home until after Valentine's Day."

Three days? "I don't have a choice?"

"Are you questioning me?" There is harshness in his voice I don't recognize. I simply shake my head.

"You can decide after the banquet on Tuesday. There will be several decisions. Everything will be fine on Valentine's Day." He holds out my suitcase to me.

"Okay." I try not to show my irritation. "I can wait a couple of days." I reach for my keys when I take my bag. He moves his hand with a tiny jerk and then takes my cell phone out of the hand I used to reach for my keys. "Dad?"

"Trust me." He walks downstairs with my phone and keys, making no noise at all. When he reaches the bottom I am still staring over the banister onto the lower level. He glances up at me then looks to where mom's "Captivity" painting used to hang. Finally, he lifts his head to the vaulted ceiling. "Trust me," he reiterates and walks into his room, where he was cleaning his gun.

It's selfish, I know, but I'm glad the waiter and his wife are arguing again. I pull the soft leggings down my calves so that my ankles are covered. The comfort of my room, pajamas, my telescope, lights off and a locked door make real life unnecessary. My situation floats away on the quietness. The eye pressed to the eyepiece blurs. I spin the focuser with a swipe of my index finger. I'm only kidding myself. I hate looking at people. I hate that they are fighting, I hate that it brings me a small measure of comfort.

I drop down to my bed and pull a few pillows on top of my face to muffle my voice.

"What's going on God?" I flex every muscle in my body three or four times until I feel tired and try not to kick my feet too much. I actually feel better after my tantrum so I roll over.

Still, a sleepless night passes and I'm already reaching for my phone before I fully wake, a habit born from the practice of checking for Truitt's email all last week. As soon as I see the empty charging station I remember. "Who was trying to get a hold of me last night?" Maybe my mom. Probably it was my dad. Un-rested and unready to rise, it is sheer willpower that propels me to a sitting position to rub my eyes.

The shower turns on in my parents' room and my dad's alarm goes off again in urgency. He must have hit snooze instead of off. After I count the three beep cycle to seventy-five, I throw back the covers and slide off the bed.

Of course he doesn't answer my knock—he's still in the shower. When I reach the alarm I have to turn on the desk lamp to figure out how to turn it off. My iPhone sits face down beside the alarm. Quickly, I flip it and slide unlock. Standard advert emails of course—but it looks like Truitt finally replied to mine from last week. It's long so I'll look at it on my computer. Four missed texts. The call was from dad, but the texts were all from Hayden's number.

This is Truitt. Please look these up.

I can't believe he texted me. He must have known I would be driving too. They are Bible verses. The effort it must have taken for him to communicate this way is enough to make me want to know them and look them up. Each verse is a separate text.

Jn 4:24, 2 Cor. 3:17 and Ps 22:3. Even with years of rapid memorization I want to write them down. I scan for a pen and paper but my dad's shower turns off.

Blood rushes and my hands feel warm and puffy as I re-read and try to commit the references to memory. When the sound of a towel is yanked from a towel bar and the shower door unlatches I give up. I try to run up the stairs without noise. Nothing like a little sneaking to feel fully awake. When I get to my bedroom I grab a pen to jot down the verses before I forget.

Where is paper when you need it? Even though I said them out loud several times, I can tell they are slipping, or I got one wrong. I grab the YWAM sheet of yellow from my Bible and scribble.

The first two are correct, I'm sure—but I only recall the chapter reference of the third: Psalm 22. I'm sure I'll know what verse he means when I read it.

My YWAM application has become scratch paper after all. I shove it back inside.

First, I open my laptop and set it next to my telescope. While I wait for it to boot, I turn the telescope and cap the eye piece. Last night was the last time I'll look through it.

The door knob jiggle startles me. "Leah? Why is your door locked?"

"I'm not covered—I was just about to get in the shower."

"Hurry up and get ready. I want to leave early," Dad says through the closed door.

"I can drive and follow in a bit."

"No." He answers too quickly. "We'll drive together. And Leah…"

"Yes?"

"Wear your hair down again for church."

I don't answer but it doesn't seem to be required because his footsteps echo down the hall until he starts banging around in the kitchen. I leave my laptop and change into my robe for showering. When I peek my head out of my room, Dad is preoccupied in the kitchen, but I pull my bedroom door fully closed behind me anyway. I shower quickly and skip the conditioner. Wear my hair down? Am I a show horse? I'll show him my hair down—in all its glory.

I hold my head upside down and brush it

vigorously with a bristle brush. The kind used to smooth straight hair. I'm still smiling at the image my hair will be by the time it dries until I leave the bathroom and see my bedroom door open. Dad is inside shutting down my laptop. "Where were you last night?"

My skin feels taut across my face and hands. "Um, I went to a home group with some college kids."

"Truitt?"

"Yes, sir."

"And what happened to your forehead?"

"I ran into a screen door."

"Truitt again?"

I don't answer, but look down. He doesn't speak so I look up. He pinches his lips together and nods. Then he closes my laptop and lifts it from my desk. "I was afraid of that."

"Are you taking it?" I try to speak softly. What was in the email from Truitt?

"You've had a little too much freedom lately."

"It was just worship with kids."

"Who else went?"

Oops. "Truitt's neighbor." I stall. My towel turban is getting really heavy. I pull my robe belt tighter.

"And?"

"Hayden and Sparrow...and Liam."

My name sounds like a curse on Dad's lips. He rants about my consorting with "that couple," an enemy of our church, Liam, and Truitt's influence, how that has led me into a demon's pit before. I'm crying before he's finished.

If only I could tell him—it was an angel in the prison and a demon in the sanctuary.

"You are naive, Leah. Do I need to remind you again, do not cast your pearls before swine?" I shake my head even though it isn't just the incarcerated he's calling swine anymore—but anyone not part of our church. "I've got so much on my mind, Leah. I can't worry about you right now. This will all be over, your mother will be back, the house will be safe, everything. Everything will be fixed after the banquet."

He leaves me again with the same admonition from last night, "Trust me."

We drive to church in silence. I rearrange my ugliest floral dress and watch my hands, trying not to flinch every time he grinds the gears of my Jeep. I didn't notice when I arrived last night, but dad's car is missing. I want to ask if he sold it or it was repossessed. Either way, it looks like I've lost my Jeep.

I wonder if my mom will notice if I never make it to Ava's house.

Probably not.

Dad slows as we pass a sign: Need Flourishing? Flourishing Faith—next right. His head bobs and he relaxes. Signs increase in frequency as we draw nearer to the church. Are we visiting someone else's church? If not, the claims of flourishing and fulfillment are lies.

Dad parks in Pastor Thompson's spot, right next to the entrance, and hops out with renewed vigor. "What's going on with your hair?"

I turn to the Jeep's window for my reflection. Every thread curls rebelliously — separate from each other. Some is still plastered, wet against my back but the top layer flits in the breeze like drunken fairies. "I don't know."

"It didn't look like that last time you wore it down, when Pastor King came for dinner."

He's stopped calling him Barkley? "Mom helped me that night."

His gaze moves from my face to my hair. What can he say? I've won. After a moment he raises his eyebrows with a "we'll see about that," expression and turns toward the church calling over his shoulder "Put it in a braid or something."

"Yes, sir." I pull the waiting hair band from my wrist and have it plaited before he unlocks the front door. He holds it open for me and when I pass him I say, "I'll start the coffee," before he can give me a job.

The signs in the foyer are ridiculous. It looks like we were sponsored by a sign shop. The fundraiser thermometer banner is the biggest, but also prevalent are T-shirts, coffee mugs, ads for Tuesday's Valentine's Day Banquet and promises of rekindling and flourishing in your marriage. The Flourishing Faith theme drips in hot pink from wall to wall.

A huge pulse of déjà vu washes over me when I enter the kitchen alone. Another audio recorder sits in the same place on the center of the counter. I scoop it up quickly and drop it into one of the large, front pockets of my dress. This one doesn't have duct tape either. I am going to have to check the extra two I left in my purse.

Once the coffee is brewing, I slip into my office and turn on the desktop computer. My dad hasn't sought me out with a task so I quickly make a new online email account under the name Petra Jones, download the audio file from the recorder and email it to myself. I leave it connected by USB to charge, hidden behind the CPU. To prevent Randall from finding anything—I'll just have to get more creative hiding stuff. Sneaking down the hall, I head to see if the recorder is still hiding under the table.

It is.

The conference room is disorganized so I straighten chairs and tables. I still don't know what dad is up to or where he went, but I won't have another chance today. I close the door, turn off the lights and stand on a table under the furthest florescent light. Using a paper towel to protect my fingers, I unscrew one bulb slightly and replace the light cover. It worked. When I flip the switch back on the bulb does not illuminate.

I replace the cover but leave a new recorder inside, next to the edge. The light won't go on, so it won't get too hot or be seen. Perfect.

Next I find the storage room and locate the box of replacement bulbs. There is only one left—probably due to our recent lack of organization since Betty left. I drop the box to its side and take a swinging-arm leap. What a satisfying crunch. I stand the box back up, straighten the corners and leave it as I found it. Now no one will be replacing bulbs for a while.

My dad's in the hall. "There you are." His face is shiny with perspiration. "Is the coffee ready? Can you start the communion cups and stuff? Plan for at least double at today's service. When the Blakes and Millers get here I'll send Marta in to help you." He turns and jog-walks down the hall with a final call of: "Learn to delegate, Leah."

It's still two hours before service starts, and I doubt last week's fiasco will fill the church, even with our mass postcard mailing and enticing signs that lead the way here. But I respond to his urgency and scurry down the hall. Miss Chan stands in front of the kitchen with a clipboard.

Learn to delegate, Leah. "Want to help me fill the communion cups?" I ask her with a smile.

The expression she returns is a scarcely controlled snarl. I laugh a little in disbelieving response before Miss Selena Chan turns and walks away. Her thin frame does not sway in any feminine manner but clips up and down like a race horse resisting restraints.

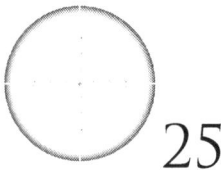

25

Noises from the gathering crowd trickle in, so I stick my head out in the hallway to gauge the number. Dad strides toward the kitchen, "How many do you have done?"

"Four trays."

"I think you'll need at least twelve."

"Twelve?"

"It's hopping out there. Full house." Dad beams. "Marta never came to help you?"

Marta does what benefits Marta—so it's funny that Dad is surprised she didn't obey. Has he not met the Millers? "I'll never get twelve done in time to do worship." I carefully guard my face so I don't show my pleasure.

"No need." Dad's preoccupied making a list in his head or something. "We hired a worship team for today...for a while." He turns to look in a cupboard. "Oh, yeah." He runs off with purpose after whatever he remembered.

I didn't want to do worship—but I'm still

insulted they hired someone else.

"Yow, Leah chil'." Alvita walks in. She's surprisingly subdued in a navy chiffon crease skirt and a snug, almost-navy suit jacket. Her burgundy lips shine the same color as her nails. "Do you need help?"

"I do. Get a few more bottles of grape juice cocktail out of the cupboard there, and the rest of the gluten-free communion disks." How different today's communion is, compared to last night's. I'm so much more comfortable with the familiar elements, and being on the preparing end rather than the receiving end—the Mary/Martha thing I guess. Alvita brings four more bottles of grape-flavored drink. I grab and open the first one she sets down, pointing to an empty tray. "Fill those with cups and then the grape cocktail. Use a turkey baster like this." I demonstrate. "There should be one in the drawer. Or it gets everywhere."

"Can do." She licks her lips and takes off her jacket to reveal a lacy white tank top with shoulder pads. Around her neck she wears a large wooden circle necklace. The off center hole is threaded by a black, beaded strand with Jamaican flag colors.

"How'd you know I needed help?" I ask after a minute.

"Don't know." She smiles but doesn't look up at me.

"It's never been this crowded before." It sounds like chaos out in the hall.

"I don't believe dat." Her accent's just as

prevalent as when she talks to Randall, like I'm part of her inner circle now.

"Why are you here today, Alvita?"

"Well, I spent a whole week cleaning with Randall so I thought I should see who it was we were serving."

Serving, not working for. If she is going to become part of the church then I want to find out if she realized what Randall had discovered when they moved the audio recorders. "His cleaning is pretty thorough."

"Haphazard is more like it. But he makes up in energy." She begins to hum "Great is Thy Faithfulness," instead of elaborate. How can I ask her without drawing attention to the devices?

"Do you only take care of Randall during the weekdays?"

"He has another aide for weekends and nights." She continues humming.

Mrs. Parker, her daughter Nora, and Marta Miller bustle in looking bewildered. They pull the coffee urn down to a wheeled cart and Mrs. Parker complains. "There's nothing in here. It didn't get made."

"I don't think we've ever made two carafes." Beside me, Alvita works steadily.

"Well, they already drank the last one," Marta says.

"If you get it started now, it should be done by the end of service," I suggest.

"Not you, Nora." Mrs. Parker says and Marta

steps backward behind them. "No one wants coffee ministry to come under women's ministry until the coffee needs to be made," she snips.

I try not to laugh at her. Mrs. Parker always wants everything to be structured under the women's ministry.

"I can do it..." And I wonder why I have the Martha syndrome.

She doesn't even offer the conventional 'Are you sure?' She just mumbles, "Anyway, I don't want to miss service."

Marta sways funny, mimicking Mrs. Parker and looks back to see if it makes me smile. It doesn't.

The urn is not heavy when it's empty, just awkward. As I lift, Alvita rushes to my side without needing a request. I refill the grounds and start the water. The machine kicks on with grinding and groans. It will take about thirty minutes for the water to heat enough.

Dad rushes in. "Oh good! You started it." He turns to our neatly-stacked, nearly-finished communion trays. "Sorry, baby. We won't be needing those today."

"What?"

"I'm sorry about your work and time, Le-ah." The way he says my name is a warning about the challenge.

It has nothing to do with my time though.

"Pas-tor King," Dad emphasizes the title, "feels that communion is too intimate, too savage a ritual and I agree with him. He doesn't want to alienate so many visitors."

Dad leaves without waiting for a reply from me, even a nod of acquiescence. Why should he? My opinion has never counted.

Suddenly I remember the unleavened bread from last night. Where did I put it? The waste, the unworthiness and the lost opportunity…

Savage. Barbaric. Intimate.

The machine gurgles and steams behind me. To my right, Alvita picks up humming again but pauses once to say, "Oh, girl—it's worse than I thought."

She walks to the table and lowers herself to a chair. "Do you ever learn to live in such a dry climate?" She laughs at herself and slips her sockless feet from her flats. White lines cover her dark skin. "I'll need to bathe in lotion to survive this five-percent humidity."

We have a bottle under the sink so I take it to her, giggling at her "Bless you."

After I wipe the counter and return the one unopened bottle of juice cocktail, I start organizing the cupboard for inventory. We'll need more supplies before next week. How did they get so many people here this week?

When guitar and drums start up in the sanctuary, the hall crowd begins to filter away. I study the unneeded communion service waiting on the counter. Should I pour the juice back into the bottles? Surely not down the drain? About the time

I decide to take it to the children's classrooms, Miss Chan's voice rises from the hall. "The bonds will be ten-year."

"Secured?" An unfamiliar man's voice asks.

"Yes, with the church's camp property."

Bonds? The church has camp property?

But they've already moved on down the hall. A glance at Alvita tells me she heard too—but she couldn't know it was all a lie. I tiptoe around the hall in time to see the group turning the corner and heading into the conference room. I want to squeal. Here's hoping the audio recorder in the florescent light or the one under the table will pick up sound.

The conference door closes and even though there is a man chasing a toddler and several wannabe hipsters sucking church-coffee from Styrofoam in the hall, I press my ear to it.

"Yes, this is a typical sized Sunday congregation." It's muffled through the door, but definitely Miss Chan and definitely a lie. How did they get all these people here, anyway?

"What are you doing?" Hailey asks. I didn't see her and Rachel sitting at the T-shirt table— probably because they both wear one and blend in. Looks like Pastor King knows what he wants to market this church. A front-line of college girls.

"Nothing." Funny that, before today, there hadn't been a new family in eight or more years. We were just a tiny, protected church of young families who grew up. In another year or so the last of the college group would have moved on and only empty-nesters would have been left.

"It is in use, if that's what you are checking."

"Yeah, that's all I wanted to know." I fumble.

"I don't know who they are." Hailey refolds a T-shirt like she's worked in a clothing store before. "Some lady who acts like she's in charge."

So it isn't common knowledge that a consultant is meeting with investors. "Pastor King hired her." Both girls study the door then, a mix of consideration and jealousy. "They're not together." I shouldn't play into the gossip—but I want confirmation of general feelings toward the Pastor.

Rachel and Hailey share smiles and whispers. Yep—the entire church sees him as the most eligible bachelor. Jane Austin wrote, "A single man in possession of a good fortune must be in want of a wife." In church culture it's, "A single man in possession of a flock."

"I need to get something out of my office," I say as I leave.

"How do you like working here all day with him?" Rachel asks loud enough for me to hear with my back to her six feet away.

I shrug, shake my head and keep walking. It works, they don't press. I reach for the recorder, charging behind my CPU. I reach again. On my knees, I grope and pat and yank the mouse and printer USB plugs to pull out my computer. The recorder's gone.

Without a glance at the T-shirt girls I speed down the hallway and surprise Alvita—still working lotion into her hands and feet. "Is Randall here today?"

"No chil'. Are you kidding? Crowds freak him out."

Each time I thought the recorder was moved by Randall, Alvita was nearby. It could just as easily have been her.

"Why are you looking at me like that?"

I retrieve the lotion from the table beside her and return it under the sink, slowly considering a reply. Since the coffee machine is hot I set a new small carafe to brew. Likely we won't need it — and it is the very last of the coffee — but if we do, I'll be a hero.

"Do you want to go in the sanctuary, hear the sermon?" she asks. Apparently she doesn't need further explanation about my expression.

Listen to a motivational pep talk full of brilliant one-liners from Pastor King? I haven't even tried to go back into the sanctuary since last Tuesday when I considered sticking a recorder in there and couldn't. What if that thing is behind the podium again? Maybe Truitt and his barbaric-fasting-worshiping group need to come perform an exorcism.

So our church can return to normal?

"Don' mek di devil fool yu."

"What?"

"It means wake up, chil'." Alvita sits on the chair with her feet planted wide and hands on her knees.

"Alvita, do you believe in the devil? In spirits?"

"Doesn't matter if I do or I don't."

The worship in the sanctuary has stopped so my dad must be moving on to announcements. "Why wouldn't it matter if you believe or not?"

She thinks a minute. "It just doesn't change a thing if you don't believe."

"You mean they're still there whether I believe in them or not?"

She nods. The coffee starts to trickle and Alvita watches it for a moment. "Why do you ask?"

I go to the table and take a chair next to her. "I think I saw something here."

"See what I mean?" Alvita lifts her hands in the air. "Whether you think or you know, either it was here or it wasn't."

Convoluted truth—just like my parents have been spoon feeding me my whole life. The scent of coffee starts to sift into the air. I rise and pull down the same two mugs I used when I made her coffee the other day. "Okay. I know. It was here," I say only loud enough for her to hear and then stare at the mugs.

Alvita retrieves the half and half from the fridge and brings it to the counter. "Because you think you saw something—"

I look up at her quickly in challenge.

"Or you saw something for the first time. Something that's always been there. Does it make you afraid?"

Seeing it wasn't what made me afraid. I shrug and start to walk away. I don't want to talk about this anymore. What am I doing telling a practical stranger? I can't expose myself, our church...and ultimately, my dad.

She grabs my wrist, she doesn't pull or squeeze but I feel bound anyway. "Perfect love casts out fear."

I actually get the chills from her words. When I look up at her, she continues, "Love God. Love people."

"Of course." I smile. What else would a pastor's daughter do? She lets me go then and I fill the mugs with coffee before the urn is finished. The brew is very dark so I only pour a tiny bit in mine and add lots of cream.

"Thank you, Leah."

"That's my first name. I go by Petra."

She smiles wide, showing her top and bottom row of teeth. Then she tells me about the first time she drank coffee.

Sitting with Alvita and laughing about stories from her childhood in Jamaica lightens me in a way church never does. Her fellowship is an unexpected refuge. By the time the closing song oozes from the congregation, I'm rested—even renewed. We migrate toward the foyer as the first of the pew-warmers bolt for the front door.

When we reach the crowded doorway to the sanctuary I scan the perimeter of the room—just in case. Nothing but the humans I expect. Alvita pushes through so I slip in after her, navigating against the stream. Dad sees me and waves us toward him and Pastor King. "Great message," he says.

"Yeah." I look to Alvita and she nods in agreement. I look away, scanning the room. I don't know why though—either it's there or it isn't. Whether I see it, or believe it, or don't.

An old lady, with fingers as crooked as her back, steps into line to greet the Pastor. Pastor King shines in the adoration of the waiting line. He jokes and mingles with the crowd until everyone, even my dad, pauses to hear everything he says. When the old lady is next, Pastor King turns left to a beautiful woman with so much jewelry she must work for one of those home-based pyramid businesses. She asks about setting up private counseling and he tells her to schedule it with the office.

The old lady adjusts her dirty coat and moves behind jewelry-girl. Pastor King turns his head to me. "Make sure this young lady gets a card so she can find the number."

"I have one." Dad pulls one of the new

business cards from a silver case in his pocket.

Pastor King still grasps jewelry-girl's hands with two of his. Tears shimmer in her eyes, rivaling her earrings. A middle-aged woman grasping hands with a big man approach us and Pastor turns away from the little old lady to greet them. The old woman looks up from her folded-over stance and patiently shifts to get in line again behind the couple.

"Do you want to speak to the pastor?" I put my hand on her back and lean over to her.

"Thank you, dear." She reaches gnarled fingers out to the air, groping. I hold my hand out to her line of sight and she clamps it. Pastor won't miss seeing her now. My five feet, eleven inches can compensate for the old woman's bent frame.

When the couple's questions about youth groups and other services are deflected with: "So nice to meet you. Come and see us again soon," I step directly in front of him, dragging the woman with me. He looks beyond us, scanning the crowd.

He inhales, deep and satisfied with a slight smile. Simultaneously—a bald man with nineteen-forty's style, round spectacles strides toward us with a determination outclassing his size. His gray suit is so shiny it looks silver. He has a long wool coat thrown over his left forearm and his right hand is outstretched.

Pastor turns directly to him. Their manicured hands shake.

"I had no idea you had this much going on

out here. My personal assistant has insisted for months that you were the one this year," the bald man speaks. "My name is Pascal Reiss."

"The people gather where God moves, Mr. Reiss." Pastor King shakes his hand and does that heel-click-bow he did so frequently the first Sunday he spoke.

"My late wife was very religious."

"Mrs. Reiss must have been a singular woman." I don't know why Pastor King feels he needs to say this, but it sure pleases the man.

"She passed near Valentine's Day ten years ago and every year I make a sizable donation in her honor."

"To honor her memory in this way undoubtedly causes her to rejoice with the angels."

I'm sure my dad's rejoicing by the way he holds his breath.

"This year, being a monumental year—a decade..." The man lets the words hang in the air just long enough for Pastor King to reply.

"Sir, shall we continue this in my office?"

"Certainly."

My dad leaves with the bald man and Pastor King.

Alvita steps nearer and gives me a hug. "See you tomorrow." She moves away and chats with a young family nearby. Tomorrow I will ask her about the moved recorders.

"Is he coming back, dear?" The old woman asks.

"No, ma'am. I don't think so." I pat her arthritic fingers.

"Oh, maybe I'll wait." She sighs.

"Did you have a need?" She probably wants a ride home or to know about our food bank hours.

"He made me think of a boy I once knew." She strains to look up at me and her eyes are light brown like young fawns in the snow white of her skin. "Jamal."

"That's nice." How long will I have to wait for my dad? I wish we had driven separately.

"I was a school teacher for fifty-five years."

"Wow." I answer somewhat automatically. I wonder how Alvita knows that family. Will she be honest when I ask her about the recorder? Wait, "Fifty-five years?"

"The last ten I've only come in one hour to read. Principal Snyder said, 'Louisa, as long as you can walk and see and speak—you have a job here.' You know, you mostly only remember the bad ones."

She looks up and smiles and I see the feistiness that kept her going to a school everyday years after her prime. She continues, "Jamal Groetsch. So hard to say his last name. His temper… when someone said it wrong. But he was a looker. Created lots of drama with the little girls." She shakes her head and laughs softly. "Sure didn't help his cause. Because with a name like that, the kids always said it wrong." She starts coughing in such a way that I lead her to a pew to rest.

A paunchy, prematurely balding man looks up from a conversation at her coughing. "How are you doing, Grandma?" He walks over to us. "We should get you back home."

She wipes her mouth with a linen and says, "That's not my home. I hate it there, with all those old people."

"She lives in a retirement facility?" An ornery gal like her doesn't belong in a home. She should be able to take care of herself since she still works.

He places a hand under the old lady's arm and she manages to her feet. "Ever since her sight started to go..."

So she can't teach any longer either. Compassion overwhelms me. I feel her loss as my own when I watch them start away. "I'm going to remember you." She lifts a crooked finger to her grandson. Are her memories on their way out too?

By the time they reach the door to leave the sanctuary I remember her words, "You always remember the bad ones." Laughing at our inside joke, I run forward, compelled externally. "Louisa, what home do you live in? And...can I come visit sometime?"

With the WoodHaven Assisted Living's name and address in my head, I beeline to my office for a pen and paper. But I forget it as soon as I walk in. Didn't I leave my computer pulled out? Unhooked? Everything is pushed in neat, I squat down. There, connected to my CPU is the audio recorder—just as I left it this morning.

## 27

As Dad, Barkley, Miss Chan and I wait for a table at a place I've never eaten — the Norwood Bistro — they become their habitual, unstoppable tricycle. No room on this contraption for me.

"I'm going to use the restroom," I interrupt them.

"Wait until we have our table," Dad says.

So I cross my arms and wait. Miss Chan is smirking but she doesn't look at me so I don't know for sure what she finds so amusing. Their hushed conversation is cryptic, but excited. It seems like we might be celebrating something. Maybe a successful first Sunday since they emotionally and literally tore apart our church. Once we are directed to a table and I return from the restroom, I sit in the only open seat between Miss Chan and my Dad, across from Barkley. I gape at the menu. How will we afford this?

"Good afternoon, today the chef has prepared…"

The waiter lists the specials. It's been awhile since I had a nice meal. With mom gone and everything, it's been some time since I had a meal at all.

"We're ready to order." Barkley sets his menu beside his bread plate. Miss Chan goes first and they look to me.

"I'll go last."

"Hurry," Dad whispers. I haven't seen more than the appetizer section but apparently everyone is famished.

It's my turn again before I've had a chance to turn the menu's page. "What were the specials?" My dad doesn't make a sound but his head lifts suddenly and he leans back and crosses his arms. "Never mind, I'll have what he ordered." I point to my dad. At least then I won't order something too expensive because he ordered it himself.

"Would you like something to drink, ma'am?"

I glance around the table to three sets of impatient expressions. "Water is fine."

The waiter leaves and Miss Chan leans in. "So?"

Barkley looks at Dad and they share a private, charged smile like parents do on Christmas morning. Dad lifts his hand and nods slightly as if to say, "You first."

"Fifty," Barkley announces.

"That puts us way ahead of schedule." Miss Chan is complete composure.

The waiter brings three sodas to the table. "Fifty what?" I ask Dad quietly.

He sighs a little patronizing noise. "A donation of fifty thousand dollars today." Because I'm focusing on not staring bug-eyed at dad, I see Miss Chan reach for Barkley's hand and squeeze it quickly before shoving both her hands under the table.

"Way ahead of schedule," She repeats and finally looks at me. Her eyes blink slowly and when they open, it's only a slit—making them look even smaller. She focuses on my feet. Her gaze travels up my legs to my body and face. Her perfectly smooth skin crinkles a bit around her nose and one side of her mouth lifts. She turns away without a word. I scoot in closer to the table so my feet are tucked under.

Apparently today's offering collection hasn't been counted, but Barkley must have been persuasive, because they all have high hopes for the building fund. I wonder how many bonds she sold.

"We'll get the AutoCAD rendition made into a poster. Visualizing the end will inspire people to contribute faster." Miss Chan smoothes her cloth napkin across her lap.

"You already have plans approved?" Things normally take forever with the bickering knights of the square table that is our church's board.

"They aren't approved with the city, yet." Miss Chan answers me but smiles at my dad. Dad pats my hand. Apparently they aren't approved with the board either. Fine. I will not ask any more questions.

Miss Chan doesn't touch her bread but my Dad devours his as though he hasn't eaten in years. I chew mine slowly, buttering each bite intensely so I have something to do while they applaud themselves and plan the "next phase." Before the food is brought I wish I had my own car again — even more so when the waiter declares the dish I ordered. "Walnut-crusted Sea Bass with cilantro…"

"I'm allergic to walnuts." I put my hand up.

"Leah, why did you order it then?" Dad is exasperated.

He heard me say "I'll have what he ordered." Dad could have prevented this too.

Now the waiter mimics everyone's impatient glare. "I just…I was rushed…I only…" No one was willing to let me have time with the menu.

"Shall I bring you something else?" The waiter is paid to be gracious I guess, but no one else at my table has any inclination.

"Yes, please."

"Would you like to see the menu again?"

"No, please bring me some kind of pasta — without nuts."

The waiter whisks away the offending dish. "Sorry, Leah. But we aren't going to wait."

"Of course, Dad. I wouldn't expect — "

But they are already eating.

My meal comes about the time they are finished so I ask for a box. When the check arrives, my dad bends to reach into a blue, zippered pouch. He's discreet, but I've seen it many times before. I've even had to take Flourishing Faith's deposit bag to the bank myself.

Dad digs for a minute and lifts several twenty-dollar bills from it and places them on the restaurant receipt.

"I need to use the restroom." Or I will scream.

"Again?"

I nod at my dad and leave before I cry in front of him. Is this the kind of wages workmen are worth?

Fortunately, The King and his advisor are gone after I'm finished splashing cold water on my eyes. Dad drives my Jeep in silence. We return to the emptiness in silence and he enters his office in, yeah…more silence.

The first thing I do is change into pajamas. Next, I pop a small portion of my leftovers into the microwave and take stock: I don't have a phone. I don't have a laptop. Mom is gone. The house is in foreclosure and Dad is not only stealing from us, but the church and finally—the pastor partakes of the benefits. Beep, beep…pasta is done. Will I partake as well?

The glop of steaming aged cheese and nuked noodles slides from the plate into the garbage disposal. The image blurs into the communion I didn't take—that I was afraid to take unworthily. I shiver.

I can't take it unworthily—does that mean I shouldn't take it at all?

I'll feel better if I talk to mom. If she pulls through, I'll be okay. It will all be okay. The phone does not have a dial tone. I hang up and try again. The lights come on the cordless phone—so it isn't the battery.

I carry it to my Dad's office and knock on the door. Click. Click. Click. He has to close out whatever it is he does in there. Apparently he paid the internet bill. "Come in, Leah."

He leans back and folds his arms over his chest. There are bags under his eyes and creases in his forehead.

"I wanted to call Mom." I hold up the cordless receiver.

His shoulders slump slightly but his arms remain crossed. "Yeah. We don't have a phone right now."

"Can I have my cell phone back?"

He bites the inside of his cheek and works it around in his mouth.

"Or can I go see her?"

"Now?"

"Yeah, I want to drive to go see her."

"No. You need to be here for the banquet."

"I'll come back." For the first time ever, it is very easy to lie.

"Too much gas. Cost's too much."

I know it wouldn't cost as much as our lunch today. "I want," I take a deep breath trying not to shake. "I want to be with Mom."

"No one has *been* with Mom in months." His anger surprises me. He jumps up from his leather chair. "You have to be here for the Valentine's Banquet. Barkley has something to talk to you about."

"What?" The guy hardly looks at me, unless it's creepy or some form of dismissal. He didn't even try to sit next to me at lunch. The last time I talked to him he questioned my interest in men under threat of my dad's job. I shake my head in surprise, disgust even.

"You said you were going to pray about it!"

"I did pray about it."

"Obviously not enough then."

I have no answer for that. If proof of my devotion to God lies in choosing the same as my dad, I'll have no adequate rebuttals.

"Go to your room."

I don't want to obey. "Can I have my phone to call Mom?"

"You're grounded. Get in your room. You need to spend the rest of the afternoon praying about your relationship with Barkley."

Dad doesn't give me the option this time. He physically guides me down the hall to my room and gives me a slight push inside. "Don't come out again tonight unless you are willing to listen to God." Dad closes the door.

Did that seriously just happen? I'm dizzy so I lower to the edge of my bed and bend over, almost laughing, almost not breathing. I can't tell if I'm hot or cold but my fingers feel tingly and fat.

The King wants to talk to me about something? Why? I sit straight quickly. It seems like he and dad have already arranged "something."

I can't face them both—I have to hide. Where could I go? Who could help me? Could I call Truitt? I'd have to reach him through Hayden. Maybe Alvita? She might know what to do. I don't even know her last name. I wish I hadn't cleaned up mom's painting—I'd like to smash the unbroken edge a little more. Captivity, indeed.

If I was able to reach Truitt, what could he even do? It isn't like he'd drive me somewhere. I roll over and crawl up into my bed, pulling the covers over me. God? Hide me.

I don't wake until midnight. When I do, I walk sleepy-eyed to my telescope and begin adjusting the lenses, automatically. This is my balm. This is my release. I need to go to the restroom before I'm finished focusing so I take care of that first. Tiptoeing back down the hall—I realize since we'll lose the house any day—Dad could find the USB keystroke recorder I left in his office.

Unless he is the one who keeps moving them.

I skedaddle as lightly as my urgent heart will allow and sneak into his office. Reaching behind the tower my fingers fumble in the haste. Finally, I distinguish the right protrusion and yank. My recorder. Dad's recorder. All-righty then. We'll see what he's up to tomorrow from my work computer.

Lucas is visiting again, but alone, and the waiter just watches television. I don't think the waiter's wife is there because almost all of the lights in the entire house are on and blinds are open everywhere. I return to Lucas. Watching him sleep, I picture him as I've seen him previously. The memory gives me a small release. I sit back on my bed and frown at the telescope. I hate this. Pain presses in my stomach like burning hunger. Even though my lights are off, it isn't dark enough for me so I unplug the digital alarm clock.

It's brighter outside my bedroom now because of the ambient downtown glow, several miles away. Even without light, I still feel exposed. Maybe someone watches me with an infrared lens. I pop up and yank the blinds closed. My legs tremble so I slide them under the covers again. The sense of exposure doesn't leave; neither does the guilt scraping at my insides. It isn't infrared. It's God who sees.

I pull my covers up over my head.

It must be morning by the sound of Dad's shower running downstairs. Who knew I could lay still and awake all night? A strange emptiness and fatigue fills me. Since I have to go to work with Dad I rise and make for the kitchen to start some coffee as a kind gesture. If I do something for him, maybe he'll let me have my phone back. I could even fake a little repentance and interest in The King...

Unfortunately, the coffee jar doesn't have a single ground left. Likewise, the coffee pot is dry as though it's been some time since it was used. Maybe he only drinks it at work these days. I stand, barefoot, studying the pantry. It will be easy to move. The same bareness inside me lines our cupboards.

I set out a navy floral dress with an empire waist, corduroy cuffs and collar, hating that I have to go but knowing I deserve it. I keep watching my neighbors and acting like my dad is in the wrong. I mean, the money was given to the church. What is the big deal if he records the deposit and goes to lunch or doesn't record the deposit and goes to lunch?

Before I shower, I lower the telescope's legs and slide it back into my closet. I will never spy again.

Dad nearly drained the hot water tank. It feels just. Why should I get a hot shower every day when people all over the world don't even have water to drink? I'm pouring it down the drain at any temperature I fancy.

I turn it all the way to cold and appreciate the misery.

I don't allow myself a towel but just pull my robe over shivering limbs. The dress sticks to my damp body. I deserve discomfort. I braid my hair without brushing or glancing in the mirror, skip the lotion and set out my least comfortable shoes. No socks today. I want pain. But nothing diminishes the ache in my stomach.

Who am I kidding? I pull out the telescope

and set it up. It is already focused for the distance to Lucas' so as soon as I angle it I can see through their window. I want more.

"Hurry up, Leah! Fix your hair today."

"Coming," I call. "Just need shoes."

When I run to my closet I knock over my craft bag. Instead of putting on the leather boat shoes that pinch a little, I begin to re-stuff the crafts. I hesitate when I pick up the scissors from the yarn pile.

Reaching behind, I lift my braid and poise the scissors at the nape of my neck. Finally, something works to make me feel alive. Alarm pushes away the emptiness. Could I do it?

The only thing worse than the shame I feel at watching others is the realization that the shame is a little less than normal.

In dread, I squeeze.

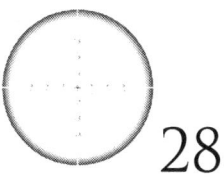

28

"Why are you wearing a hat, sweetheart?"

I finger the lacy, crocheted beanie. "I'm going to WoodHaven Assisted Living today to start a crochet class." I had that excuse ready.

"Is the lump still there?" He starts to reach for my head but I pull back.

"Nope." I finger the tender spot Truitt smacked with the screen two nights ago.

Dad shakes his head. "We have too much to do in preparation for tomorrow's banquet for you to go off today."

"I hoped to invite Pastor King to go with me." That one wasn't planned but it feels so natural on my lips I almost believe myself. Of course, that will make it harder to drive straight to Ava's but I'll figure something out.

Dad pinches his lips like he might explode with tears, pride or "tough-love parenting" relief— only it doesn't feel as good as if I'd earned it honestly. He lifts my jacket from the hall-tree storage bench and holds it out for me. Suddenly, I want to confess everything to be close to him. My feelings for Truitt, the telescope and spying, the creature in the sanctuary and why I'm scared of Pastor King. I wish I could make this pride—all I've ever wanted from him—sincerely earned. I turn and slide my arms into the plaid, purple coat and in doing this, I catch my image in the mirror. Little, errant curls are beginning to emerge from the lacy holes in my beanie.

How can he not see the lengths poking through? As I button my jacket I straighten to my full height and look him in the eyes. Do you see me, Daddy? I reach for my cap. I will show him…

"You look so much like your mother."

"But I am not my mother." One finger is hooked in the top of my cap, pulling.

"Thank goodness." He looks to the empty wall where "Captivity" hung. "A fool rejects wisdom and instruction. Your mother never yielded to reproof." He turns from me and crosses over the garage doorway with heavy steps. I am left staring at his back with the crocheted cap in my hand.

I turn back to the mirror in the hall-tree. One thing about curly hair, it doesn't need to be cut straight. The two sides are dramatically longer than the back in an accidental, funky, chin-line bob. Maybe if I keep the beanie on until it dries they will stay down. "Hello, Petra." My reflection smiles back. "Let's go see Mom." I tuck everything back inside and follow my dad out the door, mimicking his heavy steps.

Neither of us have anything to say so we drive to the church like an old married couple, like he normally drives with my mom. We stop at the bank on the way and I wait in the car. Dad takes a full twenty minutes inside and I fall asleep waiting.

"Why are you so tired? It's barely nine-thirty." Dad puts his satchel between our seats, just behind us. The blue deposit bag he brought to lunch sits just on top, but instead of being flat—empty, it bulges.

"The insomnia makes me cat-nap through the day." It's either because of my focus on the bag or the not-fully awake vulnerability that I let those words slip.

"You can't have insomnia."

"What would be a reason I can't sleep at night?"

"Disobedience." He puts his right hand on my seat back to turn and look behind us as he backs up my Jeep. I look down so I don't have to meet his eyes. Dad continues, "Or weakness in your mind. Poor planning, even." He turns forward and glances at me as he shifts into drive. "At your age, it's likely routine and diet too."

My brain is suddenly too heavy to hold up and I rest against my seat picturing the countless hours of laying prostrate, praying for sleep to come. It was my fault all along.

The Lord gives sleep to those he loves.

Leah, the unloved.

"Dad, I want to go by Petra."

Because of the silence that follows, I don't think he heard me—I even question if I said it out loud. Several cars already wait in the church parking lot, including a lighting company van and one titled Rent-a-Party.

"What is all this?"I ask.

"The Valentine's Day dinner and auction, Leah Patrice." His enunciation of my name proves that he did hear me.

I reach for his satchel to help bring stuff inside. "I got it." Dad pulls it from my hands.

Hiding a yawn, I turn and slide out of the Jeep. It's going to be a long day if I don't find an excuse soon.

Two men leave the building as we enter. Several others are coming in behind us with tables or chairs in their hands. "It's going to look great in here." Dad practically runs to the sanctuary.

I like my office, at least the idea of having my own office. But this isn't my office—whose desk and things are these supposed to belong to? A large two-tone desk and wood file cabinets fill the tiny space. There are no extra chairs, but I guess it isn't my job to entertain visitors, only direct them.

The files were dropped in the new cabinets without complete order—but I think I can right it quickly. Even the computer is new. Quickly finding the main button, I press.

"Which home are you planning on visiting?" Dad and The King crowd the doorway.

"WoodHaven Assisted Living." I pat my hat. "But I really don't need an escort."

Barkley inhales to speak but dad jumps in first.

"Nonsense." Dad looks around at the blank walls and then where I sit. "Wow, this place looks fantastic. I thought you were going to paint though." They leave, discussing the merits of painting before you add furniture.

"Dad," I jump up and strike my thigh trying to get around the huge desk and to the doorway. "What time is Alvita supposed to come in today?"

Dad turns his wrist to look at his watch but Pastor King answers. "She already came and left."

"Already left?" Dad asks before I can.

Pastor King doesn't make eye contact at first but when he does I suddenly become aware of my breathing — actually lack of it.

"I let Randall go," The King says. "It was somewhat nice, in theory, but we need to give our best to God. This is God's house. We shouldn't be cutting corners, so to speak, to save money." He turns to Dad. "I told you this was going to cost."

Dad turns and studies Pastor at that. I almost think he will respond but in the end he nods and changes the subject. "What time are you leaving, Leah?"

"I'll call and find out." As I walk back to my desk I place my feet a little more carefully to avoid another bruise. I'm getting as clumsy as Truitt.

Alvita won't be coming in today? Won't be

coming in again? I didn't even get a phone number or email. What if I never see her again?

The screen shows a "Secretary" user account. It doesn't require a password. That is the first thing I need to set up. Unfortunately, the secretary is a standard account—not an administrator. How will I install software or anything? There isn't even an email client on here. I pull up a web browser and begin to check my new Petra account but suspicion stops me. I should never log in without checking to see if one of my own gadgets is being used against me. Squatting on the floor behind the desk with a nervous heart causes me to squeal when Selena Chan asks "What are you looking for?"

"Nothing." I sit back quickly and look up at her like a toddler trying to hide.

"Nothing, on your knees, on the floor, behind your computer?" One half of her lips lift. The corresponding nostril flares lightly.

Instead of remaining on the floor, looking up at her smirk, I stand. I am several inches taller than her petite body. My hands move naturally to my hips. "I need an account that can install software."

She leans forward, almost conspiratorially. "I have recommended to Pastor King that we have a professional looking website built for us. Rollover buttons built in a Wysiwyg is fine for some things, I'm sure. But not for the future of Flourishing Faith Fellowship. Not for our goals."

A Wysiwyg—"what you see is what you get" design program. So? I'm not a coder. I need pictures to drag and drop and insert items when I build websites. I try to smile. "I guess the functionality was pretty limited."

"The functionality is secondary to the amateur design. Where did you go to college?" She smoothes her slim skirt and spends a moment picking off imaginary lint and flicking it onto the floor of my office.

"I didn't go."

My admission gives her great amusement. "The second rate staff this church hired — no wonder they needed me." She continues laughing as she leaves but turns at the final step. "Cute hat." Her laughter sounds several seconds after she is no longer in sight.

Lacking the desire to stand, I slip backward into my chair. No, I need to get out — not wait for Pastor King. I bump my thigh again in the same spot as I round the ridiculously huge desk. Even if I have to steal my keys from Dad, I'm leaving for Ava's right now — but I'll stop for my telescope and gadgets first. I'm kidding myself to think I can go without them.

Spying is a part of me. I couldn't change — even if I wanted to.

My phone and keys sit right in the center of Dad's leather satchel. I pick them both up. The money bag is gone. Undoubtedly being put to use as our "best for the Lord" on decorating the church and meals of walnut-crusted sea bass.

When I turn, I am face to face with Pastor

King. "Are you ready to go?" I'm close enough to see his eyes of black with hints of brown. Hints also of humor.

"Were you right behind me?"

"Only for a second. Which retirement home?"

"WoodHaven. Would you like to follow me?" I jingle my keys. He pauses over my anti-invite, but I don't want to wait for Dad to find us and nix the separate car thing so I start walking. "I don't know how long I will stay, and I know you have so much to do to get ready. Plus, I need to swing by my house after."

"No," he pulls my keys from my hand and tosses then toward Dad's satchel, "I'll drive us. We can go by your place first."

"Pastor King," Dad blocks the doorway, "Mark from Rent-A-Party said Selena gave him a check."

"Yes." Pastor's chin sticks out a little and he smiles, but his brows are lifted in question.

Dad continues, "I thought that we were paying all of the workers in cash—"

Pastor laughs like a two year old just tried out a new knock-knock joke. "We can't pay them in cash. All funds filter through Selena's consulting firm. That way she can track the totals and keep her commission."

Dad looks confused. "But I withdrew—"

"You'll be ready to open the new account at the credit union this afternoon?"

"I thought we were going to do that first thing." Dad is a little panicked now.

"Leah and I are leaving." Pastor looks at me with comfortable intimacy. He sets his hand on my shoulder.

"Oh, I can go alone..."

"I'm really looking forward to ministering to the elderly."

Well played—he didn't give any kind of response which I could deny or rebuttal.

"Drive safe," Dad says. As we pass him, he reaches out to me for a hug and a kiss but his left hand stretches toward the phone in my right. Like a small child I instinctively pull that hand away and turn for a fake, sideways hug. It works.

Dad is so concerned about a scene in front of Pastor the King, he lets it go. A skip hop controls my feet and in my exuberance I forget that I will be alone with the King for the morning and afternoon. But I have my phone.

"With your permission, sir, I would like to take Leah out to lunch after we visit the retirement home."

"Yes, of course." Dad answers without asking my opinion. It's all decided then. Dad walks back into his office and Pastor leads the way to the front of the building.

"Where are you going?" Miss Chan's lips wrinkle in a pouty pinch. She walks with us to the door.

"We're visiting WoodHaven Assisted Living

center so Leah can teach a crochet class."

"Where are her knitting needles and yarn?"

"Probably in the car," Barkley answers but only Miss Chan glances at me. She always makes me feel small but there is a different intensity in her gaze right now.

"When will you be back?" Her arms form a shield in front of her.

"When we are finished." Barkley still hasn't slowed his stride. He lacks the melodic intonation of normal.

"You do realize there is nothing left? We're done." Miss Chan has moved in front of us, blocking the door.

"But not finished." Pastor places his hands on Miss Chan's shoulders and moves her to the side. He opens the door and turns his handsome face directly toward me, "Ladies first."

I glance back to see Miss Chan biting her lip as if to contain words. Blotches of color rest on her cheeks.

"It's a beautiful day to spend together." Pastor reaches a black Lexus SUV and holds the passenger door open. His gallant actions are almost flamboyant. After I climb inside, he pulls the seatbelt strap and hands it to me. Once he verifies that I have buckled, he tucks in the skirt of my dress so it doesn't overhang, presses down the lock and closes the door.

"What kind of food interests you?" he asks after he climbs in and starts the engine. It takes several seconds for him to check each mirror and adjust them.

"Well, WoodHaven first." I turn slightly to see Miss Chan watching from the front door of the church.

"No, your house first. We'll run your errand."

"Fine, but it'll be fast. You can wait in the car."

"Of course," Pastor smiles and pats my hand softly. He leans to look directly into my eyes a second. "You look lovely, Leah."

I finger the wood button in the corduroy cuff, remembering the day mom and I finished sewing it. If she noticed I wasn't at Ava's, it seems like she would have come back for me by now. "I hate this dress."

His laugh sounds genuine. "But it is blue." He reaches out to touch my hand again but I pull it away. His fingers end up landing on my knee instead. My knees press together quickly in a true knee-jerk reaction. He glances at his hand as if wondering how something slipped from his grasp. "You know I love blue."

Tiny navy flowers on a canvas of white. Blue: heaven, twilight, sleep…

He turns his beautiful face to me as though I am the most important person in the world to him. "Are you comfortable? Shall I adjust the temperature for you?" He reaches for the dash but doesn't push anything.

"I'm fine." I pull out my phone. "Do you need directions to WoodHaven?"

"No, Leah," he says my name slowly as though he is trying to draw attention to the way it sounds with his accent, "I know where it is."

I don't know where it is—so this surprises me. I press the slide open on my phone and open my texts. The text from Truitt is deleted, likewise his email and contact information. I burn with irritation. Dad can't just delete my messages and contacts. I wanted to verify the verses Truitt texted me. When we get to my house, I'll grab the YWAM paper where I wrote them.

Pastor tries all sorts of small talk about the weather and other inconsequential things while I add a pass code lock to my phone. It is random enough my Dad will not be able to guess it. He may have deleted Truitt's contact information but when I start the first two letters of his name in the "To:" field of my email, it auto finishes his address.

*I need to see you tonight. –Petra*

"Who are you texting?"

I finish and hit send. "It was email, a friend sent some verses before and I wanted to get them again." I'm tempted to send one to Ava, so she can tell my mom why I'm not there but Pastor begins trying even harder to keep my attention.

"What is your favorite color?" He scoots his seat a little further back and readjusts the mirror.

"Yellow."

"What about your favorite flower?"

"I've never thought about that before." An open field of wildflowers comes to mind. Maybe an iris. Not for the way it looks but for the Coldplay song Truitt sang.

"You make me think of an orchid-lover."

I don't reply.

"Rare, fragile."

Eww.

"Something grown in a hot house that needs certain conditions to survive and should be taken care of." He can't possibly know the insult this is.

"Do you have a favorite perfume?"

"I don't like perfume."

"Got it." He is taking some kind of mental tally. "Dark chocolate or milk?"

I cock my head to the side. "What are you doing?"

"Trying to get to know you."

"It seems more like you are on the fast track to woo me."

"You aren't very much like your father, are you?"

"I don't know what you could possibly mean by that."

We sit in silence until he says, "I would very much like to woo you."

"I'm sorry." A great disappointed sigh escapes me, "I know my dad hopes for this and I hate to..."

"Do you think I'm not good enough for you?"

This question is as strange to me as the way his grip suddenly changes on the steering wheel. "I don't think that at all." I picture how classy Miss Chan looks next to him, how lovely Marta is — why is he driving so fast?

The SUV jerks and he cuts hard to the right. Crunching plastic and metal twist together in my ears. The seatbelt snaps across my chest and digs in painfully. We pull to the side of the road behind the red Volkswagen Fox coup we just rear-ended. He says a string of words pastors don't say and turns eyes on me that send cold tickles from my head down my back.

"Stay in the car." His voice sounds just like it did two Sundays ago when I wasn't sure if it was him speaking. If the seat belt weren't still cinched across me — I wouldn't be any less pinned to my seat.

Pastor reaches the rear of the red car before the teen girl has fully emerged. Not sure exactly what Pastor is saying — but her face leaves little doubt of his intensity. She shrinks back into the car. He points behind to the road then jerks a finger to his car and finally her. After a moment her lights turn back on and she pulls back into traffic, squealing her tires.

He walks to the front of our SUV and stands directly in the middle as if to cover our license plate from her rear-view mirror. His arms are crossed and his jaw contracts and tenses while he studies me. He makes no move to hide his face as he straightens, smiles benignly and methodically relaxes. Pastor walks slowly to the driver's door and climbs in. He turns the key, pulls forward and makes a risky u-turn.

"What time are they expecting you at WoodHaven?"

I swallow. Did he just intimidate a teen from reporting an accident?

"Your father needs this job pretty bad."

I turn quickly to see his face. His smile is smug. His beauty scares me a little, the confidence exuding. Probably no one tells him "No" just because of his attractiveness alone. And on the rare occasion that doesn't work—well, I just saw the ugly option.

"He's on the brink of losing everything." Pastor's hand returns to my knee.

I push it away and scoot to my right.

Pastor King laughs.

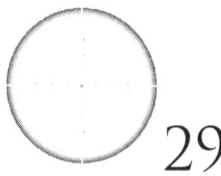29

He pulls right into the driveway. I don't know why it bugs me—it just seems presumptuous or something.

"I'll be right back."

Pastor nods and turns on the radio but keeps his eyes on me. Classical music mutes when I close the door. I feel particularly vulnerable with Mom gone. I wonder if Leland watches from his front window. Right now, I wouldn't mind.

Discreetly, I key the code into the garage door, then duck under, run through the empty garage and press the inside down button before it lifted all the way up. After I am sure it is all the way down, I slip inside.

I don't really remember what it was that I wanted to stop for even after I enter my bedroom. The telescope is positioned toward Lucas' and I glance quickly. He is there, entwined with someone again. I didn't come for this. I turn away and scan my room. My yellow dress hangs on the lip above my closet door, the bag of audio recorders sits on the floor near it and my Bible is one arm's length away on my desk.

The verses Truitt sent. That's what I came for. The yellow paper sticks out, I pull it free and lay it flat.

First, John 4:24. I find it quickly and write the verse text next to the reference on the yellow paper. "God is a Spirit: and they that worship him must worship him in spirit and in truth."

Next I write 2 Corinthians 3:17. "Now the Lord is that Spirit: and where the Spirit of the Lord is, there is liberty."

I never got the verse for the last one, Psalm 22. It starts, "My God, my God, why have You forsaken me?" That can't be what Truitt meant to send. I keep scanning, looking for the word "spirit" since the other two had that. I hope I'll figure out what he felt was important enough to actually text me. Instead of dwelling, I begin to copy the whole chapter. I only get to verse fourteen, prophecy of Jesus' death: "I am poured out like water and all of my bones are out of joint..."

"What's taking so long, dear?" I swallow before I turn around. Dear?

"How did you get inside?"

Barkley holds up my keys. The ones he took from my hand and, I thought, tossed back into Dad's satchel.

"I just needed my Bible and a few other things." I slip the YWAM paper in as a placeholder at Psalm 22 and hold the leather bound book to my chest. My hands tremble. Barkley looks around my bedroom from the pink and purple quilt-like duvet, to the desk covered in books, to the telescope and finally, to my dress.

"Is that for tomorrow?"

"The banquet?" I nod. More than he realizes because, to me, it declares my independence from him.

"I think I want my present early."

Surely I stand gape-mouthed.

"Just kidding." He walks to my window and stands next to the telescope. "But really, I'm glad you bought something like that. The one you are wearing is ridiculous. Even you said you hated that dress, Leah. Why don't you change?"

I look down at my floral print. "No. I won't be changing." I reach for my bag full of gadgets and slip my Bible inside. "I'll wear it for Valentine's Day." Of course, I'll be at Ava's.

My heart stops as Barkley bends over and looks through the telescope. "Oh?" he says. "Oh," he says again.

"I'm done, let's go. Come on. I don't need anything else."

"You have it focused perfectly on the master bedroom," Barkley says while still bent over, looking through. He stands erect and smirks at me, then bends again and watches some more. "This surprises me about you. No wonder you were taking so long," he says while watching.

Finally he stands and crosses his arms. "Put the dress on, Leah."

I shake my head no and lift my bag with my Bible to my shoulder. What if he looks inside this and sees the recorders? He'll know everything. Will he tell my dad? The church?

"I think you understand what's at stake." He bends one last time and looks through before he rises, laughing. "And I think you'll wear that dress and attend the banquet with me because anything else would…destroy your dad."

I've been staring at the dress so I look away and focus on Barkley.

"You could lose all this." He holds out his arm. "Your perfect home."

"We're already losing it." I don't care if he knows—he needs to realize he can't back me in a corner.

"You don't think Daddy is tempted to pay the mortgage off right now with what he pulled from the bank?" He raises his eyebrows as though waiting for me to understand the punch line.

The bulging deposit bag he wouldn't let me carry. "No. He wouldn't steal." Except from Mom, me, or for small things like a celebration lunch.

"That's what I thought." Barkley trails a finger across the telescope. "Of course, I never would have pegged you for a Peeping Tom." He stands still and clasps his hands behind his back, all business. "Hurry and put the dress on, Leah, and I won't tell your dad."

I'll never know what he said to the teen driver, but maybe words are only part of his persuasion. Even if I wasn't so practiced at obeying those over me — Barkley is the image of a pharaonic necropolis guard — a magnificent barrier fronting something tyrannical and sinister.

Shaking, I step into the closet behind me and pull the door closed. It is a smallish walk-in closet, and doesn't have a light, but I don't need one to switch dresses and pull back on my crocheted cap. Am I making a mistake? If I let him threaten me in this, will it stop? Will he threaten again next time he wants something? Will I spend my life wearing the dresses he chooses? I slip into tan sandals and pull the gadget bag up onto my shoulder.

He exhales. "Exactly like I hoped." Fortunately he doesn't elaborate but holds a hand out for me to walk ahead of him.

I feel exposed in the thin material but it is too late to wonder if I need a camisole or slip. It's only knee-length — what was I thinking to buy this? Not to mention the neck is a little lower than the other one — and with a bust like mine, it shows. "Where are we going?" I step toward the door, eager to leave. I don't like having a man in my bedroom.

"WoodHaven, silly." Barkley chuckles as he follows me. "I hope someday we have a place like this."

I follow his gaze to our living room then turn to the stairs. I can't descend them fast enough.

Barkley stops for a moment at the top and fixes his eyes on the last family picture we took. He steps slowly down the stairs after me with one hand on the rail studying each portrait individually.

***

Barkley is preoccupied during the drive. I pull out my phone and hold it low and to the right. I email Truitt again but without taking time to offer much explanation.

*Meet me at the church.*

When we arrive at WoodHaven, I eagerly pop the seat belt release but before I can jump from the car, Barkley's hand grips mine. I'm twisted, legs out and torso in. There is a slight struggle but his large hand pulls the phone out of my fingers. "Let's leave all the distractions in the car, shall we?"

My dad took my phone from me too. I start a retort, but the possibility of him telling my dad about the telescope and not knowing what he said to make the VW Fox driver squeal away is scarier than anything I can imagine. Any reply I might make catches in the tangle of surprise lodged in my throat. I swallow.

"Good girl."

"I need my purse, though." He opens my purse and looks through it. Barkley lifts a sanitary napkin and I feel heat rise but he doesn't pause at all. Next, he pulls out my recorder pen and clicks the button on top, inspecting the retractable ballpoint. Good thing I bought a recorder pen that really writes. Finally he lifts the handheld recorder, the first one I planted in his office.

"An audio recorder?"

Noooo, God. I plead. Assuming the only conversation ever taped was when Randall and Alvita found it—I might be safe. Good thing the other two are in my bag with my Bible.

He presses rewind, just as I did and listens to the last thirty seconds recorded. "I don't think you need to dust up there, Randall." Pastor turns to me.

"What did he find? A piece of gum under the table?" His laugh is disgusted and merciless. "Is this an interview for the church newsletter or something?"

"Yeah, it is." I answer quick.

He opens the glove box and tosses it inside. My phone though, he slides in his pocket. "I don't think you need an interview with them." He looks at me much as he did that night on my stairs when he brazenly studied my backside. "Ladies first."

I slide out sideways and turn to face him immediately, shutting the door. He is at my side in seconds and slips one arm around me with a grip firmer than necessary. "I want you to understand something." The mingling scents of him and familiar cologne provide false comfort. He wears the same scent Liam wore and bragged about. Spicy herbs and wood, a little citrus. I don't remember the name though.

I try to wiggle away but he presses the curve

between my thumb and forefinger and pain shoots down my arm. "I'm not leaving your side. Your dad thinks I'm good enough for you, and we have something planned for tomorrow night."

"I'm not..." but my voice quavers in response to the pain in my head. He turns me to him and his eyes widen with intensity like Truitt's drug-addict neighbor.

His lips mount mine in front of the building and his index fingers pinch a pressure point on each side of my jaw, effectively pinning me. Every time I pull back, pain pierces my neck and head so that I have no choice but to let him kiss my lips under the eaves in front of WoodHaven.

"Aww." Behind me, an old man in a wheel chair, and what looks like a caretaker smoke cigarettes under a dilapidated arbor.

He says it again and she replies, "Young love."

My first kiss. Too stunned to speak, and still smarting in my neck, I stumble behind him as he tugs me by the hand. Will no one help me?

"May I help you?" A younger, plump woman with a short haircut and grandma-style perm sits at the front desk. She wears matching Valentine's Day scrubs with red and hot pink hearts on a soft pink background.

"Yes, we are here to start a..." Pastor looks to me. He is so deceptively handsome. "What was it? A crochet class?"

The front desk attendant smiles and spends

more time staring at Pastor than me. She isn't going to notice his thumb resting on my hand in warning any more than my pleading eyes. "I didn't know we had anyone coming in today." She finally looks away from him and pulls out a stapled calendar. "When is it scheduled for?"

Both look at me. "I didn't have anything scheduled. I was here to visit a woman who came to our church. Her name was Louisa."

"Mel," the woman at the counter calls to a passing caretaker who wears pink scrubs and carries a plastic tub. "Is Louisa joining you today for crafts?"

Mel shifts the tub, "I believe she's already in there."

"Would you wait a second for these two, please?" The front desk lady lowers flirty eyes and then looks up at Pastor. "Sign this guest sheet and then you can follow Mel."

Pastor releases my hand and begins to write on the pink paper secured by a clipboard. The ink doesn't flow. "I believe I need another." He articulates his words with flourish and the attendant almost sighs.

"Let me find one for you."

While she takes her time giggling and rooting through a drawer—ignoring the jar of pens behind her—I pull mine from my purse. I slide the pocket clip down to record, press the top and hold it out to him. Pastor takes it, to the disappointment of the desk flirt, and writes "Mr. and Mrs. Eldfrick" on the line. He winks to the desk lady when he hands the pen back to me.

As much as I feel ridiculous doing it, I slip the still-recording pen in the front part of my dress, on the scooped bodice. The step emboldens me. We follow the waddling caretaker with the tub. Pastor doesn't offer to help; he is too busy clenching my hand. When I say, "Ow," he pinches harder.

We round a corner into a dining room-like area that has a large screen TV mounted on a wall with peeling wallpaper. Several elderly people group together at tables. Off to the side, Louisa sits alone. One hand curves over a walker and the other pats her hair. She sees me and looks confused, like she is trying to place where she knows me.

I walk straight toward her to put our connection in context. "Louisa, I met you at church yesterday."

"Jamal?" She only has eyes for Pastor. "Jamal Groetsch, I thought that was you."

"You have me mistaken, ma'am." His voice rings with melodic mocking. His left thumb presses into my left hand until it is almost numb. His right arm cups my bicep, hitting another nerve so that I cry out. "Cute, Leah." We are walking toward the exit.

The halls pass us in a blur of fading pastels. "I'm on call. There's an emergency at the hospital." Pastor announces to the lady as we pass the front desk. "We'll be back!"

"Okie-dokie," she calls with a wave.

Won't anybody help me? Does my face not show my fear? My pain? Does everybody only see what they want or expect to see?

I almost have to run to keep up with his strides. When we get outside his hand releases my bicep and reaches up behind me to pull my hair. He grabs a whole handful of my crocheted cap and curls. My eyes only see the sky above.

"Please, you're hurting…"

His handful directs my head while we are still marching to the SUV. "I don't know what the hell you think you're doing." His lips are so close to my ear I feel their moisture.

When we get to the Lexus, I resist. What if he doesn't take me back to the church? He grips tighter and my hat comes off in his hand. He looks at it in surprise and then back at my short hair. His top lip curls. "Daddy's got a bunch of surprises today, doesn't he?"

He pushes me toward the seat and pulls out the belt as he did this morning but it is entirely different this time. He removes his coat, lays it over me, locks the door and starts to walk around the front.

Quickly, I check inside the pocket for my phone and slide it into my bra. When he reaches the driver's door I unclick my seatbelt and when his foot reaches inside, I run for the retirement home. I get half-way at least before I meet the parking lot face-first. The pain comes as a blow from behind before it shoots from my hands, knees and face.

"Running is not an issue for me, sugar. I love to run." He stands and lifts me by the waist, clenching my hair again. My feet barely touch the ground and I can't get a foothold. That doesn't stop me from trying, though. I kick my legs and when we approach the Lexus, I kick it too. Doesn't anyone see us?

He opens the back door and throws me inside. I scream and kick, reaching for his face. This isn't happening. This is a dream. "Oh, God!"

"Yeah, where is your God?" He mounts me and the door closes us in. He pins both my wrists above my head with one hand and straddles me. Suddenly, I am no longer afraid of him just taking me somewhere. This parking lot is obviously just as unsafe. With a zip-tie he secures my two wrists to the handle behind the driver's seat and then my ankles to the handle behind the passenger seat. They are so tight I cannot reach the window and every time I kick or squirm the plastic cuts my skin deeper.

"Stop this! Somebody help me!" I receive a few slaps to the face. Calmly, in the midst of my screaming, Barkley removes my sandals. He wads my crocheted cap into a ball, and works it into my mouth as I alternately try to keep it shut and try to bite him.

The gagging is so horrible and involuntary that I have to blow snot from my nose to clear it and breathe. There is blood in it. The scent of his cologne, our sweat and my feet fill my senses. I farmer-blow again.

"Don't, you're getting the car filthy!" Barkley adjusts the passenger seat by sliding it as far back as it will go and then reclining it. I'm pretty much hidden. He slips into the driver seat and sets my shoes on the front passenger seat. He starts the car and pulls out. Somewhere along the way he opens the passenger side window. Then he flings my shoes out, as though I'll never need them again.

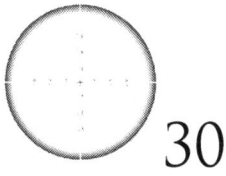30

"Dear God, thank you for this day, thank you for your provision, please put a hedge of protection around me," is pathetically inappropriate. I completely skip my normal prayer-by-rote. Nothing more eloquent than one-sentence pleas operate as my communication to God. Since there isn't anything in reach of my hog-tied hands and feet, I can't even open the door to get someone's attention. Barkley's phone vibrates and he looks at the screen while driving one-handed. An accident might be a good thing right now—if he didn't kill someone else.

"Yeah," he answers.

"No." Pause. "No." Again. "We ran into some trouble." I hear a female voice on the other side but I can't make out more than a few words.

"Well, she figured something out."

"...Reiss..." Selena's voice. The bald guy who gave a donation in his wife's memory on Sunday?

"He is still the mark."

"…about her." When her pitch escalates I hear more but make out less.

"I am not making it about her! He was still the goal."

Her answer is clipped.

"No mistaking. She ran." He cuts her off. "No—the car is not going to be damaged in any way. Yes. I know we have to take it back. I had to…she's tied up in the back."

She yells for a long time.

"Shut up, all right? You don't know what you're talking about. This doesn't change anything." And then he growls—obviously pushed as far as he would go. "Listen to me. I said this doesn't change anything. Just do your part and make sure everyone but Bryan goes home. We'll park around back."

The expletives he wove in sounded as natural as his preaching.

He hangs up. "It's not about you, Leah."

I can't answer—the cap is shoved in so far, all I can do is try to stay relaxed enough to not choke.

"Can I help it though, that your dad handed you to me on a silver platter?" He laughs. "The wild kid he didn't want polluting his precious church returns and Daddy presents his youngest virgin."

I wish he sounded unstable but he clears his throat and chuckles like our one-sided conversation is as benign as two people discussing a cute kid in the potluck line. "Okay, in the *beginning* it wasn't about you."

The car slows. We must no longer be on the freeway.

"I'll admit—" He turns sharp enough that my wrists strain against the zip ties to keep me from jostling. "—if you were interested in men at all we wouldn't have stayed past Sunday."

We are pulling into the church parking lot—I recognize the trees. Barkley turns off the Lexus and places a sunshade in the windshield. He reclines the front seat just like the passenger. With both leaning back, the tinted windows, my inability to move and now the sunshade—I am well hidden.

"Sit tight," he says calmly and shuts the door.

My jaw aches from being open. I'm stretched across the seat—but if I use the plastic zip-ties to pull up my weight...I reach my mouth. With only my thumbs I am able to dislodge the cap. Relief.

I cry. The little kid kind of great gasping sobs. I try rocking and kicking, screaming. The windows are starting to fog but I am exhausted. My phone vibrates at my chest. "Oh, God!" If I could get to it...I lift my hips and arch my back—contorting every way I can to let it wiggle from my bra. If I can get it near my mouth I can put it in my hands.

Thunk.

It lands on the floor out of reach, but face up. A blue box shows in the middle of the yellow wallpaper:

Text from Dad

*i m sorry leah. someday i hope you will find it in your heart to forgive me but i cannot wait for that after what i ve done i ve lost everything. even god.*

"That isn't from Dad." I repeat myself with a kick and jerk, punctuating each word. Dad wouldn't text the word "God" without capitalization. I'm so mad right now I could literally kill Barkley with my own hands.

But after a few hours in the car, the fight fades. I even drift to sleep. It's dusk when I wake to a blast of cold air at my feet.

"She better not have scuffed up the interior." Selena pokes at my ankles, inspecting the hand bar on the back of the front passenger seat where I'm hog-tied. The brightness of the dome light burns against my sleep-sealed eyes.

"Relax." Something cold brushes against my skin and my feet fall to the floor. I can't feel them. The driver's door opens, the dome light goes off. Simultaneously the seats lean forward, releasing me from the tomb-like oppression. I suck air greedily.

"Yeah, she's a real fighter. Can't believe you were able to catch her."

"I said, shut up."

"Oh, gross. What is that all over the back seat?" My eyes and face feel puffy from the strikes and the tears. "Seriously? You are cleaning that up."

A new zip-tie pinches my wrists before the one attached to the car is cut. "You can do it. Come back inside before you leave and get a towel."

"I'm not leaving."

"You have to get the car back." Barkley grunts his words as he pulls me from under my arms and I slide out of the car to a disoriented standing position.

"Yeah, right. And leave you here with everything? We'll do it together...*Jamal.*"

"That's not the plan!" Barkley pushes on me to move me from the car and slams the door. "You have to return the car..."

Selena slams her door too, and walks around to the front staring at me from top to bottom before she turns to Barkley. "New dress? New haircut? What did you two lovebirds do today?"

"Stick with the plan and take his car back," he says.

"She's not part of the plan." Selena pinches my arm and directs me in front of her. "We don't really need to take it back, just leave it unlocked around Fourth Street and let a couple kids take care of it." She pushes me toward the church.

If I weren't dizzy and headachy I might be able to run a bit—make some noise. I scan the completely empty parking lot.

Something that feels like an alligator bites my butt and jerks me side to side in the killing water-dance. "Breathe. Breathe," my subconscious takes over and insists. I was tired before, but now my limbs are so weak they quiver and I pant as though I've been running full-speed, several hours. Gravel pricks against my face. How did I get down here?

"Why did you do that?" Barkley constrains

his volume but his tone is menacing.

"She was going to run," Selena says with an amused cadence.

"Give me the stun gun," he says.

My legs don't seem to move anymore. Barkley sweeps me into his arms and his woodsy herbal cologne settles over me. I think I might throw up. I pray that I do. All over his suit.

"Daddy didn't like it either." Selena giggles and opens the door for us. Barkley carries me through the dark church foyer. "I'm sure she can walk now." Selena calls just before she locks the door.

Barkley doesn't put me down. I wish he would so I didn't have to smell his cologne anymore. I bring my bound hands to cover my face.

"Shhh," Barkley says. He must think I'm crying—not pinching my nose. "This isn't about you." He sets me down and I slide into a waiting chair. Selena tosses my purse and bag to the ground near the stained glass window of Jesus.

Groaning protests and "Un-uhs" in my dad's voice sound behind me. I turn quickly to see him, wide-eyed, restrained in a chair with a strip of duct tape over his mouth. I'm almost clear-headed enough to fight when a strip of duct tape goes over my ankles and then another around my upper chest, securing me to the chair back. It's just above the recorder pen, thankfully still clinging to the fabric of my dress. Barkley sets the duct tape roll on his desk, next to two passports, the stun gun, and an open briefcase of money.

Barkley leaves us and my dad squirms in panic.

"I'm okay, Dad." The dryness in my throat is as equally uncomfortable as the tender skin on my face but he needed to hear it. He stops squirming and weeps.

Out in the hall, Barkley and Selena argue. Footsteps approach loud enough to herald them.

"Is this yours?" Barkley walks toward dad and holds up one of my voice recorders.

Dad shakes his head no, slow at first and then firmer as he seems to grasp what it is. Barkley hits him back-handed.

"Whose is it?" He holds it closer to Dad's face as though Dad might be able to figure it out the owner if he got a better look.

Selena laughs. Now that I can see her, I'm not sure she is the same classy consultant Dad hired. She wears tight blue jeans, black knee-high boots with flat soles and a slim, black tank top. Her face is thin, hard and make-up free.

"What's your problem now?" Barkley directs to Selena.

She crosses her thin arms and points with her chin to me. "It belongs to her."

Barkley moves between Dad and me. "Are there more?" Each word is nearly a sentence on its own.

Behind them, Dad's frightened eyes widen. A barely perceptible shake of his head tells me an emphatic "No." Defy my dad? It's no longer my fear. I look back to Barkley. What's he going to do? Tie me to a chair?

"Probably." I shrug. Almost laughing inside. Hopefully my pen is picking this up. Fully charged, I think it is supposed to have more than sixty hours of record time. But Barkley's face changes. The number of recording hours may not matter if I don't live.

Dad looks at me scolding. But it's Selena who gives me chills. She smiles flirtatiously and struts toward me. "I'll give you only one chance."

"Honestly, I don't really remember how many I set up. I think Randall kept moving them."

Her leg lifts and presses into the duct tape at my chest. With a quick thrust, I receive a push-kick that sends me and the chair backward. I have enough warning to tuck my chin down so I don't smack my head on the ground but pain greets every inch of my back where the chair touches it. As the shock of pain clears, I notice the only noise—a wheel from the base of my chair spinning.

Barkley presses buttons on the recorder and his voice emerges from it. Soon Selena and my dad join him in what was probably a typical planning meeting. He presses another button and slams the device on his desk.

"How long have you known?"

From the ground I answer. "I'm not even sure what I know—except that my dad wasn't going to commit suicide."

"Well, after you got his text you rushed over to stop him. So maybe murder-suicide," Selena says so nonchalant, my limbs go weak.

"This isn't about her!"

"This has always been about her!" She turns to my Dad. "About him. About this church who turned away poor little Jamal. I could have directed Pascal to any church."

Judging by Dad's face, he understands. He once knew Barkley by another name—the name of a kid who needed help. I was there the day Jamal's mother, aunt, grandma—some woman—pleaded for him and my dad refused. The day I hid under the table in the boardroom.

No one broken, no one dirty was ever welcome in our church.

Liars, thieves, murderers? Nope—only white-washed sepulchers allowed.

"This church was still the best choice." Barkley slides the briefcase across the desk and closes it. "Or are you forgetting?"

"No." Selena reaches for the briefcase but he doesn't hand it to her. "We couldn't have planned it better than someone in charge with a gambling problem." They continue to stare at each other for a second and she finally drops her hand.

"You stole from that guy, Pascal, and the church?" I say for the pen.

"No. Daddy stole from the church." She lifts the audio recorder she found and looks at Barkley. "I'm going to look for more."

"Apparently, he wrote bad checks for all of this furniture, too." Barkley says with tight, scrunched eyebrows as watches Selena leave. "Oh, and the lighting company and the party rental place. They are going to be upset when their checks bounce. Bryan, you maxed out credit cards buying T-shirts and postcards. Drained the accounts so you could pay off your mortgage."

Dad groans and drops his head.

"You should be sorry. The board is going to be angry when they find out you closed the bank account without approval. What's next Bryan?" Barkley mocks and clicks open the briefcase. "Are you going to let some rough kids in the youth group?"

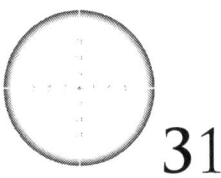

**31**

Dad looks down where I am still on my back. In his eyes resides shame. Shame like I saw in Truitt, Pastor Thompson, Liam's dad…my mirror. He closes them.

"Jamal?" I ask.

Pastor's head pulls up but he doesn't turn or answer.

"Did you ever stutter?" He sang Amazing Grace like a believer right after his story of stuttering—were they both false?

He still doesn't answer.

"Come and help me." Selena stands in the doorway of the pastor's office wagging the recorder.

"Why do you think there's more?" Barkley asks. "Do you think the pastor's daughter spends time in spy shops? Recording conversations? She moonlights as a Peeping Tom?" He looks up at me with a sudden epiphany-smile. "Hold that thought." He jogs away.

"Is Selena your real name?" Even if I die, I

want as much info as possible recorded. She huffs, incredulous and humored. Selena takes the briefcase from the room but returns a moment before Barkley.

"Spying? Yep. Recording conversations? Yep." He lifts the other recorder. "What else have you been up to?" Barkley looms over me while I'm on my back with duct tape holding me to the chair. My hands are rubbed raw and still zip-tied in front of me. Dad starts to protest and squirm.

Closing my eyes, I brace myself for another blow or a kick. Nothing happens. His slacks rustle and his footsteps lead away. Barkley stops at his desk and pulls out the computer. He squats on the floor and inspects the sides, then focuses on the USB ports. Lifting the keystroke recorder, he shows it to Selena.

"I'm supposed to believe that she's known all along and has been tracking us?" Selena's voice is screechy.

"You don't believe it?" Barkley juts the keystroke recorder out at her. He charges toward me. "What is this thing?"

"A wireless mouse connector, maybe?" That was what I first thought it looked like when I bought it.

"What are you trying to pull on me?" Selena says to Barkley.

"What am I trying to pull?" Barkley towers over her and though he is lean and lithe, I know his strength from the way he carried me. "Do you think

I planted this on my own computer?"

"Well, you instantly knew where it was. Even though you wouldn't help me look earlier." Selena takes a step back and straightens as if to maximize her height. "And you happened to have another recorder in Pascal's car." I can't see Barkley's face from behind him but his slowness in reply seems to encourage Selena. "I'm thinking of the conversations we've had in there."

Barkley grabs for her arm.

She pulls it back and holds it away. "I'm not your charge."

"Come with me then. Look on every computer. Under every table."

"Sure, and then I'll believe that every one you stumble across is on accident." But she follows him out of the room.

I bought four audio recorders and three keystroke recorders. I had a keystroke recorder on both Dad's home and work computers and one on the Pastor's. I had audio under the table in the boardroom and one on the picture frame in here. I think that was the first one moved, which I found in the kitchen. I moved it to the light fixture in the boardroom. The second time I found one moved—I still have no idea where it came from. There are two unused in my bag. Hopefully they won't find the one in the light in the boardroom. That only leaves the pen recorder hooked on my shirt at my sternum.

Dad fidgets, trying to get his hands free. I follow suit.

Barkley moves into the room like a water buffalo on land. He's fast, but I hear him before I see him. He pulls the duct tape from Dad's mouth and my dad answers with a low-pitched scream.

"Are you the one who planted these?" He holds up a recorder I don't recognize.

Dad works his mouth and lips with facial stretches and expressions.

Barkley backhands him. "Answer me!"

"I didn't plant them. That is just for recording meeting notes so the secretary can type them later."

He pushes Dad back with both palms but when Dad's chair crashes to the floor like mine he lands on his right side, away from me. I turn my head up and I can see his duct taped hands—his arms would be hurt or broken if he'd landed backward. I can't see Dad's face.

"Maybe Selena planted them all!" Dad calls out.

"Yeah, right!" Selena answers.

"Well, she took the briefcase out of the room when you went to the car." Dad is quick to reply. Barkley walks to Dad's chair and pushes the leg of it with his foot. It turns Dad's whole body so that his face is toward me. But we are upside down from each other. Dad tries to make eye contact, maybe to reassure me. I look away. "Then she brought it back before you returned."

"Shut your mouth!" Selena starts toward him but Barkley blocks her.

"Did you?"

"No!"

Barkley looks at me. "Did she?"

I nod—just a little though.

Barkley walks over to the briefcase and lifts the lid. "Did you think I wouldn't notice?" His voice is lyrical, amused.

"No, I just..." Selena points at me. "I just don't know what you've got going on in your head right now—the way you keep changing things."

"You still think this is about her?" Barkley moves toward Selena with the focused eyes and body language that all the girls lap up like dogs.

"I think it's been about her all along."

"Go and get the money."

Selena pauses for a moment. He picks up the briefcase, "We'll split it all, now."

They both turn and leave with the briefcase.

"What'd they do to your hair, Leah?" Dad asks like he doesn't really want to know.

Curls and frizz block my eyes, but I look through the strands to his face. "I cut it this morning."

There's silence, not even the sound of breathing. I angle my head and try to watch his face without him seeing.

"You cut it?"

I nod.

"This morning? When you were wearing your hat?"

I can't help it, a little huff escapes. He's so

shocked I wish I'd shown him this morning. Maybe this whole day would have been different. I'd be locked in my bedroom, grounded!

"And that dress…why are you wearing it? When I saw it in your room I thought it was pajamas. You know your mother and I…" Dad looks toward the stained glass of Jesus with outstretched arms before he corrects himself. "Well, I wanted you to keep your hair long and feminine and only wear modest clothes."

My head jerks up and I have no problem looking at him without hiding all the anger inside. "So I could catch a godly man like Barkley?"

"I thought he…he was supposed to be…"

We both sigh. What is there to say? We all thought.

"I only wanted what was best for you." Dad finally redeems the silence.

"Is this what's best for me?" I lift my duct-taped ankles. The pent up words and challenges are starting to cause tears in me.

"I didn't foresee this."

"You didn't try to foresee anything."

"Honor your father!"

"I have honored you!" I can't control my volume. "In almost everything I have obeyed and deferred to you. Looked to you. Trusted you!"

"You know," Barkley's voice startles me. How long has he been standing there? "It isn't like Leah is so pure. She isn't so far above us." He licks his lips and his eyes shine.

I wore the dress for Barkley but he will tell Dad about the telescope anyway. I try to distract him. "I never thought I was too good for you. Why do you keep saying that?"

"He's just shocked that anyone would turn him down." I crane to see Selena. Was she here all along, too? "What do you think this means?" She hands a paper to Barkley.

He reads quietly but his lips move. "Leah," he begins aloud. "I need to talk to you about the recorder you were charging. I thought it belonged to the church. I needed to borrow it. This may be important. You aren't answering my email. Please call. Josiah."

"So I went to her computer and found this." Selena holds up the USB cable I used to charge the recorder on the Sunday it went missing. "And look at this." She inserts it into the first recorder they found. Her voice takes a malevolent tone. "Perfect fit. Who is Josiah?"

I focus on the hem of my dress slipping up my thighs and try to pinch my knees tight to keep it from going further. God, make them leave Josiah out of this.

"He's the tech geek who records..." Barkley and Selena look at each other suddenly as Barkley says the last word, "services."

"The audio kid?"

"Well, he left a number. I suppose we could call him. Then swing by and see." Selena reaches for the briefcase, opens it and removes a gun no bigger than her hand. "This loose thread is your fault."

"Then we'll deal with it."

"No—all the recorders are mine!" I squirm and my yellow dress slides up to the top of my thighs.

"I knew it." Selena is smug. "What have you recorded?" She holds the gun out in my direction and suddenly it doesn't seem so small.

"Meeting notes and interviews for the newsletter."

"Why was he concerned about it? Think it's important?" She grabs the paper from Barkley.

"I …" I look to Dad. He will find out after all—but if I am to die, I'd rather keep Josiah protected. "I was spying on people." Barkley will believe me. "I took random pictures and Josiah must have found my camera. He probably wanted to exhort me privately before taking me in front of the elders…" I can't believe how plausible my story is.

"Stop. I hate the way you people talk." Selena wags the gun then presses her fingertips to her temples—the gun temporarily points away from me and toward the ceiling. "I don't believe you. It makes more sense for the kid who records services to walk around recording everything. If there are pictures or audio, he has them."

"No." Barkley says slowly with his eyes trained on my dad. "Leah does spy. At her house she had a telescope set up to watch the bedroom of her neighbor."

I make sure not to see my dad's response.

Selena takes her hands down and levels the gun at me. "If we don't need to visit Josiah, if it has been you all along—prove it."

I want to bargain—to verify that they will leave Josiah out of it. But it seems better to not act like I care about him so much. "There is one more recorder in the burned out florescent light in the boardroom, and maybe a few things in my bag." I lower my head to look at the pen on my blouse. "That is all."

"I'll go to the boardroom," Barkley says.

"I'll check her office."

When we are alone, Dad's face morphs. He starts to cry. "I failed you."

"No." I try to stop him.

"Yes," he gags out the word.

I don't even recognize him—I've never seen his face show a hint of remorse or humility and this brokenness transforms him. "No, Dad. You didn't fail me." I don't care if I'm lying, I don't want to see him in this pain. "Stop."

"No, Leah. It needs to be said. I couldn't see anything but the money. I knew I was losing everything, even though with each bet I only saw the possibility of winning. I never could see you— couldn't even see your mom."

"Why didn't you stop gambling when you started to lose?"

"It was like I became a different person. Someone else took over—I was just a hostage in the tank running over my own life." He grunt-yells, and strains at the duct tape around him. Then, resolved, regains control of his emotions and tears. "And now look at what it has done. It drove you to spy on me and others to protect yourself."

My laugh surprises him. "Actually, Dad, I wasn't leaving recorders around the church because I'd uncovered some kind of plot. I'm just nosy. Voyeuristic."

"That's not voyeurism. Voyeurism is sexual—watching people," Dad says.

He still doesn't see me for who I really am.

"And it's illegal," Barkley says. "Naughty girl. Maybe I'm the one too good for you, princess. Confession is cathartic, don't you agree?" He holds a new audio recorder.

"I do," Selena responds. "Are you done with her now?" She asks Barkley.

"She is in thine hand. Do with her as it pleaseth thee," Barkley quotes Abraham when he spoke of Hagar and touches Selena's elbow tenderly. Selena turns away from him, smiling like she is in control—like she has him wrapped around her finger. Behind her, he wears a similar expression.

They both seem to think they are playing each other.

"Finally," she says. "Help me lift her." She squats by my chair back while my dad bargains and protests.

Selena doesn't need him though. My chair

lifts and almost flies forward so that I hold my taped legs out for balance. She pulls the back of the chair and as I am wheeled from the room my limbs quiver with unspent adrenaline. The tears begin to flow. "No! Dad?"

It is good I can't see my dad's face because the anguish in his voice as he calls my name absolutely terrorizes me. "Why? Where are you taking me?"

Selena doesn't answer. She pulls me backward down the hallway of the church where I grew up. Where I learned "Dear God, thank you for this day, thank you for your provision, please put a hedge of protection around me." Where I played, modeled annual Easter dresses and held babies. Where two of my siblings were married before they moved as far away as possible.

We enter the sanctuary — my personal oxymoron. Closing my eyes, I block the possibility of viewing what evil spirits await me. I feel myself mentally cocooning, I can't fight this. God, I can't.

Barkley tramps up the aisle, arms swinging, lip curled. "Are you sure this is all there is?" He sets the recorders on the stage in front of the pulpit.

"Why would I tell you?" I ask.

"She told me she left two at home. Both in her room," Selena says. "One of them incriminates you."

"Okay." He breathes obvious relief. I look up in surprise, first to Selena, then to Barkley. He meets my gaze and something inside of me starts to shake and panic at his expression of lust. Without looking away from me he says to Selena, "Go to her house and get them, I'll wait here."

"Suddenly you can do demolitions?" She answers quick and wipes her hands on her pants. Barkley continues to stare at me until she walks in between us. "Yeah. It isn't about her?"

He turns a charming smile back to Selena. I can't see her face but I've seen the responses in college group to his suave grins. She's probably melting. It's confirmed when she reaches out and grabs him for a kiss. Their kiss is unlike any I've ever seen except through a telescope.

"I need thirty minutes tops. So drive fast. Look under her pillow." Although, with this lie of hers, I realize she is not falling victim to his charms but actually controlling him.

Why would I contradict Selena's lie—to keep him here? I don't want him to look at me like that even one more time.

Selena starts walking toward the door but it only takes Barkley a few steps to catch up with her. "Take the Lexus," she directs over her shoulder. Her sexy stride is so subtle and unlike her normal walk I wonder if he picks up on it.

They share a few muffled words. More arguing. The lights go off.

My stinging wrists and ankles, aching from sitting in the chair, my sore back—it is all replaced by the tiny shiver that starts in my limbs and grows to overcome me.

I'm alone in the dark sanctuary.

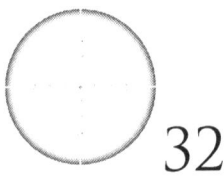32

If a spiritual being enters this room, I know I cannot hide by being quiet but I try to slow my breathing for the silence anyway. My eyes adjust and scan, trying to decipher every outline. If I can't figure out what a shape is, I watch it with wide eyes until I can.

Light shocks my retinas. Something approaches. I scream and Selena laughs.

She carries a jug of bleach and several other chemicals. She sets them on the front row in the sanctuary and sits next to them. Slowly, methodically, she opens a box containing a cell phone, removes the phone and charger and plugs it into the wall. She leaves and turns the lights off again. She plays with me.

Everything looks different from before. I can't remember that silhouette. My breathing becomes panicked again. Little moans escape and it makes me more afraid that I can't hide in silence. What if that creature is in here still? I keep thinking

I'll see him sitting in a pew or waiting at the pulpit.

When the lights flick on again, I'm disoriented and blinded. This time I keep my eyes closed tight until she speaks.

"This was in your bag with the other recorders."

I squint as she sways down the aisle with her eyes trained on me while carrying my leather, initial-embossed Bible. Her scrawny arm doesn't hold it out—it's probably too heavy for her. Still, it looks as if she's keeping it as far from herself as possible. When she is within ten feet, she flings it. "I'm sure you don't want to be without it." Her sarcasm doesn't cut like she intends it. I do want it.

The Bible lands upside down and open, near my feet. The tiny communion bread piece, still wrapped in a paper towel, lands on top of the yellow YWAM sheet where I wrote Truitt's verses. She laughs and leaves. The lights go off.

My Bible lays so close, yet my feet are still bound together by the duct tape and I cannot reach it. The lights are gone and I cannot see it. I study the area it landed until my eyes adjust again and I can make it out. The yellow color helps. Near enough to see the pinch of bread—but not near enough to touch, partake. This is the symbol of God and my life.

"Lord, I'm ready to meet you." He knows this, but I have to say it. And I have to say it different than my usual formula-prayer. "I've always wanted my eternity to be with you. I'm sorry I wasted my mortality without you." That's what I have done, wasted every chance to truly take communion with him. Ingest him and let him infiltrate the secret places. I have to swallow for the tingle of saliva puckering at the thought of the stale corner of yeast-less bread. I want so bad to have God inside me.

Do not take communion unworthily. I think the point is to get right with him and take it — not walk away or wait. Now it's too late.

A creak sounds. It is just the building swaying in the wind. Another sound from the other side of the room. Is that a shape? God help! Suddenly I need to see the whole chapter of Psalm that Truitt sent — how did it start? Why art thou so far from helping me, and from the words of my roaring? He knew I would need it. I should have memorized it!

My toes strain and I start to reach and jerk. The chair moves. I don't care about silence anymore. I'd rather cover any other noise in the room so I jerk my chair and wiggle until I am rocking and scooting. What did Alvita say? It doesn't matter if I believe in spirits or I don't, because either they are or they aren't — regardless of what I see.

Well then, I don't care what else is here. My bare foot reaches the paper. With my toe I press down and try to slide the paper toward me. At first, the bread and paper towel ride on top but then the paper slips from underneath. I pull the sheet directly in front of me and rest my feet over it.

The lights burn again and I call out in anger. Selena enjoys my pain and walks to the wall where she'd plugged in the brand new cell phone. She makes a show of turning it on with her index finger and takes a deep breath.

"Nine, one, one," She says the numbers as she dials and closes her eyes.

There is a pause.

"Oh my, God. Oh, I'm so scared." She cries into the phone. "Someone is breaking into my house." Selena squats and whispers, really getting into it. "He's driving a Lexus." She rattles off a license plate then my street and house number. The phone call is real.

"Help me!" I scream to get the operator's attention.

"Don't, Leah. He'll hear you." Selena yells into the phone. "My daughter is with me. Oh God! He's coming upstairs!" She clicks the phone off and powers it down. "Thanks, honey. I knew you'd be a good girl." She drops the phone. Just before she leaves, she adds, "Like usual."

I burst into tears realizing I helped her plan and it is several seconds after she's gone before I comprehend: the lights are still on. With my hands and arms taped I cannot reach to wipe my eyes so I continually blink. The YWAM paper stares up at me, mocking my dissatisfaction with a simple life.

I use one foot to slide the paper up onto the other foot, and pinch it with my toes to turn it over.

John 4:24 God is a Spirit: and they that worship him must worship him in spirit and in truth.

2 Corinthians 3:17 Now the Lord is that Spirit: and where the Spirit of the Lord is, there is liberty.

I know what Truitt was pressing—my incapability and failure when it comes to worship. That's the furthest possible issue from my immediate concern. The chapter on Psalm is what I need. I skim it: Be not far. Trouble is near. O my God, I cry by day, but You do not answer; And by night, but I have no rest.

David couldn't sleep either! I am not alone.

Thank you God. I needed this. I want to die with your words on my lips.

Read the whole thing.

More than just an internal sensation, it feels like a clear command from my own mind. I start at the beginning and on verse three my whole body lights. He inhabits the praises of Israel. He inhabits praise. I start over and read it again. Praise was the common thread, not spirits.

He lives, I know.

He is everywhere, I know.

But he dwells in praise.

"Where are you?" Barkley's voice sounds in the hall.

Selena calls out my own question. "Why are you back?"

"You thought I wouldn't check, that I

wouldn't notice? Where's my money?" He calls her by a curse.

Half a dozen shots of gunfire echo in the hall just outside of the sanctuary. Now I wish the lights were off.

"Leah!" It is a horror-cry in my dad's voice and sounds very far away.

I throw my feet down with a sudden burst and I'm able to pitch my chair sidelong. My jerking and wiggling do not completely muffle the struggle and screams outside. I don't stop until I have somehow managed to twist and squirm my mobile prison near the front row. One last jump-jerk-roll...and I am slightly wedged under the front row of chairs. I can't move my chair at all now, but at least I'm sure I will not be seen if someone opens the door. The smell of bleach burns my throat. On the seat above me sit the chemicals Selena brought in.

Several minutes go by in silence after the gunfire and scuffle. Twice, the sanctuary doors open and close, but no one enters.

Just when I begin to hope they shot each other at the same time, an explosion reverberates, followed by a rattle in the windows. Another smaller bang sounds and then the piercing screech of fire alarms.

My head aches from the high-pitched shriek of linked fire alarms that seem to echo and answer themselves. It combines with the bleach-scented air — but within minutes it is worse. I smell smoke.

A caustic scent—unlike the mountainy smell of wood smoke—it's a chemical fire. Another realization combined with a physical confirmation of Goosebumps. Demolitions. That's why Selena brought the bleach and other chemicals in here. And I am stuck under them.

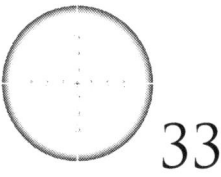

33

Wood and flame quarrel with each other through cracks and roars. The temperature rises. Perspiration dampens my face and any part of my body touching another. I don't see flames yet, but I am wishing my hands were at least free to pull a cloth over my mouth. Maybe this way it will be quicker.

"I don't belong here?" It is the same undefined figure who stood behind Barkley nine days ago. His outline shifts like taunting flames in front of the glass podium.

I want to shrink inside my frame to hide. Oh, God. Let me die quick. Scouring my mind, only bits of verses are found—though you pass through the fire, or is it the valley? When the waters overtake…I wish water would overtake right now. The only Bible story that I can think of is when a man brought his son filled with a demon and the disciples could not cast it out. After Jesus cast it out, he told them why they couldn't… my mind begins to shift and flicker. I cannot finish the thought.

The alarms scream in my ears. Or maybe it is the demon. I open my eyes; his shifting shadow is opaque, like the smoke. "I live here!" he says.

"But you don't belong," I answer quietly. God! I just want to be with you in heaven—why do I have to see this? Let me die.

"You're a fool. I've dwelled here a long time."

But Jesus lives inside of me. Is saying it in my mind enough? The disciples were unsuccessful. I shiver with cold, as though I'm not trapped in a burning building.

"Get used to the burning!" he screeches.

"No," I whimper. I won't listen to this. I love God. I trust his word that I will be with him in heaven for eternity!

But do you trust me here on earth? Take my hand, Petra.

The maniacal shrieking seeks to split and divide my mind. I have to discern who is who by the truth of what is said—not where the sound comes from. Unite my heart, God. Unite my heart to fear your name. Acrid breaths sting my throat and nose.

"Yes. I trust you here. I trust you in this." Who else do I have but God? If he has my eternity— he has this life in his hands as well. He even has the transfer, the release from here to there!

I dwell in the praises of my people, daughter.

"Then I worship you!" And I do. Lovely,

lovely, God. The song that bursts forth is so heartfelt, so sweet. I begin to scream it. He is God! I will trust.

Another shape shines in the dark. I notice it long enough to understand it is just another servant. He clashes with the demon and I sing louder — completely throwing myself into the splendor of God. I don't recognize my own voice any more than the words and joy that lift me…it is ecstasy.

Finally another figure approaches and I laugh at how much I am not alone. God — you send so many to usher me into your presence? Only, this shape is fat. He trips.

"Good thing you were singing so loud, I couldn't find you."

Truitt lifts me — still bound to the chair — in one swoop. My stomach drops from the speed of it. I weep. God, I wanted to be with you.

"Shh, Petra," Truitt says. His lips touch my forehead. "I've got you now."

Somehow he maneuvers me and the chair through the hall, past a sprawled-out Barkley and through the shattered glass that used to be front doors. When the night air hits us, I start coughing. My hacking becomes uncontrollable, but I can still hear sirens off a-ways. He sets me down hard and begins to tear and struggle against my duct tape. A police cruiser peels into the parking lot. "The Lexus is still here!" I wiggle and struggle against the tape.

"You're not helping. Sit still," Truitt yells.

"Selena is still inside — with a gun. My dad."

Everything I yell is punctuated by the nearing fire truck horns. "My dad!"

The cop squeals to a stop and leaps from his car.

Truitt still kneels beside me with his hands on my ankles. He tries to tear at the tape but I moan in pain. He sets to finding the end and starts unpeeling it. "Where is your dad?"

I can't answer for the sobs but I look at the church framed in smoke. It doesn't matter; the cacophony of confusion, horns, sirens, and roaring would smother anything I said.

Another police car pulls in. Truitt grabs my face with his palms and moves just inches from me. "Is your dad inside?"

"Yes."

Truitt turns and bolts for the front door.

"Truitt!" But my cry is drowned by a long honk from the fire department as they pull into the parking lot. They are followed by two more cop cars.

"I'm tied up!" I call out when the first cop is close enough to hear. A second cop runs toward me. The firemen barrel out of the truck and begin unrolling hoses, hoisting axes and other items with the organized precision of a stage performance.

"Where did the man go?"

"He went in to get my dad."

"Is anyone else inside?" The second cop arrives.

"Truitt, my dad, Barkley and Selena. She has

a gun."

They lift my chair into the air and the way I jerk up and down with their running—I pray the duct tape holds me to it.

One of the policemen says to a fireman, "Four people inside, possible firearm or more hostages. Unsafe to enter."

"My dad is tied up!" But they don't look at me. "Truitt went in after him—he doesn't know where he is. I should have told him!" I start kicking and jerking and my legs break free. This gets a few people's attention.

"Hold still," a female cop says. "I'll cut the tape. Are you okay? Do you need medical attention?"

An explosion resounds and when it stops I am still screaming "No." Everyone turns to or runs toward the side of the building to get a better view. Heat surges from Flourishing Faith, no longer speckled with fire and smoke but blazing from behind.

God help. I run to the pastor's office stained glass window. "Daddy."

I'm not sure what I see inside at first, movement, lights and darkness. Then I realize and duck in time. A chair flies through, shattering Jesus. I stand up and begin pulling down the triangles of glass depicting clouds. Just as I break away Jesus' feet, my dad's unconscious face moves toward me.

Truitt hoists him, still attached to the chair, forward and I lift my hands to catch. Two firemen reach above me and bear his weight over my head. Another two arrive and I press against the building to stay out of their way. Truitt fills the window. He is sweaty and dirty with streaks of soot racing across his cheeks from his eyes. Before he lifts a leg, he searches wildly. When he sees me, his jaw drops in a moaning-type sob of relief. He climbs out to the reaching arms of the firemen.

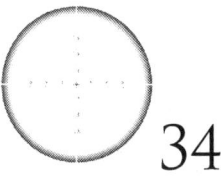34

Truitt spasms with coughing as he's lowered to the ground. They cut my dad free, lift him and take him to a gurney by the ambulances. After I say thank you to Truitt, I will run to ride with my dad. Only—Truitt no longer coughs. His eyes, red and distracted moments ago, are closed, his mouth slightly open.

Spray from the hose mists my face. The firefighters drag Truitt away from the building until they are met by two paramedics with a long backboard.

"One...two..." They lift Truitt to the board and flank him, checking for pulse.

"BVM," one commands and the other unzips a large black bag.

While one is unpacking a bag, the first paramedic begins pressing on Truitt's chest, counting loud and fast. He presses so hard I am sure he'll crush Truitt's rib cage. It may be my fear creating the noise, or it's real, but that was definitely a crack. They place a plastic mouth piece attached to a blue balloon-like ball over Truitt's mouth.

My arms don't seem attached to me—they feel as if they float somewhere nearby. I must have swallowed smoke or something for how queasy my stomach feels. When I turn to see where they took my dad, my vision blurs with tears. An ambulance is leaving the lot with lights and siren and I am not with my dad. I fall to my seat and turn back to Truitt. His shirt is ripped open, exposing his chest and stomach. Two off-white squares are stuck to his chest and ribs.

The machine attached to the pads on his chest has a woman's voice, "Analyzing rhythm."

"Stand back," says one.

"Clear," says the other.

The machine beeps and Truitt's whole body jerks.

You'll take them both God? And make me live?

Do you trust me here on earth?

God, I trust you.

Take my hand Petra.

Even in this?

A beep. Truitt jerks, arched-back and stiff-legged.

God doesn't answer because I already know—even in this. If I don't have enough faith in him for the stuff on earth, can I really say I have assurance for the biggest thing of all—my eternity?

So how do I take your hand, God?

Hebrews 13:15.

My head drops. They return to pounding the CPR on Truitt, counting aloud. Fire roars and water sprays. Men yell. I weep.

Okay, God. Where else will I go? I lift my hands and look up. You have the words of life.

My recording pen still hangs in my dress between my breasts. I click the recorder off and write the verse on my hand. Hebrews 13:15. As soon as I cap the five, the paramedics roll Truitt to his side and he pukes. The mess looks like charred blood, but he coughs several more times and gasps a beautiful, labored breath.

They roll him back onto the board and strap him in, continually stopping to check him and his growing responsiveness. I walk to their supply bag and take the handles.

"You'll ride with us?"

I nod, lift the bag and follow to the ambulance.

The shorter man drives and the one who rides in the back with Truitt and me sets another mask on Truitt's mouth. "Oxygen," he says. He has thick curly blond hair and a narrow, pointy jaw.

I take Truitt's hand and try to stay steady as the ambulance weaves and jolts. If I still had my phone I would look up my verse. Several people are waiting for us when we arrive at the hospital. They have a gurney ready and Truitt's board is placed on top. When they move into the ER, I am prevented from following.

I stand awkwardly staring at the closed door. "Do you need to get looked at?" The blond paramedic says.

"No, I'm fine." But I start coughing.

The shorter one reaches toward me and I look where he points. The back of my left hand has Heb 13:15 scribbled. I need a Bible, but that can't be what he means. I turn it over; both palms are caked with dried blood. Some dripped down my arms and has dried there as well. Ahh, from pulling out the stained glass window—it starts to hurt. Soot and blood are all over my yellow dress. I cough again.

"I'm fine," I try to say, but this time it is through chattering teeth.

"Yes, you're going to be fine," he says with surreal calmness.

"I'll get a blanket," the short one, I think, says. First I'm dizzy, sitting in a wheelchair, next I'm sleeping in a bed covered with heated blankets and pillows under my feet and knees.

"Hi there, I'm Sara, your triage nurse." Sara is large with small teeth and narrow set eyes. She wears scrubs with cupids and white Dansko clogs. "I'm going to take your blood pressure."

"I need to know if my dad and Truitt are going to be okay." Sara lifts my arm from under the blanket. She turns it over and looks at the blood. "Then we'll clean you up."

"Can you tell me about the man I came with? Truitt Ridgemann."

"I don't know anything right now—but I'll

find out in a minute, all right?" Sara affixes the blood pressure cuff and holds out a small device. "I'm going to take your temperature." She slides it into my ear. I cough. "Are you having any difficulty breathing?"

"Really, I'm fine." I start to sit. "I just need to know about the men I came in with."

She looks at me blankly. "I'll clean your hands up too."

"Not yet. I need to keep this," I hold up my hand indicating the verse.

Her already small eyes shrink as she lowers her lids to study me, "Let me finish taking your vitals…"

"No." I pull off the sleeve and sit up. "I'll do whatever you want after I see Truitt."

"Wait here," she says and leaves. I'm about to go and poke my head into each room looking for him myself when she comes back.

"Come with me."

I follow Sara down the hall and around the corner. She points to a door and I brush past her. Inside, my dad lies on his back—looking smaller than normal. He is hooked up to a mask and has his eyes closed. I place my hand on his arm and jerk away. My fingers are like ice. He opens his eyes. There is so much relief and love in his expression. He puts his hand on my cheek to wipe my tears and I cradle the hand, trying not to press or bump the tubes taped to him.

"I'm fine, Dad," I say it several times before

he relaxes enough to look like he believes me.

He lifts his mask. "Your hands. You need to see a doctor." He points to the dried blood I haven't cleaned up yet.

"Not gonna happen, Dad." His head jerks back a little in surprise.

"Is the mask comfortable?" A black man asks as he enters.

"Yes, but I want my daughter—"

"Then I need you to keep it on," he commands.

Dad's eyebrows are pinched, he starts to lift from the bed and he's giving me the "look." I say to the nurse, "My dad wants me to get checked out too." Dad lays back and relaxes at my obedience. I stand. "But, I assure you—I'm fine," I say this to the nurse but look at my dad. "Besides, I'm not doing anything until I see Truitt."

I'm not even afraid to see what dad thinks of that. He can be ticked at me for the rest of my life. I give him a quick kiss on his forehead and start to leave. "Which room is he in?" The urge to cough rises but instead of giving in, I step away and try not to clear my throat.

The nurse glances back at my dad but if he detects anything, he keeps a professional face. His badge has his picture over the words "DeJuan, R.N." He smiles at me and I feel like we share a secret.

"I came here with a man in an ambulance."

"I know who you're talking about." He leads

me back near the room I was originally in and walks inside. Just before I enter, I say, "DeJuan, could you bring me a Bible?"

He glances from side to side, hurriedly. "If I get a sec."

Truitt lies on his side, conscious, eyes open. He has tubes in his nose—not a full mask like my dad did. He smiles wide as soon as I enter, and I cover the distance with quick steps.

"Hey there," he says.

"I'm so glad to see you." I want to be down near him but the only chair is by the foot of his bed. Instead, I squat so my eyes are closer to his eye level. I look up a little into the grassiness of the color. The whites are red-streaked. "Thank you," I say.

"Your hair, I love it." He takes my hand and presses a kiss to the back of it—his movements so natural, so unassuming and informal. He holds it to his cheek and then kisses it again.

As he releases, he sees the verse I wrote. "What's this?"

"Something God gave me."

Looking into my eyes he says, "By him therefore let us offer the sacrifice of praise to God continually, that is, the fruit of our lips giving thanks to his name."

I point to the scrawled letters on my hand in question.

"No matter where I look, that verse keeps popping up." He closes his eyes for a second and smiles to himself. "God is trying to tell me something."

The sacrifice of praise. Continually. The fruit of our lips giving thanks. "Sorry, Truitt, that was for me." We share a smile. "Say it again," I ask of him. He does, and I try to repeat it with him.

Truitt turns my palm over.

"Oh, no. Are you hurt?"

"The blood is dried. I feel like I have been singing the words 'I'm fine,' for an hour now. Really—I'm fine."

"Well, if you want to sing something else— I'd love to hear that song you were singing in the sanctuary." He rolls to his back and I stand. "It was so…"

Our eyes meet and he looks at me with an intimacy I well recognize—even though no one has ever looked at me this way before. "…amazing, beautiful, lovely." Truitt reaches for my hand again and places the back against his mouth. He isn't talking about the song. "Happy Valentine's Day."

I don't know the exact time, but it is Tuesday. Dad was right. Everything is fine now that it's Valentine's Day.

"Will you sing it?"

"I don't remember the song." Warmth and chills compete from different areas of my body. "I was preparing to meet God. It was just something that came out."

"And you don't know what you said?"

"I remember singing, but not words. It was

more like…audible emotion."

"I'm so glad it wasn't—he didn't—you didn't…" A tear drips down Truitt's cheek and he pressed his eyelids closed.

I squeeze his hand. "I'm glad too, Truitt." And I mean it.

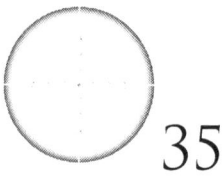35

My hair is so much curlier without the weight—it looks even shorter than it actually is. Shorter than when I cut it myself.

"Your father's going to pitch a fit."

"I know, Mom." I turn my chin and study my reflection from another angle. "I'm not actually that concerned. It's just a Monroe piercing. It's not permanent, like a tattoo or gauges." I finger a few more curls into place. Since I don't really wear make-up, it's nice to add a little sparkle.

"He's still going to..." She trails off and her hands shake as she tucks in her shirt and then un-tucks it.

"Are you nervous?"

"No."

I look past her to the messy apartment we share. Well, she shares with me. At least until I leave for Hawaii.

Thank you, Jesus.

"You're wondering if I'm nervous about

church or seeing your father in jail?" Mom looks frail and old to me, but maybe that's just because I've been taking care of her now for months. Still, Mom and I have an agreement not to try to rule each other.

"Both," I say.

Even though church is in a park and the jail is just a white-collar facility, I still think it's too much for her to have two "firsts" on the same day. Praise God Dad was exonerated of Barkley's murder. My recorder pen wasn't admissible in court—but it was the proof Mom needed to believe in him, and to paint again.

She licks her lips and rubs at some reddish watercolor smudged on her arm. "Yes. I am nervous."

"It's going to mean so much to him that you come." I reach for my cell and keys. "You have no idea, Mom." The very idea that a man who saw prisoners as swine—unfit for visitors to bring light, love, relief—is now in prison needing just that. Yeah. She has no idea.

Mom looks down. This must be the guilt stage of her slow grief-processing. "When does Truitt get back?"

"Thank the Lord, he got back last night." I quiver a little and touch the foreign object in my tender lip. "He's meeting us there."

"I don't think I'm going to go to your church yet." Mom slips her bare feet from her flats and leaves them in the middle of the floor. She reaches for the remote.

I bite my lip in decision. I can't live her life. God—please help her, give me the words.

"Do you want me to pick you up on the way out to see Dad?"

"Call first." She focuses on the television.

My phone buzzes. It's an email from Truitt.

"I have something I want to give you."

I bet I can guess what it is. We have an agreement to not text, but email works just as fast. I slide my phone down into my jeans pocket.

"Mom, I'd like it if you picked one: church or jail." I laugh to myself a little at what the options sound like. I'm not going to control her; she just might need a little…prompting.

"You would?" She looks up.

"If you had to choose, which would it be?"

Mom presses the remote and the television turns off. "Church," she whispers without looking away from the enormous, old television someone donated to our cause.

Thank you, Father.

Oh, well. Maybe next week, Dad. "You'll love sitting outside, Mom." Since Selena made off with all the money our church had and the building itself was unsalvageable—they sold the land to pay for outstanding debts. But when God is present, starting with nothing can be a beautiful thing.

"Liam is getting really good." I can tell she doesn't believe the kid she knew now leads our dismembered band of misfits and barbarians. "I listened to him practice this week. He's talking about the demon-possessed guy who was a cutter and lived in the caves."

"A cutter." She shakes with a disbelieving smile.

I don't believe it, but Mom rises from the couch and slips one foot into a shoe. I continue, "Think about this: when Jesus cast out the demons, the town asked him to leave. Isn't that crazy?"

"I know the story, Petra." Dad will never call me that but Mom took to it immediately.

"I'm sure there isn't a story in the Bible you don't already know, Mom—but when Jesus prepares to leave the guy, all healed; he wants to go with Jesus. Jesus tells him no. Doesn't that seem...unloving?" Liam said it so much better. But she's listening and we're almost at my Jeep.

My Jeep: the only thing not in Dad's name, lost to my parent's bankruptcy and Dad's embezzlement charges.

"It does seem unloving." She climbs into the passenger seat. "I've always thought it was weird Jesus just abandoned him like that."

"That's the thing," I start the engine and slowly navigate through our apartment complex's parking lot. "Jesus didn't abandon him. That man was Jesus' gift of love—provision—for a town that rejected him."

"They rejected him and God still provided." Mom stares out the window as she works on that.

"Isn't that the whole point?" I ask her.

"While we were sinners, he died."

"Sure, he brings the sinners in and the prodigals home. But then we have to live with each other." We drive in silence until she finally adds, "We forget we were saved once."

She's right and I remember Alvita's point. "The religious were the only ones Jesus ever cussed at."

We pull up to the park. It was chilly a month ago, but May is a gorgeous time to meet outside. "Don't forget, Mom. God left a provision for the religious when he sent Peter to preach to the Jews."

Tingles run up my arms.

Do you love me?

You know that I love you.

Feed my sheep.

"So, Petra." Mom emphasizes my name. "Are you going to start preachin' to the choir?"

"No way. You already know everything." Mom smirks when I say this.

Truitt smiles from the far side of the group and starts walking toward us. Behind him, Alvita lifts a hand to wave. God, I love that woman.

I look at Mom as I round the front of the Jeep, and say to her, "The church: the most dangerous mission field of all." Then I hum the "Jaws" movie theme.

Mom laughs. "Since there is no more risky place than a group of lukewarm Christians."

"Where it's more than your life you stand to lose," I counter.

Her eyes fill with tears. "It could be your marriage, your faith...your sanity."

I study her for a moment. "Only because sometimes it's harder to live for him than die for him."

Mom nods and looks up at Truitt while he approaches, "He's lost weight," she says too loudly.

"He has a little, I guess." I thought it was just that it'd been two weeks since I'd seen him. Two weeks since he drove to California to make peace at the grave.

"Look, Mom, there's Damon and Laura." Of all the people I never expected would sit and listen to Liam preach — well our old pastor and his wife are just one of dozens.

Laura sees me pointing and starts toward us. When she recognizes my mom she runs with her arms open. My mom makes a sound and then starts to meet her. Thank you, Lord.

"How was the trip?" I ask Truitt.

"Needed." Truitt's mouth is tight as he approaches.

"You have something for me?" I hold up my phone.

He gets a wicked grin then. I try to step back a little out of his reach.

"Yep," he grabs my elbows and pulls me close. His feet stumble and his hand clenches my arm as he steadies himself — but our knees still bang and I drop my phone. "This is cute." He points at the faux diamond stud in my lip with a jerk of his nose.

And in his kiss there is fine wine.

"YOU ARE A HIDING PLACE FOR ME;

YOU PRESERVE ME FROM TROUBLE;

YOU SURROUND ME WITH

SHOUTS OF DELIVERANCE."

PSALM 32:7 (ESV)

# BOOK CLUB QUESTIONS

1. Most people have never seen the slaughter of an animal for food—much less a sacrifice. Depending on your background and your culture, the word "sacrifice," can bring connotations of anything from a bloody ceremony to going without cream in your coffee. What does sacrifice mean to you? Describe something you have personally sacrificed.

2. What does Hebrews 13:15 tell us to offer in sacrifice? Why do you think the word sacrifice is used to describe a something verbal—that you must say it?

3. When Leah and Truitt were praising God through song, he warned her with the verse Isaiah 29:13. Have you found it possible to go through the action of praise, yet keep your heart removed?

4. Christ also quoted that verse in Isaiah in Mark 7:7. It's easy to say that you love worship if you love singing—but is it still possible to worship in vain even if you love to worship? Share an example if you can.

5. You may know from passages such as the Lord's Prayer in Matthew 6:9-13 that we are to forgive others. Now read Matthew 5:23-24. If we remember someone has something against us, what are we supposed to attempt *before* we leave our sacrifice?

6. I know as a parent, I am most content when my children are not only tolerating each other, but enjoying each other. What did David have to say about unity in Psalm 133:1?

7.  In Zephaniah 3:9 Why does God purify their lips?

8.  How do you think your relationship with other Christians affects your worship? If nothing comes to mind, spend a moment in prayer.

9.  There are many different kinds of people. Humans can be loud, subdued, outgoing, private...continue the list by describing both yourself and people that annoy you. Also think of people who please you, or draw you into worship.

10. Other than singing, what actions are listed in Psalm 95?

11. Do you believe God created us to be different? Explain or list verses.  How should/can all the different kinds of people approach God:
    In worship? Should it be the same for everyone?
    In our hearts? Should it be the same for everyone?

12. There is a quote in the movie Chariots of Fire, "I believe God made me for a purpose, but he also made me fast. And when I run I feel His pleasure." Share a way you worship God besides singing. If you're not sure, think of something that gives you a great deal of joy even if it is simple, like making a meal or buying someone a cup of coffee.

13. We don't always come to God happy, but we can always praise. Write a few positive or negative emotions that would match the following actions as

listed in Psalm 95. You could have both represented
in each action.
Shouting
Singing
Kneeling
Bowing down

14. According to John 4:23-24, God is seeking true
    worshipers. What else does it say about God?

15. It is good to take note when Christ says we must do
    something, or do it a certain way—specific
    instructions from him aren't negotiable. How does it
    say we must worship God?

16. How would you know if you believed a lie about God?

17. In what ways can your truthfulness about yourself
    affect your approach to God?

18. Why would God want honesty about yourself
    apparent in your relationship to him?

19. How do you define being in the spiritual realm?
    Worshiping in the spirit? What is the difference
    between worshiping in the spiritual and physical
    realms?

20. If you are worshiping the true God, in spirit and in
    truth—should it matter what genre of songs the
    worship leader is playing?

21. Are you allowed to seek out music that pleases you in your worship to God? Why or why not?

22. Do others need to be as affected by your favorite music as you are? Do you need to be conformed to someone else's preferred music or worship-style?

23. Return to Zephaniah 3:9, use New American Standard Bible (NASB) if possible. As we stand shoulder to shoulder with the body of Christ; each with different personalities, tastes and preferences, what is the one thing that should unite us in our worship?

24. If you are worshiping in spirit and in truth, and sharing grace with those you are worshiping with, could it be considered a living sacrifice to God?

25. Is there anything that currently prevents you from worshiping God?

# ACKNOWLEDGEMENTS

Writing is lonely, I couldn't do it without the people God strategically brings. I'd like to thank my husband and three adult/near adult children for their encouragement and critical input. One thing I never anticipated was that my children would one day improve and edify me.

You wouldn't be holding this book if weren't for my writing group: Lisa Phillips, Heather Woodhaven, Kristine McCord and Becky Avella. All fabulous writers themselves, they sacrificed their own time to read, edit and cheer.

Lisa Buffaloe read the very first version. I never could rewrite it enough to make Truitt tolerable for her — but she helped me anyway.

My mom and sisters read the story and offered enough support to keep me going, just as they keep me going in other ways.

Lori-Ann Whyte patiently answered all my questions about Jamaican culture, dialect and idioms. Anything that's inaccurate, I messed up.

Heather Woodhaven, Lisa Hess and Andrea Graham helped with the book club questions and verses.

Mick Silva offered timely and encouraging words, the kind that writers need.

Peter Leavell gave a talk in the book's infancy about the meaning of colors — and I saw yellow.

I'd also like to thank Ray Ellis, for always answering procedural questions and Julie Winslow for edits and ideas that bolstered me in the home stretch.

May the Lord shine his face upon you all.

Hilarey Johnson teaches martial arts in Idaho with her husband and three children. She keeps a larger than normal, urban garden with chickens.

When she isn't writing or getting lost, she loves to cook foreign foods and read redemptive fiction. Someday Hilarey hopes to time travel.

She blogs infrequently at Hilarey.com.

Made in the USA
Middletown, DE
09 June 2015